The Unfortunate Fursey

Mervyn Wall was born in Dublin in 1908. He was educated at Belvedere College, Dublin, at Bonn in Germany and at the National University of Ireland. For fourteen years he worked in the Irish Civil Service, and from there he moved to Radio Éireann. In 1957 he became Secretary of the Arts Council, a post he held until his retirement in the mid-1970s. Best-known for his novels and short stories, Mervyn Wall also had many of his stage and radio plays produced and gained a reputation as a radio critic and newspaper and magazine contributor. Among his best-known novels are *Hermitage* (Wolfhound Press), the prize-winning *Leaves for the Burning* and the comic classics *The Unfortunate Fursey* and *The Return of Fursey*. Mervyn Wall died in 1997.

The Unfortunate Fursey

Mervyn Wall

WOLFHOUND PRESS
Celebrating 25 Years

Published in 2000 by
Wolfhound Press Ltd
68 Mountjoy Square
Dublin 1, Ireland
Tel: (353-1) 874 0354
Fax: (353-1) 872 0207

Originally published by The Pilot Press.
Published by Wolfhound Press in *The Complete Fursey* (1985).

 Wolfhound Press receives financial assistance from The Arts
Council/An Chomhairle Ealaíon, Dublin, Ireland.

British Library Cataloguing in Publication Data
A catalogue record for this book is available from the British Library.

ISBN 0-86327-729-2

10 9 8 7 6 5 4 3 2 1

Cover Design: Sally Mills-Westley
Cover Illustration: Áine Duggan
Typesetting: Wolfhound Press
Printed in the Republic of Ireland by ColourBooks, Dublin

To
Denis Devlin
remembering many a lively evening

Chapter 1

It is related in the Annals that for the first four centuries after its foundation by the blessed Kieran the monastic settlement of Clonmacnoise enjoyed a singular immunity from the visitation of imps and ghouls, night fiends, goblins and all sorts of hellish phantoms which not unseldom appear to men. Within the sound of its bells the dark operations of magic were unknown, for no witch, sorcerer or charmer could abide the sanctified air. Other religious settlements were sadly plagued by disembodied spirits, demons, lemuses and fauns snorting and snuffling most fiendishly in the darker corners of the corridors and cells, and it was not unusual for a monk to be seriously injured or lamed as a result of their mischiefs and devilments. Philomaths of the profoundest erudition century after century poring over the great elephant folios in the library, shook their heads and warned their brethren that they could not expect to be always immune from such visitants, and that if the Prince of Darkness did but once gain a footing, he would be aflame with the thwarted malice of centuries. But the monks put their trust in the blessed Kieran and in their own sanctity, and it may have been their presumption in this regard that at last opened the door to the pestilential demons which towards the close of the tenth century thronged to Clonmacnoise from their horrible and shadowy dens.

The holy place had its first indication that its defences had been breached when one evening in early April Father Killian, who had the care of the monastery brewery, emerged from his place of work to take the air for a few minutes before returning to the main building for vespers. He had worked diligently all day, and the night air was pleasing to his heated face. It was a dark night, and he experienced some difficulty in finding his way between the cells and huts to the palisade which surrounded the settlement. When he reached it at last he stood for a time looking across the fields towards the river invisible in the darkness. It was very quiet: nothing was to be heard but the regular grunting of a monk in a nearby cell, who was plying his discipline with more than usual determination. Suddenly the moon came from behind a cloud, the river flashed silver, there was a blast of pestilential wind, and Father Killian became aware of a huge swarthy cacodemon sitting on the palisade some paces from where he stood. The face of this hideous spectre was turned back to front, and it was crunching and eating red hot coals and other dangerous matters with its teeth.

Father Killian, knowing that it was always ominous to see such a creature and that it was best not curiously to meddle, would have taken to his heels if only his legs had obeyed him, but they were paralysed with terror, which was by no means allayed when the hellish goblin, swinging itself suddenly from the palisade, took up a position beside him, and in an ingratiating manner began to tempt him to deny God and curse the Abbot. When the startled monk found his voice it was to begin a devout recitation of the psalms, whereupon the demon seized him by the throat in a fearful grip and well-nigh throttled him. He lifted Father Killian and flung him against the base of the round tower thirty yards away, and then letting out a hideous yell the creature vanished in a foul black smoke, leaving behind him so intolerably stinking and malignant a scent as is beyond all imagination and expression.

The fiend's parting scream brought the monks from their cells like a swarm of bees, and compressing their nostrils between their forefingers and thumbs by way of protection against the horrid and noisome stench, they made their way through the murky smoke to carry the unconscious Killian back to the monastery.

Two hours later the Abbot Marcus, returning to Clonmacnoise by boat from a day's fishing on Lough Ree, found the settlement in turmoil. The entire community crowded around him as he took his chair in the chapter house, and the white-faced Killian was carried in and propped against a wall where the Abbot could see him with convenience. The Abbot listened with some impatience to the chatter of the affrighted monks before sternly dismissing them to their beds; and then, having ascertained that Father Killian was capable of speech, he helped him to a chair and slowly drew the story from him.

'Hm!' said the Abbot, 'how can you be certain that it was not the false impression of a timid and fretful imagination?'

Father Killian assured him that it was not, and showed his bruises and the mark of the fiend's nails upon his throat.

'I still don't believe it,' said the Abbot; but seeing the indignation in the monk's face, he added charitably:

'You are the best brewer we have ever had in Clonmacnoise, but I have thought of late that from excess of zeal you are inclined to overwork. That might perhaps account for your hallucination. I think I will take you out of the brewery and put you in charge of the poultry, where you will find the work more agreeable to your present nervous state.' And the Abbot Marcus, who was renowned far and wide for his kindness, assisted the still dazed Killian across to his cell and into bed, and left him with a promise to remember him in his prayers.

On the following morning a dish of broken food was put into Killian's hand, and he was led into the poultry house, while the brewery was committed to the care of a father of noted piety, who many years before had made a vow never to drink anything but water. The Abbot assembled the community and lectured them gravely on their childishness and their lack of faith in the blessed Kieran. When he had brought his address to a firm and dignified finish, the monks and novices dispersed to their daily tasks somewhat reassured, though an inclination to glance over their shoulders remained with them during the day.

About the hour of sunset a sudden shower of fish, which fell from the heavens like hail, occasioned the Abbot certain disquiet. During the night hoarse coughs and deep sighs were heard in the passages, followed by the barking and baying of giant dogs. On the following morning an octogenarian monk made his way into the Abbot's presence with the help of two sticks to complain of the presence in his cell during the night of an evil spirit in the form of a beautiful harlot, bravely dressed, who with mincing gait and lewd gestures had tempted him to fornication. This sequence of inexplicable events forced the Abbot to the conclusion that the monastery was badly haunted.

During the day he read up the subject in the library with the help of the apprehensive custodian, and at nightfall every monk, student and novice was assembled in the great church. As he faced them and looked at their white faces strained and tired from lack of sleep, the Abbot felt an immense pity for his spiritual children. A shudder passed through the community as he took for his text the words from the thirteenth chapter of Isaiah: 'Fauns, Satyrs and the hairy ones shall dance in their palaces.'

'The day of battle is at hand,' began the Abbot. 'The Evil One has gained entrance to the holy city of Clonmacnoise.' He went on to warn them of the sinuous cunning of the Fiend, who has a myriad devices at his command, and whose minions might be expected to appear in the guise of goats, hares or horned owls. If in their cells they were to hear most lamentable moan and outcry proceeding from some invisible source, they might shrewdly suspect a manifestation. If an evil spirit did manifest itself, they should be armed to address and speak to it, and should adjure the spectre in the name of God, if it were of God, to speak; if not, to begone. 'Should a ghastly apparition suddenly confront you, be not over-confident in yourselves and presumptuously daring, but fervently recommend yourselves to God. A valiant warrior of Christ is always armed with the buckler of faith and the breastplate of hope. Dread particularly the fiend who appears in another guise, fascinating your senses and deluding you with glamour. A stoup of holy water is most healthful and efficacious, and a sure protection against the malice and attacks of unclean spirits.' At the conclusion of the sermon holy water and books of exorcism were distributed to all.

The monks went slowly to their cells, their minds filled with apprehension. Before long, restless spirits could be heard groaning and sighing in the passages. About midnight the first explosion occurred. Father Leo had observed a pale, bleeding wraith, which crooned softly as it attempted to draw and switch away the quilt and blankets from his bed. As he did not deem its answer to his adjuration satisfactory, he gave it a slash of holy water, which caused it to explode and disappear through the ceiling in a sheet of flame, setting fire to the thatch in its passage upwards. An unearthly silence followed; but before long other distant rumblings were heard, and soon the monastery was filled with smoke, noise and the smell of sulphur.

When the bell rang for matins the monks came from their cells a little haggard and shaken, but with renewed confidence. Everywhere that the enemy had manifested himself he had been defeated. Father Sampson had spent the night struggling with an incubus, but as Sampson had been a wrestler at the court of the King of Thomond before he entered the cloister, he had been well able for his adversary. Brother Patrick had been caused annoyance by a huge black dog, hideous to look upon, barking at him from a corner of his cell. As Patrick had been too terrified to reach for the holy water, the demon had remained until the crowing of the first cock; but the lay brother had suffered no inconvenience other than loss of sleep; and Brother Patrick remarked philosophically: 'I wouldn't have slept in any case.' Other monks had been scandalised by the presence of damsels of excessive comeliness, who had succeeded in divesting themselves of the greater part of their clothing before the fathers could find the right page in the books of exorcism. A suave gentleman of swarthy aspect, thought to be the Prince of Darkness himself, had actually had the audacity to try to tempt the Master of Novices and had got very much the worse of the encounter.

The Abbot, who again spent the morning in the Library and was beginning to find the subject interesting, assembled the community once more and warned them of the further evil sleights and tricks the Fiend might be expected to have at his command. He admonished them particularly to beware of complacency, an injunction which most of the brethren were inclined to think unnecessary. During the afternoon the Abbot was grieved to receive applications from many of his monks for permission to leave the monastery for varying periods in order to visit sick relatives and aged parents whom the applicants accused themselves of having sinfully neglected for many years. He sternly turned down all such representations, and the applicants set themselves to the business of learning the exorcisms and adjurations by heart, and looked to the oncoming night with doleful foreboding.

For fifteen successive days Clonmacnoise was haunted horribly. It became commonplace for a monk on turning a corner to be confronted by a demon who saluted him with cuffs and blows. Hydras, scorpions, ounces and pards frequented the cells, and serpents filled the passages with their hissings and angry sibilations. The nights were hideous with a horrid hubbub, a clattering of wrenching doors, and the howls and shrieks of invisible beings.

On the sixteenth day a sullen deputation of elderly monks awaited on the Abbot.

'It's not the look of the demons I mind,' said Father Crustaceous. 'A sentence or two of Latin soon disperses them. It's the lack of sleep.'

'I don't mind the ones on two legs or even four,' said Father Placidus, 'but I can't abide loathly worms and dragons.'

'The long and short of it,' said another hard-bitten veteran, 'is that we're of opinion that it's time for you in your capacity as Abbot to take these hellish sprites and bind them to the bottom of Lough Ree.'

There was a general grunt of assent. The Abbot did not appear to have heard the last remark.

'The learned Gaspar Diefenbach has written at length on the subject,' he murmured absently.

'There is a sort of feeling in the monastery,' said Father Crustaceous grimly, 'that our affliction by these fearful demons may be due to a lack of proper sanctity in high places.'

The Abbot's fingers played nervously with a heavy folio of Cornelius Atticus.

'I will not do anything with unbecoming haste,' he said shortly. 'I must give some time to reflection and prayer.'

Muttering, the deputation shuffled out of the cell.

Two days later, before the Abbot had completed his meditations, the haunting suddenly ceased. A free and balmy air pervaded Clonmacnoise; an expression of relief, almost of gaiety, manifested itself in every face, the monks went about their work with a lighter tread. Credit was generously given to the Abbot, for it was believed that the deliverance was due to his prayers. No doubt he had taken the matter up very seriously with the blessed Kieran, who, after all, could scarcely turn a deaf ear to the representations of his own abbot; and, of course, everyone knew how powerful was the influence exercised by Kieran in Heaven. In anything touching Clonmacnoise he was sure to be called in for consultation, it would be discourteous to ignore him when great decisions were to be taken affecting his own foundation. The Abbot, though he said little, seemed to be satisfied that he had managed things very well with Heaven, so that it was with considerable chagrin that he listened to the halting story of a wretched lay brother, who three days later threw himself on his knees at the Abbot's feet.

Brother Fursey possessed the virtue of Holy Simplicity in such a high degree that he was considered unfit for any work other than paring edible roots in the monastery kitchen, and even at that, it could not be truthfully claimed that he excelled. The cook, a man of many responsibilities, was known on occasion to have been so wrought upon by Brother Fursey's simplicity as to threaten him with a ladle. The lay brother never answered back, partly because in the excess of his humility he believed himself to be the least of men, and partly because of an impediment in his speech which rendered him tongue-tied when in a state of excitement or fright. So it came to pass that for three whole days the wretched lay brother kept his alarming knowledge to himself through sheer terror at the thought of having to face the Abbot. While all Clonmacnoise believed that the satanic hordes had taken their departure, one man alone knew that they had not.

When the settlement had first been plagued by demons, Brother Fursey, in common with everyone else, had been strongly moved to perturbation and alarm, but when night after night had passed, and the first week had crept into the second, without his having been maltreated or belaboured, or even seeing a demon in the shape of beast or bird, he happily concluded that his soul was too mean to excite the avarice of Hell. So while the rest of the community sweated and prayed, Brother Fursey, convinced of his own worthlessness, slept blissfully beneath his blankets; but on the very first night during which the others were untroubled by devilish manifestations, the door of Brother Fursey's cell was suddenly and violently flung open. The lay brother started into a sitting position and fixed his eyes on the open doorway with some misgiving, for he knew that it was unlucky for the door of a chamber to open of its own accord and nobody to enter. He had been sitting thus for some time when an ungainly creature of the gryphon family ambled in from the corridor and, casting a disdainful glance at the startled monk, sat down in the centre of the floor. It wheezed once or twice as if its wind were broken, and gloomily contemplated the resultant shower of sparks which fell in every corner of the cell. Appalled at such a foul sight, Brother Fursey fell back against his pillows. When he roused himself again, he felt that he was like to lose his wits, for a seemingly endless procession of four- and six-legged creatures of most uninviting aspect was shuffling in through the doorway and disposing themselves about the cell. An incubus followed, and clambering on to the bed, seated itself without much apparent enthusiasm astride on Brother Fursey's chest. The lay brother was by this time so nigh driven frantic by fear that he scarcely noticed the galaxy of undraped females of surpassing loveliness who assembled in a corner and appeared to be exchanging gossip while they tidied up their hair. Lastly there entered a black gentleman who walked with a slight limp. He carefully closed the door behind him and, advancing to the head of the bed, saluted the lay brother politely. Brother Fursey's brain simmered in his head as he tried to remember the form of adjuration, but the only words that he could bring to mind were those of Abbot's injunction: 'Be not over-confident in yourself and presumptuously daring.' The sable gentleman signed to the incubus to give place, whereupon, grunting horribly, it slid off Brother Fursey's chest and, waddling across the room on its bandy legs, seated itself astride the prie-dieu. The dark stranger sat on the side of the bed and addressed the monk with affability.

'You have no occasion to be alarmed,' he said. 'You must regard this as a friendly visit.'

Brother Fursey's eyes rolled agonisingly towards the stoup of holy water on the adjoining table.

'Now, now,' said the Devil, shaking his head reprovingly, 'you mustn't do that. Even if you can nerve your arm to stretch it forth from beneath the bedclothes, I would point out that in the past fortnight myself and the children have acquired considerable dexterity in skipping out of the way of a slash of that nasty, disagreeable stuff, especially when it is cast by a shaky hand. Now,' he continued, 'I expect that you are mildly exercised as to the reason for this seemingly discourteous interruption of your sleeping hours. We had no choice, Brother Fursey, we had no choice. Never in all my experience as a devil have I encountered such obstinate sanctity as exists in this monastery. The boys are half-blinded with holy water and completely worn out. They need a rest, a little while to recuperate before returning to the fight, newly armed with the experience they have gained, the next time to succeed and to wipe out forever this sickly plague-spot of womanish men and chanting monkdom.' Here the archfiend grated his teeth horribly, and lightnings danced in his eyes; but he glanced down in a manner by no means unfriendly at the wisp of hair and the two button-like eyes above the quilt, which was all that could be seen of Brother Fursey.

'To compress the matter into a nutshell,' continued His Highness, 'I admit that my forces have been worsted in the first encounter, but I am not the sort of demon to retire with my tail between my legs and meekly allow the victory to my opponents. My troops are in need of rest and re-armament, that is all. What with the smell of incense, the splashing of holy water and the sound of the Latin language, there is no safety for any of us in this settlement elsewhere than in your cell, where due to the happy chance of your having an impediment in your speech, we are in no danger of being suddenly ejected, by a string of Latin or a shrewd adjuration, into the outer air, which is a different sort of place entirely. If I were to withdraw my legions altogether for recuperation to a clime more salubrious and more welcome to their natures, that dull fellow you have for abbot, would be up to some game such as the sevenfold circuit of the bounds of the settlement with chantings and bells so as to render our return difficult, if not altogether impossible. I intend keeping a foothold in Clonmacnoise until I clear it of its pale inhabitants. Your cell is our sanctuary. You, my dear Fursey, are our bridgehead.'

For a few moments there was silence broken only by the chattering of the monk's teeth. Then a choking sound became audible from beneath the quilt. The black gentleman withdrew a pace with some distaste.

'I beg of you,' he said coldly, 'to give over your attempts at prayer. You know well that your fright is such as to render you incapable of the formation of a single syllable. We are both men of the world, and a ready acceptance of the position will do much credit to your commonsense and make for mutual respect. And now, to show you that I am not ungenerous, but am willing to repay your hospitality, I should like to do something for you. Purely as a matter of accounting and to keep my books straight, I shall, of course, require your soul in exchange. It's not a very valuable soul, its market value would be small; but you won't find me haggling over the price. Are you perhaps a lover of beauty?'

The demon waved his hand, and a queue of desirable females began to move monotonously across the cell from the door to the far wall, where they disappeared through the plaster. The monk gave vent to a deep groan and closed his eyes tightly. When he re-opened them with due caution his visitor was regarding him with professional interest.

'You have been a long time in a world of wattled huts and whitewashed cells,' he said. 'Do you never long for the freedom you once had, to climb the hills and move through the woods just as you please? The breeze was pleasant when you were a boy, the forests were full of mystery, and you had a great liking for paddling your feet in the fords of rivers. All the length of a summer day you had to yourself, with no one to say "Fursey, do this," or "Fursey, do that".'

Immediately a bird call was heard and the gurgling of streams. A silvan sounded a few hesitant notes on a rustic pipe, and the cell became full of heavenly fragrance and sweet odours. The demon studied the lay brother's reactions in his staring eyes and twitching forehead. It was all he could see of the monk, who had the bedclothes drawn up to the bridge of his nose.

'I'm afraid your tastes are vulgar,' said the fiend with some disappointment. 'What about a mighty reputation as a warrior?'

Brother Fursey became aware of the clash and clamour of battle, the heartening burst of trumpets, and the brave flash of coloured cloaks as swords were wielded. At this point the lay brother lost consciousness, for his was a timorous nature, and he had always been adverse to violence.

For three days the wretched Fursey crept about the monastery as in a trance. He spoiled hundreds of edible roots and pared large slices of flesh from his thumbs. He would certainly have fallen foul of Brother Cook but for the latter's exceeding good humour resultant on the departure of a poltergeist which had made itself at home in his cell and whose least prank had been to heave him out of bed several times during the night. It was only at the close of the third day that Brother Fursey gathered together his wits and the remnants of his courage. He came faltering into the Abbot's presence and knelt at his feet. It took the lay brother a long time to stammer out his story. The Abbot heard him in silence sitting brooding in his great chair. At length he arose, uttered a sigh; and raising Fursey, bade him return to the kitchen. Then he summoned the elder fathers to council and when they had assembled, he went down on his knees before them.

'I accuse myself,' he said, 'of spiritual pride. In my foolish presumption I imagined that my wretched prayers had been efficacious. The clearance of the greater part of the settlement from fiendish visitants has, in fact, been due to the stalwart piety of you, my fathers, and of the rest of the community.' Then not wishing to cause his monks further embarrassment by the sight of their abbot so humbling himself before them, he got to his feet and resumed the abbatical chair. Alarm, and then consternation, manifested itself on every face as he related the lay brother's story. There was some toothless whispering among the fathers and a great nodding of bald heads, then Father Crustaceous spoke.

'None of us is without sin,' he said, 'and a man's sins concern only himself and Heaven. Let us proceed at once to consider how Brother Fursey may best be relieved of this intolerable burden, and these execrable fiends be dispersed and scattered for once and for all. No doubt your lordship can now make arrangements to surround and lead them into captivity, preparatory to binding them securely to the bottom of Lough Ree.'

The Abbot coughed.

'I am but a poor sinner,' he said, 'in sanctity the least among you. Many a man excelling me by far in piety has in the course of such an operation been torn into small pieces, and the pieces dispersed no man knows where.'

'If such should be your fate,' said Father Placidus, 'you would be assured of a martyr's crown. Your saintly successor would certainly not omit to plead at Rome the cause for your canonisation.'

'These matters are not easily put into execution,' remarked the Abbot diffidently.

'It should at least be attempted,' said Father Crustaceous.

'But how will the monastery benefit by my demise and subsequent canonisation, if the suggested operation be not efficacious in scattering the dread sprites that infest it? My saintly successor would be in an even worse plight with the horrid example of my failure before him.'

The Master of Novices rose to his feet. 'Fathers,' he said, 'this discussion is getting us nowhere. I am responsible for the spiritual care and well-being of our novices and students. I cannot but rejoice that the female demons who have displayed themselves with such disregard for decency in the cells of our impressionable youth, now restrict their disgraceful activities to one cell only, and that cell the cell of a lay brother so grounded in piety as to be indifferent to their hellish charms. Let us leave well alone. Brother Fursey is winning for himself a celestial seat. Would you deprive him of it? Who knows but that the sufferings which he is at present enduring, may not result in his speedy demise and assumption to his Heavenly reward? He seems to me to be a man of poor constitution. With Fursey's happy translation Heavenwards, the Archfiend will no longer have a foothold in Clonmacnoise.'

'Is there not a danger,' asked Father Placidus, 'that Brother Fursey, being subjected to such an assembly of the batteries of Hell, may before his constitution fails him, succumb to the unhallowed suggestions of the Evil One, and even form a compact with him detrimental to this holy foundation?'

'But,' said the Novice Master, 'I understand from our lord the Abbot that this lay brother is a man of such resolution and so charged with the seven virtues, that he laughs to scorn the most insidious temptations that Hell has been able to devise.'

'That is generally true,' said the Abbot. 'According to what Brother Fursey has related to me, only one suggestion of the Fiend appeared to him to have been even sensible. With more than diabolical cunning the Father of Lies represented to Brother Fursey the attractiveness of murdering Brother Cook by creeping on him unawares and tipping him into the cauldron of Tuesday soup. But as soon as this devilish suggestion was insinuated into Fursey's mind, his mental agony was such that he for once succeeded in bursting the bonds which impede his speech, and he called aloud on the blessed Kieran for aid, which aid was forthcoming with such little delay that the desire to kill faded instantly from Fursey's mind beneath the outpouring of grace which drowned and overwhelmed his soul. I think we may safely assume that now that Brother Fursey is aware of this chink in his armour, he will be forearmed to resist any infernal promptings in this regard to which he may be subjected.'

'Nevertheless,' said Father Placidus, 'a word to Brother Cook would perhaps be not amiss. He should not turn his back to Brother Fursey, and it would be no harm to remove any choppers that may be lying around the kitchen.'

'A good cook is hard to come by,' muttered Father Crustaceous.

'It is agreed then,' said the Master of Novices, 'that the heroic Fursey continue to hold at bay the powers of darkness until his happy demise (which will deprive the Archfiend of his only foothold in Clonmacnoise) or until the blessed Kieran intervenes powerfully on our behalf, whichever be the shorter. In the meantime the community should address itself urgently to prayer.'

'And,' added Father Crustaceous, 'our lord the Abbot will no doubt make every effort to increase in sanctity, and in the intervals of his fastings and scourgings he will continue in his studies as to how demons are best fastened to the bottoms of lakes. Is that the position?'

'That is the position,' said the Abbot shortly, and he dismissed the council.

When Brother Cook was informed of the grievous temptation to which his helpmate was exposed, he generously urged that it was not fitting that a man of Fursey's piety should be called upon to perform the menial tasks of the kitchen. The Abbot, however, insisted that Brother Fursey continue his offices among the edible roots, whereupon the Cook respectfully petitioned for a transfer to the poultry house, where Father Killian, who had never fully recovered from his grim experience, was not doing as well as might be desired. The Abbot curtly refused, and there was much grumbling in the monastery at the deterioration in the cooking, due to Brother Cook's difficulty in keeping his mind on his work, and the fact that he spent most of his time with his back to the wall watching Brother Fursey.

A week passed, and a certain uneasiness began to pervade the settlement. It was true that Brother Fursey's hair was now white, but he showed no signs of dissolution; and it was not doubted but that the imps and ghouls were steadily recruiting their strength for a renewal of the assault. Every morning he was questioned by the Abbot as to the previous night's experiences, and he stammered out his story to the best of his ability. On Thursday he had been offered the crown and robes of the King of Cashel; on Friday efforts had been made to beguile him with mellifluous verse and the promise of a reputation as a man of letters. On Saturday he had to be carried on a stretcher from his cell to the refectory; for Satan, losing all patience at the unfortunate lay brother's lack of interest in a shower of gold, had handed him over to four poltergeists to work their will on him: but by nightfall Brother Fursey had sufficiently recovered to be able to limp back to his cell with the aid of a borrowed crutch. The monks began to be horribly alarmed.

Father Crustaceous sucked hard at his one remaining tooth.

'There's nothing for it,' he said. 'Father Abbot must set about binding them to the bottom of Lough Ree. What's he hesitating about? Is he afraid they'll spoil the fishing?'

The old men rose with one accord and stumped and hobbled to the Abbot's cell.

'I won't do it,' said the Abbot violently. 'That's final. But,' and he fixed his eyes on Father Crustaceous, 'I have under consideration the allotting of the holy task to a father of greater sanctity than myself.'

Father Crustaceous' mouth fell open. There was an uncomfortable silence, which was broken by the suave voice of the Master of Novices.

'I imagine matters can be arranged more suitably,' he said, 'and with satisfaction to all. We must expel Brother Fursey from Clonmacnoise before the horrid strangers that frequent his cell, feel that they are strong enough once more to assail us. When Fursey is gone, their foothold will be gone. There is no time to lose.'

Every face brightened.

'Do you think it quite fair?' began the Abbot.

'Is he not a harbourer of demons?' asked Father Placidus hotly.

'Fair or not,' said the Master of Novices, 'we must consider the good of the greater number. Remember our innocent, but perhaps imaginative, novices subject at any moment to the onset of a bevy of undraped dancing girls.'

Father Crustaceous uttered a pious ejaculation.

'So be it,' said the Abbot, and he turned away.

Within a short space the astonished Fursey found himself led to the great gate that opens on The Pilgrim's Way. The Master of Novices pointed out to him his road and indicated that he was never to return. Brother Fursey wept and held on to the other's cloak, but the Novice Master broke his hold, and left him with his blessing and the present of a second crutch.

On the side of the hill Fursey sat down in the heather and turned his red, swollen eyes to where the towers and cells of Clonmacnoise lay cluttered in a little heap beside the river. Lucifer came and stood beside him.

'If it would afford you any satisfaction,' said that personage, 'I will rive one of the round towers with a ball of fire. I regret that I am not allowed to damage the churches or cells.'

'No,' said the ex-monk, who now that there was no urgent necessity for him to speak, found that he could do so with reasonable fluency. 'I wish you'd go away. You're the cause of all this,' and he burst into a fresh fit of weeping.

The Devil hesitated. 'What are you going to do?' he asked.

'What can I do?' moaned Fursey. 'No religious settlement will admit me with the reputation I've acquired.'

'The world is a fine broad place,' said the Devil.

'What is there in it?' asked the ex-monk. 'I looked at it long ago and left it.'

'There are women, riches, fame and sometimes happiness.'

Fursey raised his voice in a howl. 'Are they there for a white-haired old man with a broken hip?'

'I'm sorry about the hip,' said the Devil. 'I assure you there was no personal ill-feeling.'

'Have you not shown me such numbers of luscious and agreeable females that henceforth all women that I shall meet, must seem to me hideous and in the highest degree undesirable? What are the little wealth and distinction that must be wrested from the world, to me who have rejected showers of gold and the thrones of kings? Demon, you have undone me.'

Lucifer regarded him not unsympathetically.

'You should have come over to my side in the beginning,' he said. 'I'd have made you abbot of that place, and we'd have wrecked it together.'

The ex-monk emitted a dolorous moan.

'Give over this unmanly plaining,' said the Devil with some impatience, but Fursey's only answer was: 'What will become of me? What will become of me?'

'To live, a human being must eat,' remarked the Devil sagely. 'The best thing you can do is to go down to the city of Cashel and there secure for yourself employment suitable for you having regard to your age, sex, physique, education, normal occupation, place of residence and family circumstances.'

'I'll have to go to Cashel anyway,' replied Fursey. 'It's the only place this road leads to.'

'Cashel is a fine big city,' said the Devil meditatively. 'It has a hundred and twenty-two wattled huts as well as the King's House and the new thatched palace the Bishop has built for himself. You'd be assured of employment in such a teeming centre of population.'

'The trouble is that I'm not much good at anything except washing and paring edible roots,' replied Fursey. 'They never trained me to anything else.'

'Nonsense,' said the Devil encouragingly. 'Surely a man of your ability could milk a cow without pulling the teats off her.'

'I suppose so,' said Fursey without much conviction.

'Well, come on,' said the Archfiend. 'What are we waiting for?'

'I trust that you are not coming with me?' said Brother Fursey, his voice betraying some anxiety. 'I'd prefer you wouldn't, if you don't mind.'

'I have no choice,' said the Devil. 'As you yourself indicated just now, Cashel is the only place to which this road leads. So of necessity myself and the boys will bear you company. They're waiting below around the bend of the road, a whole acre of them, an acre of the choicest and most variegated demons that have ever been brought together in this holy land of Ireland. You will travel in style, with an entourage the Emperor of Constantinople cannot boast of. Besides, I have a little business in Cashel. An acquaintance of mine is being subjected to ill-treatment in that city, and I must see if something cannot be done to alleviate her distress. She's a very fine old lady. Fifty years ago there wasn't a handsomer woman in the territory. She's a little broken in the wind now, I'll admit, and somewhat spavined. You must make her acquaintance, my dear Fursey. I have no doubt but that the two of you will find that you have much in common.'

The ex-monk groaned as he placed his crutches beneath his aching armpits and painfully made his way to the road, while the Devil strolled beside him discoursing affably on the beauty of the countryside, the gentle greenness of field and tree, the flaming yellow gorse and the hawthorn in pink and white blossom. As they walked along the crooked road towards the bend where it curled over the hill, the vast sky, woolly with cloud, shed its mild sunlight down upon them.

'It's the first day of May,' said the Devil. 'I must admit that it's good to be alive.'

He was silent for a moment, listening to the stumping and grinding of Fursey's crutches on the stony road and the heavy breathing of the ex-monk who was inexperienced in such work. Then his face darkened.

'The old lady is being most foully ill-treated,' he said, 'by a villainous oaf of a bishop, a most uninviting fellow, gaunt and hungry-looking, with a smell of grave-mould off his breath that would turn your stomach. I don't fancy him at all. Himself and the King are intent on burning her as a witch. Did you ever hear the like?' said the Devil, and a hard note crept into his voice. 'If there's one thing I can't stand,' he said, 'it's superstition.'

Chapter 11

On a morning of sprightly sunshine and breeze a friar of huge stature came along the southern road towards Cashel. The dust that powdered his sandals and robe indicated that he had come a long way. He had a mop of wiry ginger hair, which seemed pale in contrast to the fiery red of his face. Indeed, only for his dress, which proclaimed him a man of God, the flaming hue of his countenance and his nose blossoming in the centre of it, might have led one to believe that he was addicted to the pleasures of the table and to the sorry joy that is derived from the consumption of strong drink. It would have been an unjust judgment; for the mighty fires that raged in Father Furiosus proceeded from love of God and the desire to smite at Evil wherever it might raise its ugly head. He was a man of powerful frame; and you had but to observe the great knotted fist clutching a heavy blackthorn stick, to have it borne in powerfully upon you that the Church Militant was no empty phrase.

At the wicker gate in the palisade he brushed aside the guard who diffidently enquired his name and business, and proceeded on his way without deigning to reply; but he had only advanced a few paces into the city when a rabble of dogs came tumbling from the alleys and doorways, and precipitated themselves in his direction, snarling hideously. Scrubby and raffish curs who were investigating distant rubbish heaps, hearing the din that betokened a stranger within the gates, immediately abandoned their researches and came tearing towards him with bared fangs. The guard at the gate and those citizens who were in the immediate vicinity, hurriedly took refuge in the neighbouring cabins, from which they peered in morbid expectancy of seeing the newcomer torn to pieces. But the older and more case-hardened canines pulled up suddenly in full career, for a second glance at the broad-shouldered friar lightly swinging his blackthorn stick as he strode confidently on his way, seemed to persuade them that they had misconstrued the situation. They circled him once or twice and grudgingly wagged their tails as if to convince him that their actions had been motivated merely by friendly curiosity; but a few of the younger and less experienced dogs came within his reach growling fiercely, until the friar, without pausing in his stride, with a few deft backhanders of his blackthorn, scattered them in all directions yowling piteously.

As Father Furiosus made his way among the hundred-and-twenty huts that constituted the city, he noted appreciatively the signs of prosperity and happiness on every side of him, the peat smoke billowing from the doorways of the cabins, the crowing of the city's cocks and the tuneful grunting of its pigs. In a couple of minutes he had traversed the settlement and found himself at the northern gate. Here he paused and raised his finger to indicate to the armed guard that he wished to converse with him. The soldier came running to his side, bowing abjectly.

'Tell me, fellow,' said the friar, nodding towards a fine new building which stood on a slight eminence, 'is that the palace of your wise and enlightened monarch, the mighty Cormac Silkenbeard?'

'Oh no, sir,' replied the solider, 'may it please your reverence, that's the new palace which good Bishop Flanagan has built for himself.'

Father Furiosus turned to admire the edifice. It was a building of generous proportions, thatched with the best of seasoned reeds and fronted by a pair of bronze doors so wide that four churchmen could walk through abreast without undue difficulty.

'It actually has what they call an "upstairs",' volunteered the soldier with considerable awe in his voice, 'the first "upstairs" that was ever in Ireland. It means, as it were, that there are two houses on top of one another. There are rooms up there in the air where you can walk about if you want to.'

'Dear me,' said the friar sententiously. 'One of these days science will certainly over-reach itself. And does not certain danger attend the ascent?'

'They say not, your Holiness,' replied the soldier. 'The Bishop does have a class of ladder of the finest polished elm-wood, which brings you to the "upstairs" through a hole in the roof.'

'It's a fine building,' said the friar, adding thoughtlessly: 'It must have cost a power of wealth to build.'

'Yes,' said the soldier with a slight sigh.

The friar turned and indicated a large building at some distance. 'And I suppose that's the King's House?'

'It is,' replied the soldier.

'That's all, my man,' said the friar, dismissing his informant, who with a grovelling bow ran back to his post.

For a moment or two Father Furiosus contemplated the King's House, its thatch decayed and diseased, and one of its walls supported by a manure heap. He smiled slightly, then he turned his steps to the incline which led to the Bishop's Palace, reflecting as he went that it was well to assert at all times and in all things the superiority of the Church to the State.

The great bronze doors of the Palace were opened by an Anglo-Saxon slave boy, who on hearing the friar's name and condition, ushered him into a spacious hall strewn with sweet-smelling rushes. The Bishop, he explained, was out in the stockyard at the back of the palace inspecting the episcopal herds, but would be informed at once of the friar's arrival.

Father Furiosus had not long to wait before the lean figure of the Bishop slid through a doorway, and advancing noiselessly across the hall, held out his hand for his visitor to kiss. When the friar arose from his knees he was graciously waved to a seat on a bench that ran along the wall. After the exchange of the usual civilities about the weather, the Bishop politely enquired whether the friar had lunched.

'Indeed, no,' replied Father Furiosus with a sigh that seemed to come from the hollow depths of his stomach. 'I have but even now arrived in your splendid and interesting city.'

'Then you must lunch with me,' said the Bishop. 'I am about to partake of my mid-day collation. I keep but a poor table: perhaps that is fitting in a man of God. I trust that you will honour me by sharing my humble meal.'

Father Furiosus protested that food was a thing to which he seldom gave a thought, but he arose with alacrity and followed the Bishop into an inner room. They seated themselves, and at a command from the Bishop discreet serving-men placed before them two quart-pots of ale and a jelly of smelts.

'I trust that you have at least breakfasted,' said the Bishop.

'I did,' replied the friar, 'but sparingly. In a cave on the road about ten miles to the south there lives a gentle anchorite with whom I stopped to exchange the time of day. We passed a pleasant hour in godly conversation. He pressed me to partake of a couple of his crusts and obligingly smashed them for me with his mallet.'

'It's all very well for the anchorites,' said the Bishop. 'They use up none of their energies sitting at the mouths of their caves all day, but a man like yourself who has to be about God's work, needs more solid sustenance. Eat up, there is a second course. A dish of lampreys is to follow.'

The grateful friar needed no second invitation. As they ate and drank in silence, Father Furiosus was enabled to study Bishop Flanagan, whose reputation as a man of God was only second to his own.

Those who did not like the Bishop, whispered of him that he was a man from whom every graceful attribute seemed to have been withheld by Nature. He was spare and stringy, and his Adam's apple was in constant motion in his scraggy throat. His underlip was loose and twitched as he looked at you, but it was not from nervousness, for the way he held his head and the unrelenting gaze of his eyes close placed above the long thin nose, betokened his pride in his exalted rank and his determination to exact from all the respect which was his due. The odour of sanctity was clearly discernible from his breath and person.

When the dish of lampreys had been carried in by two undersized serfs the Bishop replenished his ale-pot and leaned across the table towards the friar.

'Father Furiosus,' he said, 'I want you to know how honoured I am to have under my roof-tree a man of your great reputation and sanctity.'

The face of Father Furiosus clouded, as it always did when he

heard himself praised. It came to him that he should not have
drunk his second quart of ale so rapidly, for there was a tear in his
eye for which he could not account. However, he bent towards the
Bishop and answered huskily:

'Please don't say that, your lordship. I know that I have quite
unworthily acquired such a reputation, but it never fails to grieve
me to hear such sentiments expressed. I am at once overwhelmed
with the consciousness that there does not walk the roads of Ireland
a more depraved sinner than myself.'

'Tut, tut,' said the Bishop, 'how can you say that?'

'Listen,' said the friar vehemently, clutching Bishop Flanagan's
arm. 'When I was young I led a most wicked and dissolute life. I
blasphemed God and cursed my parents, and gave myself over to
every infamy. I was a wrestler at the court of the King of Thomond.
I rejoiced in circuses and the godless company of acrobats. Thank
God, I kept myself free from the taint of women; but in all else I
was a lost soul. I was a gambler, a drunkard and a singer of songs. I
rejoiced in poetry. But on the day of my greatest triumph when I
broke the back of Torgall the Dane, God spoke to me, and I heard
Him even above the applause of that wild court. "Vanity of
vanities," He said, "and all in vanity." I heard Him, but I heeded
Him not. But that evening when the moon was out I was approached
by a lively and engaging female with an invitation to take a walk
with her along a country road. By ourselves actually, and by
moonlight! Then did I know indeed that I was trembling on the
brink of Hell, and I fled from that court, first to the hills, and then
to the monastery at Glendaloch. But you probably know the rest.'

The friar flung his great bulk back into his chair despondently.

'You didn't stay,' said the Bishop gently.

'They wouldn't keep me,' said the friar. 'A little dispute with the
cook about the porridge being cold one morning. Unfortunately I
crippled him.'

'It was a pity,' said the Bishop.

'It was the same in every monastery I entered,' continued Father
Furiosus gloomily. 'My ungovernable temper was my ruin. In
Bangor I deprived the doorkeeper of the one eye he had, and I
killed a scullion in Clonfert. I pleaded with the Abbot that his skull

was thin, but they turned me out.'

The friar seemed sunk in intolerable dolour until the Bishop replenished his tankard.

'God's ways are not our ways,' said Bishop Flanagan, 'perhaps it was for the best. See all the good that you have been enabled to do.'

'Yes,' said Father Furiosus, rousing himself to drink deeply. 'I became a wandering friar, and as God has given me a spirit that fears neither man, dog nor devil, I have perhaps done some little good. I make my way from settlement to settlement wherever I think my services may be needed, and I assure you it is a sturdy demon or necromancer that can stand against me. I have become expert in demonology and in detecting the darker acts of sorcery. On my way from town to town I clear the lovers from the ditches and the doorways, but that's in the nature of a sideline.'

'Nevertheless, even if it be but a sideline, you have done a man's part in preventing the hateful passion of love from spreading throughout this land.'

'I have a strong arm, thank God,' said the friar.

'Where have you come from now?' asked the Bishop.

'From the town of Cork,' replied the friar.

'Business, I suppose?'

'Yes,' said the friar, 'a bad case of werewolves. Some thirty citizens had disappeared leaving no evidence of whither they might have betaken themselves. A heap of skeletons, picked clean of flesh, was found in the backyard of a town councillor. This, as you may imagine, gave rise to suspicion, and I had him watched. It transpired that three town councillors were involved. Every evening at sundown the spirit of the wolf took possession of them, and they repaired to the forest. They were small, paunchy men, and to see them coursing through the woods, naked and on all fours, was a remarkable sight.'

'It must have been,' remarked the Bishop. 'What did you do with them eventually?'

'We hunted them with hounds and spearmen, and deprived them of their lives,' replied Father Furiosus gloomily. 'It's the only thing to do with a werewolf.'

'Is there no way,' asked the Bishop, 'whereby a werewolf may be detected in the early stages of his affliction?'

'Yes,' replied the friar, 'when a man first becomes a werewolf, he often betrays himself by going out and fighting with all the town dogs. I don't know if that perhaps happened before my arrival. The people of Cork are singularly uncouth, and such behaviour might not have been deemed in any way extraordinary.'

The Bishop arose from the table and led the way back to the hall.

'I hope,' he said, 'you will be able to stay a couple of days in Cashel. We have need of your services here.'

'I was on my way to Clonmacnoise,' replied the friar, 'which, I hear, is much abused by disembodied spirits and satanic creatures of the craftier sort, and I had looked forward to greeting again an old fellow-wrestler at the Thomond Court, a Father Sampson, who is now a monk in that monastery; but hearing that Cashel was enduring sundry molestations and the worst horrors of witchcraft, I turned aside to place my experience in such matters at your lordship's disposal. In what way are you troubled here in Cashel? Is it by wily imps teasing the besotted natives or have strange and terrible happenings come about through the detestable workings of a witch? Tell me all. Do not fear that your lordship will alarm me. I am hardened by many a fight with the Evil One and by many a lonely midnight prayer.'

'I am walking over to the King's House,' said the Bishop. 'If you will accompany me, I shall relate to you the story of our afflictions.'

They passed out through the bronze doors, out into the pleasant sunlight. As they walked down the hill towards the litter of huts, groups of townspeople, when they saw the Bishop, removed their hats and even fell on their knees, while little children ceased their play and crept out of sight.

'You must know,' began Bishop Flanagan, 'that our minds have recently been exercised by certain untoward happenings which gave rise to the conviction that there were sorcerers in the neighbourhood. For many nights King Cormac Silkenbeard had been deprived of his rest by the hideous caterwauling of a platoon of cats, who mustered on the roofs surrounding the royal dwelling, and there raised a clamour so uncouth and deformed that it was speedily doubted whether their behaviour did not proceed from the operation of a powerful spell. On the fourth night, King Cormac told me, he had drunken deeply of brown ale in an endeavour to forget his cares; and, enraged by the persistence of the persecution to which he was being subjected, he seized his sword and rushed out into the garden in his night attire. To his horror he beheld several felines engaged in what appeared to be animated conversation, while on the wall sat a brindled tom of monstrous size with gleaming eyes and large white eyeballs, who grinned sarcastically at the King and waved his paw in derision. There could be no further doubt but that these were enchanted cats; and on my advice, two conjurors and a ventriloquist who had come to the town for the annual fair, were immediately seized. As they persisted obstinately in denial, they were put to the question.'

'With favourable results?' asked the friar, whose professional interest was aroused.

'Yes,' said the Bishop with satisfaction. 'After three days' application of the best available monkish tortures, they agreed to admit anything. Further proof of their guilt was afforded by the fact that no sooner had they been apprehended by the King's men, than the enchanted cats ceased to trouble the royal repose.'

Father Furiosus nodded approvingly. 'It's a well-known fact,' he said, 'attested by all the Fathers of the Church, that when the officers of justice lay their hands upon a sorcerer, he is at that moment bereft of his execrable powers.'

'Unfortunately,' said the Bishop, 'the two conjurors and the ventriloquist, having been crippled in the course of the judicial examination, had to be carried to the stake. The burning was a colourful ceremony, but I should have wished that they could have walked.'

'It's more impressive certainly,' agreed the friar.

The Bishop's face darkened, and his underlip twitched alarmingly.

'But evil powers did not cease to trouble us,' he said. 'Not long afterwards, the city was subjected to a plague of fleas whose inordinate fierceness and voracity far exceeded the experience of the oldest inhabitant. They appeared to make a particular set on me and on the canons of the Chapter; and this impiety, together with their exceeding briskness in evading capture, convinced me that their activities were not of nature, but proceeded from the damned art of witchcraft.'

Father Furiosus nodded gravely while the Bishop scratched his buttock reminiscently.

'I had two mathematicians burnt,' continued the Bishop, 'but it did little to abate this strange and grievous vexation. Next, an army of mice started to march up and down the streets of the town in an orderly company without stragglers. You can imagine our alarm, for we knew that such an extraordinary purposeful march could not but presage evil. Such persistent persecution, we felt, could only be the result of spells of peculiar malignancy. We were concerting further measures when once more the King was struck at, this time through the medium of enchanted beer. His secretary set down in writing an exact record of the King's experiences, and it is at present in my possession. King Cormac one evening after supper innocently consumed six quarts of a particularly delectable ale, and was at once filled with vague and disagreeable sensations. He sat for a long while gnawing his beard while his terrified servants hurried over to my palace in search of spiritual aid. When I arrived with my book of exorcisms the unfortunate man had begun to laugh and frolic, and was shouting the most villainous and the lewdest language that ever man heard. Under exhortation his sportiveness abated; he sunk down in a swoon of gladness and lay a great while like as he had been dead. His limbs being rendered unserviceable by the malignant potency of the spell, he had to be carried to his couch by six servitors, where he lay unconscious while a choir of monks in the corner of the room chanted throughout the night the psalm, "*Ad Deum cum tribubarer*". Under this treatment he recovered towards morning; but marvellous to relate, remembered nought of his frenzy.'

Father Furiosus shook his head gravely. 'Faith,' he said, 'is the best buckler against such invasions. Is King Cormac perhaps a man in his mode of life indifferent to heavenly things, and careless of the well-being of the Church? Does he contribute regularly to the support of his pastors?'

'Indeed, yes,' said the Bishop, 'he is a faithful son of the Church, who never fails to enrich with a tithe of one-third of the spoils of war the abbeys and religious settlements of his kingdom, so that they have grown to an exceeding sleekness, reflecting the highest credit on him.'

'He seems to be a right and proper prince,' said Furiosus meditatively. 'It would appear that we must look elsewhere for the cause of these stubborn manifestations. I am not inclined to believe that they proceed from the malice of demons: firstly, because they are not in character; and secondly, because I have information that all the demons in Hell are at present at Clonmacnoise, where some weeks ago they succeeded in penetrating the defences raised by the prayers of the blessed Kieran, and where they are exercising every species of wile and violence to win the good monks from their duty. Are there any other ventriloquists, mathematicians, acrobats, charmers or reciters of poetry in the neighbourhood? If you wish I will institute an inquisition of likely persons. As you know, I am licensed by the Synod of Kells to search for conjurors.'

'No,' said the Bishop, who had been waiting impatiently for the friar to have done, 'they have all fled. But,' and the Bishop's underlip vibrated with satisfaction, 'I believe I have in custody the *fons et origo* of this dismal and abhorred business.'

'Indeed,' said the friar, somewhat crestfallen.

'Yes,' said Bishop Flanagan, 'four days ago the sexton of Kilcock Churchyard, a worthy fellow, came to me and laid information denouncing as a witch an impoverished hag of advanced age, known locally as The Gray Mare, who resides within a stone's throw of the sexton's house. He had frequently seen her at night out on the hillside struggling with a cat; and recently, while he was watching her over the fence which separates their land, her body changed, horns appeared on her head, and she went on all fours like an animal. He has also, he avers, seen her changed into a horse and walking on her hindlegs; but it was not until last week that his suspicions were really aroused by the sight of her astride a broomstick, on which she ambled and galloped through the air, flying by his house with such velocity that the wind of her passing did raise much of the thatch from his roof.'

'Hm,' said Father Furiosus, 'it has all the signs of a bad case of sorcery. I trust there is no reason to suspect that the sexton in laying the charge was actuated by malice?'

'Well,' admitted the Bishop somewhat reluctantly, 'I understand that there is some dispute between the two, something about a boundary fence and a trespassing goat; but the sexton is a worthy man, and he was very positive in his accusations.'

'How did you proceed?'

'We seized the witch and formally accused her of being a companion of hellhounds, a caller and a conjuror of wicked and damned spirits.'

'How did she react to these charges?'

'She at once lodged a countercharge against the sexton, accusing him of being a damnifying sorcerer himself; but, at his own request, his legs were examined by the canons of the Chapter, and his knees being found horny with frequent praying, he was immediately acquitted.'

'Yes,' said the friar, stroking his red jowl thoughtfully, 'things look bad for this woman you call The Gray Mare. Did you put her to the torture?'

'No,' said the Bishop regretfully. 'She is old and frail, so that we were in fear lest she should die before the day appointed for her burning. We did, however, walk her up and down for three days in the approved manner, thus depriving her of sleep and rest; and in relays we continuously questioned her, but it was of little avail. Under this treatment she admits everything we suggest, but no sooner is she permitted to sit down than she speedily retracts it all. Indeed, she is a witch full of craftiness and wile.' The Bishop's eye gleamed fanatically, and his voice became shrill. The friar watched the jerking underlip fascinated.

'But we will tie her to a strong stake of faggots,' said the Bishop, his voice rising almost to a scream, 'and we will burn her, as is right; and from her mouth will be seen to issue a swarm of sorceries and lies and other hideous devilries.'

Father Furiosus waited respectfully for the Bishop's anger to abate before he again spoke.

'When is the burning?' he asked.

The Bishop's face darkened.

'I regret to say that the date is not yet fixed. Some of the canons of the Chapter, quite foolishly it seems to me, still entertain doubt as to her guilt. They seem to be not altogether convinced of the sexton's bona fides on account of the dispute about the trespassing goat. So I have reluctantly consented that one more trial be made of her. We are going to swim her this afternoon in a pool in the River Suir two miles from the town.'

'An excellent test approved by every writer on the subject,' said the friar, rubbing his large red fists with satisfaction. 'If the water rejects her; that is, if she floats, it is sure proof that she is a witch. If she sinks, God has plainly manifested that she is innocent.'

'You wouldn't be so punctilious about the fine points of the matter,' said the Bishop sourly, 'if you had been subjected to the attentions of a myriad of enchanted fleas of a dexterity and agility altogether out of the course of nature. However, here we are at the house of the noble Cormac Silkenbeard.'

The Bishop knocked at the door with his pastoral staff. It was opened at once by a serving-boy whose face fell at sight of the churchman.

'Is your royal master within?' enquired Bishop Flanagan.

The youth did not reply, but seemed to be experiencing the liveliest consternation.

The Bishop gave him a sharp look and pushed by him into the royal kitchen. Father Furiosus followed.

It was a spacious room furnished with several spits and a shining array of bronze vessels; but what riveted the friar's gaze was the extraordinary sight of an aged gentleman, apparently naked, sitting bolt upright in a species of ornamental bath set in the centre of the earthen floor. The tub was so short that the old gentleman had of necessity his knees drawn up to his chin. An immense silky grey beard concealed most of his person. He was chortling, evidently in huge enjoyment of a stream of warm water which a serving-man poured from a watering-can on to his bald head. His back was to the door, so that the first indication he had of the presence of visitors was when the Bishop accosted him with a voice of thunder.

'What is this I see?' demanded Bishop Flanagan, 'in the Royal

House of Cashel, a scene reminiscent of the worst excesses of the Roman Empire!'

The serving-men retreated hurriedly from the room, and a blush of shame could be seen creeping down the back of the monarch.

'Get out of that at once,' commanded the Bishop harshly.

'I can't,' said the King feebly. 'I'm jammed. It's rather short, and I do have to be lifted out.'

'This is a grievous sight,' continued the Bishop harshly. 'I bring to visit you a stranger, a powerful man of God. I tell him the King of Cashel is a man of beautiful thoughts and pregnant principles, and what does he see in the Royal House — every evidence of lax, unrestrained and vicious living.'

The King's hand shook as he made a weak attempt to spread his beard so as to cover as much of his naked chest as possible.

'Where did you get that device of the devil?' demanded the Bishop.

'It was sold to me by a travelling salesman from the Eastern World,' replied the monarch humbly. 'He had a fine share of talk, and he tempted me by urging that all the best people in the Byzantine Empire have them installed.'

'Yes,' thundered the Bishop. 'And where is the Byzantine Empire now? Rotten with heresies! You didn't think of that?'

'No,' replied Cormac, 'I didn't think of that. I'm only a poor king,' he added plaintively, 'broken with the years and surrounded by damnifying witches trying to bring about my final undoing.'

'The first thing is to remove you from that slough of sin,' said Bishop Flanagan. 'Father Furiosus, maybe you can be of use here.'

'Certainly,' said the sturdy friar, rolling back his sleeves. He grasped Cormac under the armpits and lifted him without difficulty from the bath. He held the king in the air for a few moments expecting him to stretch out his legs and stand, but Cormac kept his knees up to his chin, his legs still cramped by the sudden fright induced by the arrival of the Bishop. The friar placed him gently in a sitting position on the floor. Bishop Flanagan kept his eyes modestly averted until a towel had been draped around the monarch.

'I cannot understand,' commented the Bishop, 'how a man of your upbringing, education and position can be unaware of the heinousness of such conduct. It was in the effeminate steam of the bath-house that the strength and resolution of Rome evaporated, leaving her a prey to the barbarian. God has made the human body to exude natural oils and vapours, and you would defy the divine economy and undo His work by impiously washing them off. I tremble for your immortal soul, Cormac. Indeed, I do not know if anything less than excommunication will meet the case.'

At the sound of the dread word King Cormac was gripped by a fit of trembling.

'I confess my sin,' he said abjectly. 'Perhaps a small offering to the Church, maybe two bullocks —?'

'Forgiveness is not a commodity that can be bought,' replied the Bishop haughtily. 'Nor is it wise for a sinner to be niggardly with God.'

The King groaned. '*Four* bullocks,' he suggested. 'They will be driven over to your stockade before sundown.'

'Well,' said Bishop Flanagan, 'I don't wish to be hard on you, particularly as you have recently been subjected to operations of a magical character far from pleasant. I shall send over the absolution when the four bullocks are delivered. You must surrender the bath, of course, that we may burn it with due ceremony.'

'I am most willing to follow any course your Holiness indicates,' replied King Cormac humbly. 'May I now be permitted to resume my clothing? This earthen floor is grievously chilly and unfriendly to the buttocks.'

'Yes,' said Bishop Flanagan, 'and when that office is performed, you may join us in the sun-room.'

The Bishop led the way from the kitchen, down a passage, and through several spacious apartments. He and Furiosus met nobody. This very much surprised the friar, who had expected to see the entire personnel thronging around the Bishop to receive his blessing and to beg the favour of kissing the good man's hand; but instead, Furiosus was conscious of gently closing doors and dim footfalls, as if the inmates were most anxious to keep out of sight. There was silence in every corner of the Royal House, but it was not the silence of a deserted place; it was the tingling stillness in which one feels that behind every door human beings are standing motionless, almost afraid to breathe. Father Furiosus shook his red mane angrily. He was a straightforward, downright man; and these fancies disturbed him.

On the floor of the sun-room sat two of King Cormac's daughters. The younger was stringing a set of multi-coloured beads, and the stones, jasper, amethyst and cornelian, lay heaped in her lap. Her sister had let down her hair. It was of the colour of gorse and lay tumbled in brilliant profusion over her shoulders. Squatting back daintily on her slender haunches, she was combing it with long, rhythmic strokes. Bishop Flanagan started on seeing the two girls, and instinctively averted his eyes; but Father Furiosus, who had as much sense of beauty as one of the royal bullocks that was shortly to change its allegiance, stared stolidly at the spectacle.

An important feminine conversation was in progress.

'You glanced at him,' giggled the girl who was stringing the beads.

'I did not,' replied her sister, tossing back her yellow head.

'I tell you I saw you. You glanced across when you thought he wasn't looking.'

'And I tell you again that I didn't.'

The dialogue lost itself in a series of titters, which terminated abruptly when Golden Head, glancing around, caught sight of the Bishop and the friar standing in the doorway. Her face grew scarlet. She dropped the comb and, springing to her feet, bundled her hair into a silken cap, which she hurriedly pulled down over her ears. Her sister, no less alarmed, grabbed her handful of stones, dropping one or two in her haste; and rose to her feet. They curtsied deeply as Bishop Flanagan walked into the room. He gave them a curt nod, and then seemed to lose himself in thought until an irregular lump of amethyst gave him a purple wink from the floor. He touched it with his foot.

'You've dropped one of your baubles,' he said harshly.

The girl stooped hastily to pick it up, and she and her sister slipped unobtrusively from the room. The Bishop took four paces across to the wall and then turned to gaze gravely at Father Furiosus.

'This is serious,' he said at length.

The friar looked at him enquiringly.

The Bishop's eyes had narrowed, and his Adam's apple was in motion in his throat.

'You heard what they were talking about?' he asked darkly.

'No,' replied the friar.

'Men!' said the Bishop. He seated himself carefully, keeping his eyes fixed on Father Furiosus, who sat down too and waited for enlightenment.

Bishop Flanagan's brow was furrowed, and his face had the set expression of a shepherd who discerns in a thicket the grey snout of a wolf. His grip tightened on his pastoral staff. He rose to his feet again and began to walk to and fro.

'I must talk to their father,' he said weightedly. 'It's high time those girls were married or in a cloister. The eldest is seventeen.'

Father Furiosus grappled with the problem.

'Do you think they'd make good nuns?' he asked at length.

'I do not,' said the Bishop. 'Marriage is the only thing for it. Fortunately, I know of several elderly, stolid farmers with some share of the world's goods. I'll make a list of four or five, and the girls can have their choice. Women are feather-brained creatures and are apt to make difficulties unless they are allowed the exercise of a choice. I'm sure I don't know why, but it's an undeniable fact.'

Furiosus sat back lost in admiration of his companion's organising ability.

The Bishop gave vent to a long-drawn sigh.

'Did it ever occur to you to wonder why God created women?' he asked. 'It's the one thing that tempts me at times to doubt His infinite goodness and wisdom.'

The friar shrugged his shoulders and exhaled noisily to demonstrate that this was a problem far beyond his limited perceptions.

'It's a thing that I've long since given up trying to understand,' he replied. 'I assume with a blind faith that they are in the world for the trial and affliction of man, that his entry into another sphere may be the more glorious for the temptations that he has successfully withstood in this.'

'It was a hard measure,' muttered the Bishop. 'God's hand was heavy on mankind the day that He created woman.'

'Are you afflicted much by the antics of women in this neighbour-hood?' enquired Furiosus politely.

'The situation was bad when I came here first,' said the Bishop, 'but I cleaned up the city pretty quickly. Why, it was actually the practice of merchants to display articles of women's underwear on their stalls during the monthly fairs, to the grave detriment of morals.'

'That was bad,' said the friar. 'Some of these merchants have no care that such garments powerfully affect youth, giving rise to unmentionable thoughts and desires.'

'Exactly,' said the Bishop. 'However, I organised the pious, God-fearing women of the settlement. They went in a body to the merchants and threatened to withdraw their custom unless such raiment was kept under cover and not displayed before the gaze of men.'

'Excellent,' said the friar.

'Love-making was also rife, but the threat of ecclesiastical censure generally proved sufficient.'

'I find a blackthorn stick and a stout arm most effective,' said Father Furiosus diffidently; 'but then I am not favoured with your lordship's eloquence and your powers of excommunication.'

'In extreme cases of failure to conform, in this as in other things, I have recourse to the civil authority, who deprives the offender of his livelihood,' replied the Bishop. 'I'm proud to say that there isn't in all the land a cleaner or more God-fearing diocese than this.'

'I can well believe you,' said the friar.

The two men of God sat for a little while in silence. The friar's gaze wandered around the room. Beneath one of the benches lay a couple of beads from a necklace, and in the centre of the floor were the broken fragments of a comb on which the Bishop had trodden in his striding to and fro. It was a pleasant three-walled room. The fourth side was open to a tiny garden of grass and half-a-dozen apple trees. The room was built facing south so that full advantage might be taken of the sunlight, with which it was now agreeably flooded. The furniture was simple, a few benches and stools. There were no hangings to be injured by rain or rough weather. It was only when the skies were mild that the room was used at all. The friar noticed these things and listened dreamily to the birds that hopped from branch to branch of the apple trees, letting fall their little tuneful notes and whistlings. A wagtail fluttered through the air and alighted at the Bishop's feet.

'Birds,' said the Bishop suddenly.

'Yes, your lordship,' said Father Furiosus, arousing himself from his thoughts.

'Next to women,' said Bishop Flanagan, 'there is nothing more productive of evil than birds.'

'Indeed,' said the friar, rather surprised. 'I'm rather fond of them.'

Bishop Flanagan bent a disapproving gaze upon his companion. 'Then you are wrong,' he said roughly. 'Birds are inciters to laziness and easy living. They work not, neither do they spin. Their silly singing is a distraction to good men at their prayers and meditations. The very waywardness of birds is an encouragement to man to take pleasure in the deceitful beauty of this world instead of fastening his gaze upon his heavenly home. I'm surprised at you, Father Furiosus. I tell you we can never be too much on our guard against these things that appeal to our senses. Besotted poets are always bleating about birds and bird-song. Isn't that enough?'

'I suppose you're right,' agreed the friar grudgingly.

'Of course I'm right,' replied the Bishop severely. 'I've had every tree around my palace cut down. Until I did so, I had no peace from their incessant chirruping.'

The wagtail took a little run of half-a-dozen steps, wagged his tail up and down for a second or two, then raised it almost vertically, disclosing to the Bishop's gaze a little feathered backside. He cocked his eye as if to see how the Bishop was taking it, before fluttering away into the trees.

Bishop Flanagan's face grew red. 'Did you see that?' he said savagely. 'Deliberate disrespect for a Prince of the Church! Maybe now you'll believe in the depravity of birds.'

Before Father Furiosus could think of an answer King Cormac entered the room. Now that he was clothed in his royal robes of saffron and blue he appeared to greater advantage. The golden circlet of Cashel environed his bald head, and he carried himself with greater assurance, almost as if he and the Bishop were equals. He was not a tall man: in fact he was stumpy; but he was broad-shouldered and sturdy, and he held himself well for his age. One hand rested on the handle of a short iron sword strapped to his side, while the other played in and out of his immense snowy beard. Sometimes he fingered the silky tip at waist level; at other times, when he fondled his chin, his hand and arm were lost to sight as far as the elbow.

'God save all here,' said the King courteously.

'God save you kindly,' answered the two ecclesiastics.

Cormac dropped on one knee and kissed the Bishop's ring.

'When we met previously this morning,' said the Bishop, 'the occasion did not seem to me suitable for the formal introduction of Father Furiosus, who, as a scarifier of conjurors and demons, is at the summit of his profession.'

Cormac withdrew his hand from his beard and held it out to the friar, who gripped it in his huge freckled fist.

'It's an honour,' murmured the King; and going to the door he clapped his hands. Four slaves entered at once, bearing three foaming pots of mead and a reserve basin lest anyone should crave a second helping. The Bishop and the friar immediately addressed themselves to the consumption of this delectable beverage. By the time each had emptied his second pot the conversation had become general. The final arrangements for the witch-dipping, which was the business that had brought the Bishop to the Royal House, were speedily disposed of. Father Furiosus related as an item of gossip how in the recent war in the east the King of Hungary had put into the field a battalion of vampires recruited in his Transyllvanian dominions. They had wrought great havoc among the Byzantine troops in the mountainous Danube country, until the Emperor formed a special shock brigade armed with small wooden crosses, sharpened stakes and mallets; and sent them into battle with a baggage train composed exclusively of cartloads of garlic. The opposing forces had at first experienced difficulty in making contact with one another, by reason of the marked disinclination of the Imperial troops to fight otherwise than by day, while the unholy legions of Hungary only came out at night. But, God be praised, the warriors of the Christian Emperor had at last prevailed, due to their superior mobility; the vampire soldiery being much encumbered in their forays by the necessity of bringing their coffins with them, in which to bivouac between sunrise and sunset.

The King nodded his head sagely. 'Mobility is of the first importance in mountain warfare,' he said. 'By the way,' he continued, turning to the Bishop, 'has your lordship heard this strange rumour of the motley company that has been seen on the northern road, and which appears to be coming towards Cashel?'

'I have not,' said the Bishop, somewhat nettled that anyone should have news before himself.

'They say that a collection of grotesque animals such as have never before been seen in these parts, is on its way hither. It seems to be some sort of gigantic circus. It is led by a gentleman in black, probably the ringmaster, and by a man in the habit of a monk who proceeds with the aid of crutches.'

'The habit of a monk!' ejaculated Father Furiosus. 'Surely your informant is mistaken. Probably the gentleman referred to is of foreign extraction; and his alien clothing has given rise to the error. No doubt he is the capitalist who finances the undertaking. I have seen such menageries at the great fair at Tara.'

'Circuses are a great occasion of sin,' said Bishop. 'Does rumour report whether there are women travelling with this gang of mountebanks?'

The King coughed diffidently and looked as if he wished he hadn't introduced the subject.

'Well, yes,' he said hesitantly. 'In fact, my informant stated that they were present in large numbers.'

'You're holding something back,' said Bishop Flanagan sternly.

'I don't wish to offend your lordship's ears,' said Cormac, looking rather frightened, 'but it's said that many of the women in the troop are insufficiently clad considering the rigours of this climate; in fact, that many of them have no apparent clothing at all.'

There was silence except for the loud beating of the King's heart. Then the Bishop threw himself back in his chair.

'Stuff and nonsense!' he said. 'Who told you that fantastic story?'

'A travelling gypsy woman who came around to the back door this morning to beg for a bite of bread. She insisted that she had seen the concourse herself.'

'A woman!' Father Furiosus laughed suddenly and relaxed his giant limbs. 'I never knew a lying story that was not traceable to a woman. King Cormac, I'm afraid you're a very gullible man. You'll find that there's nothing more than a band of tinkers with a dancing bear and, maybe, a couple of performing dogs.'

'No doubt, no doubt,' said the King, much relieved at the easing of the tension.

Bishop Flanagan permitted himself a rasping laugh as he bent over to pour the dregs of the mead from the basin into his mug.

'The very idea!' he said. 'Women without clothes in my diocese!'

*   *   *

It was late in the afternoon when a solemn procession of monks and laymen left Cashel by the northern gate and moved slowly along the road towards the bend in the River Suir two miles beyond the town. At the point where the river curved there was a deep pool only a stone's throw from the hut in which The Gray Mare was said to have practised her dark sorceries. The procession was headed by a column of hooded monks walking two by two and chanting hymns of the most doleful character imaginable. The funereal responses to each sombre anthem filled everyone with mournful thoughts of dissolution and doom. The very birds stopped their play-acting in the trees and huddled together to watch the gloomy train of humans who moved slowly forward as if fatalistically impelled, trampling with unnoticing, indifferent feet the wild pansies and primroses and all the tiny flowering things on the grassy edges of the track. The general body of clergy followed, red-faced, burly men with an occasional gaunt ascetic among them. Close behind came the canons of the Chapter, rotund and mostly out of breath. Father Furiosus walked alone, his blackthorn under his arm, seemingly impatient of the slow pace of the procession. Then, preceded by a choir of youthful ecclesiastics singing '*Ecce Sacerdos Magnus*,' came the Bishop, distributing blessings every few yards to the onlookers left and right. A high cart followed, in which sat the notorious Gray Mare, tied hand and foot. The cart was surrounded by twenty-six marching soldiers, the entire armed forces of Cashel. Behind it rode King Cormac in his war chariot; and a long line of similar chariots followed, bearing the great men of his kingdom, famous warriors, rich landowners and the two members of his Civil Service. A large concourse of persons of low birth came after, out-of-step and quite incapable of keeping in rank. The procession tailed off in a horde of children and barking dogs.

The Gray Mare, a very old, spent and decrepit hag, perched high in her cart, seemed to be experiencing a certain feminine pleasure from the fact that she was the centre of attention. She leered at nearly every group of onlookers standing by the roadside, and shouted a greeting, addressing them all as acquaintances, which might perhaps have been excused in her as she was very nearly blind. Those whom she hailed did not at all appreciate her friendliness, but crossed themselves hurriedly and hastened to explain to one another that they had never seen her before in their lives. It was thought very ill of her to display levity in the course of a religious ceremony of such antiquity and importance. It was contrary to all custom: witches and conjurors in such a situation invariably comported themselves with the greatest seriousness. Old men shook their heads. It was a great mistake, they said, not to have put her to the torture. It would have induced in her a frame of mind more in keeping with the occasion. And accompanied by the clangour of the handbells carried by the clergy and the lugubrious chanting of the monks, Church and State in awful solemnity wound their way in a long, thin serpent under the fresh green of the trees, along the stony track, and across the Maytime fields, while the object of it all sat high above them, grinning and cackling half-wittedly, and to all appearance having the time of her life.

The spot appointed for the witch-dipping was at a point where the river curved forming a tranquil backwater. There was an open field capable of accommodating a large number of spectators. The proximity of the thatched cabin where The Gray Mare had lived made the spot selected for her trial peculiarly appropriate. The fields rose from the river's edge to a low line of hill, so that from this point the road ascended and crept over the summit about two hundred yards away, where it was lost to sight.

A crowd of countrypeople had already assembled along the river bank, and as the procession wound into the field, they fell on their knees, bowing their heads to receive the Bishop's blessing. When he had passed, they sprang to their feet and greeted The Gray Mare's cart with catcalls and a shower of sods and stones, most of which struck the surrounding soldiery. When the two horses drawing King Cormac's chariot cantered into the field with the gallant monarch standing erect, his white beard streaming behind him in the breeze, a great shout of welcome went up. While the monks and secular clergy formed themselves into two squares facing one another, a high chair covered with purple and cloth of gold was placed in the centre to accommodate the person of the Bishop. He seated himself, and the canons of the Chapter draped themselves in a semi-circle behind him. A small chair had been set up for the King, and he took his seat surrounded by the officials of his household, his secretary, the commander of his armed forces, the master of the kitchen and the royal doorkeeper. Four slaves stood in readiness to run messages. Some paces away sat the Civil Service on two small stools which they had had the forethought to bring with them. The landowners and the few warriors who had survived the wars of the reign, stood alongside. The general public was kept at a respectful distance, and six of the soldiers guarding The Gray Mare were detached to keep them in order with the butts of their spears. The Gray Mare herself, now that she found herself at the water's edge, seemed to have lost a great deal of her light-heartedness. She sat on the grass muttering to herself and rubbing her wrists and ankles, which had been untied by direction of Father Furiosus. The friar had been authorised to conduct the proceedings in virtue of his long experience of such matters and as a graceful compliment to him as a visitor to the city.

The ceremony began with prayer, at the conclusion of which Bishop Flanagan imparted his blessing to all. Then the elder of the Civil Service arose and read the indictment from a series of wax tablets. These were passed up to him as required by his junior from a heavy box in which they were neatly filed. The Gray Mare was asked whether she pleaded Guilty or Not Guilty, but no answer was forthcoming as she had impiously fallen asleep during the prayers with which the ceremony had opened. All efforts to awake her proved unavailing, and Father Furiosus explained that it was in no way to be deemed obstinacy and held against her, but was no doubt due to the fact that she had not been permitted to sleep during the previous three days and nights while the judicial examination was in progress. A sigh of relief arose from the crowd, who had feared for a moment that she was already dead, thus cheating them of their entertainment. Father Furiosus directed that a plea of Not Guilty should be entered; the Civil Service sharpened a fine stake of wood with his hunting knife and made the entry in a neat hand on a fresh wax tablet. A short argument developed at this point: the Bishop intervening to urge that the silence of the accused should be construed as an admission of her guilt, that the dipping should be abandoned as unnecessary, and The Gray Mare carried back immediately to the town for judicial burning. The Bishop's suggestion found great favour with the crowd, who expressed their agreement at the top of their voices until most of them were hoarse, but Father Furiosus was able to quote numerous passages from the Fathers to prove that his procedure was correct. The Bishop sat back in his chair, an unusual flush in his sallow face. The friar then addressed the crowd and indicated that he would break the back of the next man or woman who impiously interrupted the proceedings. He returned to his place and bowed to Bishop Flanagan, who with a slight movement of his hand directed that the ceremony should continue. The friar, thereupon, delivered an oration on the damnable nature of witchcraft, pointing out that it was laid down by Moses that no witch should be permitted to live. He underlined his discourse with numerous quotations from the Scriptures and from the Fathers of the Church proving the existence of witches and setting out the proper methods for their disposal. He concluded by explaining clearly the nature of the present proceedings, and reminded his audience in forceful words that The Gray Mare was not yet a proven witch. She was merely undergoing trial. They had adopted a sure method of ascertaining whether or not she was guilty, a method proved on countless occasions, a method never known to fail. If, when thrown into the water, the water rejected her; that is, if she floated, it was certain proof that she was a witch, and she would be handed over for burning to the secular arm, as the Church itself never polluted its hands with blood. If, on the other hand, she visibly and truly sank, it was proof of her innocence; and she would be released to return to her home without a stain on her character. The friar concluded his peroration with a stern command to the crowd to maintain order and not become excited. His speech made a powerful impression, and the atmosphere was tense as he turned to supervise the final proceeding.

As it wasn't deemed fair to throw The Gray Mare into the water in her present somnolent condition, she was awakened with difficulty by the judicious prodding of the soldiers' spears. Father Furiosus then ordered that she be stripped to her shift; but while this was under way, an unexpected difficulty arose: it was discovered that she didn't wear one. After much sifting of his memory for a precedent, the friar consented to her being immersed in such clothes as she had on, a careful search having first been made to ensure that she had no heavy stones concealed so as to defeat the ends of justice. Her shoes were removed and her hands and feet tied crossways, the right hand to the left foot and vice versa. During these preparations some of her old spirit seemed to revive, and she laughed immoderately, complaining in a cracked voice that the soldiers were tickling her. Finally a rope was tied around her waist. Two soldiers were given the loose end and instructed to hold it tightly, so as to be able to pull her out again when directed to do so.

At a command from the friar she was lifted by brawny arms, a queer little bundle with her grey hair streaming behind her. On no one of the hundreds of faces that were bent upon her, was there sympathy apparent. Every face expressed the same feelings — loathing and strong religious emotion. As Father Furiosus with sure dramatic instinct delayed the final command, the tension became so palpable as to be almost unbearable. All at once he raised his two arms high above his head. The crowd held its breath.

'Now!' he shouted, bringing his arms suddenly down to his sides. The soldiers swung back and heaved. The crowd drew in their breath with a loud penetrating hiss as The Gray Mare flew through the air, rolling over and over. The Bishop and the King had risen to their feet, and every neck was craned as she struck the surface of the water with a mighty splash. She immediately disappeared from sight.

A disappointed howl arose from the crowd.

'She's sunk!'

Indeed, there didn't seem to be much doubt about it. Father Furiosus counted a hundred. There was still no sign of The Gray Mare.

'Pull her out,' commanded the friar. 'God has clearly demonstrated that she's innocent.'

'Wait,' said the Bishop. 'Give her a bit longer. It's better to make sure.'

Father Furiosus gave him a quick look. 'I'm not going to have murder on my soul,' he said roughly. 'Pull her out.'

The two soldiers bent their weight upon the rope to the accompaniment of hoots and angry shouts from the crowd. She seemed to be a long way down, for there was still no sign of her.

'Pull harder,' shouted the friar savagely, and he gripped the rope himself. The howling of the crowd arose in a crescendo, and they broke their ranks, knocking over the few soldiers who tried to restrain them. Men and women rushed to the river bank, picking up stones as they ran.

'Get back,' shouted the friar furiously, as he strained at the rope.

The Gray Mare's head suddenly broke the surface. Her mouth opened, a stream of water came out, followed by a feeble curse.

At that moment a sudden terrified cry pierced the air.

'Look at the hill!' someone screamed.

So insistent was the cry that everyone turned. About two hundred yards away where the road wound over the hill, stood two figures, one a graceful man clothed in black and the other a monk leaning on a pair of crutches. It was not these two that had caused the alarm, but a motley crowd of dreadful creatures that were topping the rise for hundreds of yards on either side of the road.

Cacodemons, black and grey, lumbered along. Minotaurs, leopards and hippogriffs came into sight peacefully cropping the grass in the neighbouring fields. Centaurs cantered back and forward. A legion of imps came leap-frogging across the rise. Furies and vultures flew from tree to tree. A moving sea of scorpions crept along the shallow ditches, interspersed here and there with a brace of cockatrices or a hippogiraffe.

For one moment the human beings by the river bank stood petrified. Then someone raised a shout:

'The demons from Clonmacnoise!'

Immediate panic ensued. The rope that held The Gray Mare was dropped, and she sank once more to the bottom. Soldiers and people ran blindly in all directions; some in their frenzy were so foolish as to run into the river. Bishop Flanagan was one of the first to fly. He sprang into the royal chariot with such agility and determination that he knocked the unfortunate Cormac out the far side. The Bishop seized the reins and would have left the King behind only for the devotion of two slaves who bundled Cormac back again just as the Bishop made off in crazy career across the fields. Chariots were driven into ditches and gates, and a score of serfs and underlings were trampled underfoot. Father Furiosus made a gallant attempt to stay the panic, until he observed on his left an outflanking movement by a squadron of poltergeists, variegated in hue, but mostly yellow and green; and from seven to nine feet in height. From their drooping shoulders their long arms swung obscenely, the fingers nearly touching the ground. Their faces were creased with unholy smiles. Father Furiosus took one look at this hideous apparition, and jumped into the last chariot. In the space of two minutes there was no one in sight. Even those who had been bruised and wounded by the horses' hooves made their escape, some on their hands and knees, with astounding alacrity.

Brother Fursey stood in the middle of the road propped up by his crutches, and gaped down at the extraordinary spectacle. At one moment the road and fields seemed to be full of people running madly in all directions, the next moment there was no one to be seen. While he was trying to understand this remarkable pheno-menon, the Devil touched him gently on the arm.

'At this point,' he said, 'our ways part, but I want you to know what a pleasure it has been to have made your acquaintance; and I want to thank you again for your company, which has done so much to relieve the tedium of the journey. I will not flatter you by saying that you are in any way remarkable as a conversationalist, but I can assure you that I have rarely met a better listener.'

He took Fursey's listless hand and shook it warmly.

'I am speaking no more than the truth, my dear Fursey, when I say that I have acquired a great affection and genuine regard for you. If at any time I can do anything for you, you have only to call on me. I am to be found in the flesh in the Devil's Glen in Wicklow, where myself and the boys are now repairing for a much needed rest. One last thing before I go — I want to direct your attention to the fact that an unfortunate fellow creature of yours is at this moment in process of drowning in that pool in the river where you saw all those people. I need say no more — you are a man and a Christian.'

Brother Fursey turned and found himself alone. Nowhere could he see even one of the ghastly host that had accompanied him for the previous three days. The fields and hills were deserted. He could hardly believe his good fortune. A great lump came in his throat and nearly choked him. He hurried forward with tears of thankfulness streaming from his eyes, but the scraping and thumping of his crutches seemed to him to beat out in rhythm the Fiend's parting words: 'You are a man and a Christian — a fellow creature is drowning.' A loud sob came from his throat as he realised vaguely that some duty had been laid upon him when his one desire was to get as far away as possible. He didn't know what was required of him, nor did he wish to give the matter any thought. In his hurry his crutch slipped among the loose stones on the road, and he fell heavily. As he lay sprawling, groping blindly for the crutch, the words came into his mind again: 'A fellow creature is drowning.' He clambered painfully to his feet, hesitated and groaned aloud; then turning towards the river, he made his way slowly across the fields. Soon he was standing on the trampled grass at the edge.

Chapter III

Fursey stood motionless, gazing out over the flood of brown, bog-stained water that moved by impassively. At this point a narrow mudbank extended into the river forming a backwater in which the water circled ever so slowly, eddying slightly as it rejoined the main stream. Nothing was to be heard but the tiny flap-flapping of the wavelets against the bank on which he stood.

'There's nothing here at all,' he said to himself. 'This is very remarkable.'

His eye fell suddenly on a rope lying along the grass, and trailing over the bank into the river. Beyond the rope a stream of bubbles rose delicately and broke on the surface of the water. This seemed to him even more remarkable, so he hurried over and began to haul in the rope. It was heavy work, especially when one was trying at the same time to maintain an upright position on a pair of crutches; so after he had tripped himself twice, he abandoned the crutches and, seating himself on the grass, pulled at the rope as if his life depended on it. He was greatly amazed when a little old woman tied in a ball, bobbed up on to the surface and came drifting towards him. At first he couldn't reach her; but he hit on the expedient of passing the armpit of one of the crutches over her head, and so by hooking her under the chin, he was able to yank her up on to the bank. His strong, rough fingers quickly untied the ropes that bound her feet and hands. She lay to all appearances dead, and the ex-monk, not knowing what to do, gazed down at her in mingled pity and horror. He did not for a moment doubt but that this was more of the Devil's work, and he was swept by a flood of fierce indignation against that suave personage.

All at once he remembered an incident that had occurred at Clonmacnoise the previous year. On the feast day of the blessed Kieran, after the usual banquet at which ale and mead had been consumed in great quantities, little Brother Patrick had insisted on going for a walk along the bank of the River Shannon. The great river flowed past the settlement, and the diminutive monk insisted that he wanted to look at the full moon, which, he said, reminded him of his mother. Brother Fursey and a few laughing lay brothers went with him. It was a good thing they did, for the voluble Patrick had not gone very far before he fell into the river. His frightened brethren managed to fish him out and carry him back unconscious to the monastery. Father Sampson, who was knowledgeable in such matters, had immediately swept them all aside and, seizing the damp and bedraggled Patrick, had flung him across the gatepost where he worked on the lay brother's back with a see-saw motion to the vast admiration of the group of half-tipsy monks. In a few minutes Brother Patrick had come back to life, laughing uproariously and still talking about his mother.

The recollection of this event had no sooner crept across Fursey's mind than he seized The Gray Mare and laid her across a granite boulder so that her head and legs hung down on either side. After a moment's thought he placed his hands carefully on her back below the ribs, and began to exert pressure, rhythmically swaying himself back and forward on his crutches. Nothing happened for a long time. Fursey's difficulty was to remain awake. He had not had a full night's rest since the awful evening when the legions of Hell had first ambled into his cell at Clonmacnoise; and the see-saw motion of artificial respiration induced sleepiness. Twice he tumbled backwards, but he picked himself up and resumed his good work without even pausing to examine his bruises. At long last he was rewarded by a low cry from the old woman. He redoubled his efforts, and she began to scream. Fursey paused and carefully turned her over. She was a strange sight with her old grey locks plastered to her head. She looked up at him with bleary eyes.

'I'll admit anything you want,' she gasped. 'Why don't you burn me and have done with it?'

While Fursey was wondering what this strange speech could mean, she lapsed once more into unconsciousness. He began immediately to chafe her hands and feet vigorously. When he looked at her face again he was delighted to see that her eyes were open and were fixed upon him. He began to laugh immoderately.

'What are you trying to do?' she asked savagely. 'Rub the skin off me?'

This surprised Fursey greatly, and he was looking down in wonder at his large rough hands when she struggled feebly into a sitting position and aimed a blow at him. The startled Fursey retreated a few paces and stood looking at her with dumb reproach. A lump came into his throat; he felt that his eyes were about to fill with tears: he bowed his head, and turning, started to hobble away. A cracked voice called after him:

'Where are you going?'

Fursey turned. 'I don't know,' he answered.

'Who are you?' she asked.

'Just a stranger who brought you out of the water and back to life.'

The Gray Mare turned this over in her mind for a few moments, and when she spoke again, her voice was more gentle.

'You're some class of a monk?'

'No. I was once, but not now.'

'They thrun you out?' queried The Gray Mare.

'Yes,' answered Fursey, the pink blood gliding into his cheeks.

The old woman emitted a throaty cackle.

'Was it creepin' after some high-steppin' young female you were?'

'Certainly not,' replied Fursey indignantly. When he remembered all the high-stepping young female demons that had crept after him, his indignation increased.

'Certainly not,' he repeated. 'Nothing of the sort.'

The Gray Mare seemed to have lost interest in his affairs. She was peering short-sightedly to left and right.

'Are they all gone?' she asked in a loud whisper.

'I don't understand,' said Fursey. 'There's no one here, if that's what you mean.'

'Dirty pack of murderers,' muttered the old woman. 'They'd have left me to drown.'

'Well, you're not drowned,' said Fursey. 'May God and the blessed Kieran have you in their keeping,' and he turned away once more.

'Mister monk,' called out the old woman.

'Yes?'

'You can't leave me here to catch my death of cold in my damp habiliments,' she said coaxingly. 'You've a kind face, mister man. Do me another kindness, and I won't forget it to you. Would you ever carry me up to my little house beyond on the hill? I doubt if I could get there by myself, I'm that weak.'

'Certainly,' said Fursey.

It was a nightmare journey. It is bad enough to have to climb a hill on crutches, but it is infinitely worse to have to do so with an old woman on one's back. The Gray Mare seemed to think it was all a great game. She belaboured Fursey with her fists pretending he was a horse, all the time crowing and cackling and exhorting him to 'gee-up.' The unfortunate Fursey stumbled on his way, gasping and grunting, sometimes choking and sometimes weeping from sheer misery. At length he stood at her door: how he got there he never knew.

'Carry me in,' commanded the old woman.

Fursey ducked his head and struggled in through the low doorway. It was an ordinary kind of cabin with a great hole in the centre of the roof to let out the smoke. The Gray Mare slid off his back and leaned against the table, her wet garments clinging to her skinny frame. She shivered violently as she began to speak. Fursey did not hear what she said. He half-closed his eyes as the walls of the room swayed sickeningly: he saw the floor coming up to meet him, and he was conscious of falling heavily.

When he awoke he was in darkness and lying on a hard pallet covered by a ragged blanket; but he did not mind how hard his bed was, provided he was allowed to lie still and rest his aching legs and back. He was conscious of distant crooning and muttering: while he was wondering about it vaguely, he fell asleep again. And so for an interminable period he slept and awoke and dozed, blissfully at peace. He was fully awakened at last when a door was opened, and the light from another room fell across his face. The Gray Mare was standing in the doorway grinning in at him.

'Are you awake, mister man?' she croaked.

'Yes,' said Fursey, sitting up. 'I'm awake.'

'Maybe you're hungry and would like something to eat?'

'Yes,' said Fursey eagerly. 'I'm hungry.'

'Well, come and get it,' she said, and she went back into the far room.

Fursey got off the bed wonderfully refreshed, and followed her. It was only when he was standing by the table in the outer room that he remembered that he had forgotten his crutches. He staggered and held on to the table with both hands.

'What's wrong with you?' queried The Gray Mare. 'You're not going to go unconscious on me again?'

'I've forgotten my crutches,' said Fursey. 'I can't walk without them.'

'Nonsense,' replied the old woman. 'You've just walked in here without them. You don't need crutches.'

'I assure you that I do,' replied Fursey earnestly. 'My hip was smashed by a poltergeist.'

'Arrah what,' said the old lady, 'the lad only sprained it. I cured you while you slept. You did me a kindness, and I told you I wouldn't forget it to you. Just try, and you'll see that you're able to walk.'

Fursey was accustomed to obedience, so he immediately relaxed his grip on the table and essayed a few steps across the floor. To his huge delight he found that he could walk. To convince himself of the genuineness of this astounding miracle he started to run up and down the kitchen.

'I can walk,' he cried. 'I can walk.'

'Stop running,' said the old woman. 'You'll upset the pot. Sit down there and have something to eat. You should be hungry. You slept the whole night through and most of to-day. It's already late in the afternoon.'

As Fursey seated himself he observed on the table what appeared to be a small wax image of a man. The light from the smoke-hole in the roof fell directly upon it, so that he could see it clearly. A little tuft of white hair was tied to the head, and it was partly wrapped in a piece of thick brown material similar to the habit he was wearing. A dead snail pierced by a thorn lay on its hip.

While Fursey was still gazing at the image The Gray Mare suddenly snapped it from the table and turned her back. A moment later she went to the fire and threw something in. Then she kneaded the image between her skeleton-thin hands until it was just a lump of shapeless wax, which she put away carefully on a shelf. She seated herself at the table opposite Fursey and sneezed once or twice. In answer to his polite enquiry, she explained that she had caught cold as a result of her immersion in the river. Fursey looked from her to the bare board between them and then back at her again, wondering with a sinking heart whether there was any food in the house. She seemed to guess his thoughts.

'What would you like to eat?' she asked.

'Whatever you're having yourself,' replied the ex-monk politely.

The Gray Mare stretched up her hand, and Fursey noticed for the first time a rope which hung from the rafters. Raising his eyes he saw that the end of it hung loosely over a beam in the roof. The Gray Mare jerked the rope three times, and to Fursey's astonishment a flagon of ale, two loaves of bread and four pounds of choice beef slid down the rope, apparently from nowhere, and settled themselves in a neat pile on the table. While he was still gaping up at the rafters, thinking that it was a very inconvenient place to keep the larder, The Gray Mare arose and, going to a hole in the wall, took out a couple of wooden goblets, which she brought over to the table. She shook a family of red spiders out of one of them and placed it in front of Fursey. The spiders ran hell-for-leather over the table in all directions, but she recovered them without difficulty and carefully stowed them away in an old stocking that hung from a hook in the wall. Fursey realised with a sigh that he had lived so long in the cloister that he was quite unaccustomed to the ways of ordinary people, so he carefully suppressed any manifestation of surprise.

Before long they were eating and drinking merrily. Fursey thought she was the pleasantest person he had ever met. Women as they had existed in his imagination, and as he had seen them from afar, were creatures endowed with an evil comeliness in order to tempt men; but this amiable old lady was so hideous that she was not like a woman at all. He could converse easily with her and found it pleasant to do so, as conversation with a woman was a new experience for him. Never, he felt, had he met such kindliness and understanding in a human being. Before he had finished his first goblet of ale, he had told her of his incredible experiences in Clonmacnoise and his resultant misfortunes. She listened with the greatest interest, punctuating his monologue occasionally with a murmur of sympathy or with a violent sneeze.

'One of the things I wonder at most,' he said, 'is the fact that while I was in Clonmacnoise I had the most awkward impediment in my speech; but now it's gone, and I can speak with reasonable fluency.'

The Gray Mare nodded her head sagely.

'That's easily accounted for,' she said. 'The impediment was frightened out of you. You went through so much that it's doubtful if anything can ever frighten you again.'

It made him uncomfortable, however, to hear her uttering harsh words about his late brethren in Clonmacnoise, as she did on hearing how he had been finally expelled from the monastery. He shifted uneasily on his stool, knowing that it was unlucky to speak ill of the clergy. In any case it was the demons who were to blame. In this strange world things like that just happen to a man; no one can help it. What else could the monks do but get rid of him? He was glad when she launched into a mumbling and toothless account of her own trials and sufferings.

He was appalled at human depravity when he heard of the bitter enmity which the sexton of the neighbouring churchyard bore her on account of such a small matter as a wandering goat. He crossed himself when she assured him that the sexton was undoubtedly a sorcerer. He could scarcely believe his ears when she told him how the wicked sexton had actually had the effrontery to denounce her to the authorities for crimes which he had himself committed. He became frightened when he heard how human beings had 'walked' her up and down for three days and nights without sleep, how human beings had taken her and thrown her into the river, and how human beings, even when her innocence had been fully demonstrated, had nevertheless picked up stones to kill her. It frightened him to think of the kind of world it was in which he must in future live, and he longed to be back in the quiet and safety of the cloister. It was with an aching heart that he told himself that he must put Clonmacnoise forever out of his thoughts.

The Gray Mare was muttering to herself as she gathered a little pile of crumbs together with her skinny fingers.

'And you were really innocent all the time?' asked Fursey.

She shot a quick look at him.

'Didn't you find me at the bottom of the river,' she replied gratingly. 'Isn't that sure proof that I'm not a witch?'

'Yes,' said Fursey. 'I've always heard that that's sure proof.'

She started up suddenly.

'The sexton,' she said. 'He'll be renewing his attack, and here I am wasting my time gabbling, instead of making preparations to meet him.'

She hurried over to the fire and began to stir a huge pot that hung over the embers. Then she lifted down a cobwebbed jar from the shelf and, taking from it a handful of amber grains, she threw them into the liquid, which began at once to bubble and spit angrily. Bending over the cauldron she began a low chant. At that moment there was a clatter of horses' hooves on the track outside the door.

'Hallo there!' shouted a loud voice.

'Who's that?' hissed the old woman.

Fursey went to the door and opened it. Three horsemen had reined their steeds on the road about fifty paces from the door. To his astonishment Fursey recognised the Abbot Marcus, who was being helped from his horse by a huge red-faced friar. On a bony nag sat an ecclesiastic in the dress of a bishop. He was gaunt and sallow, and he gazed at Fursey sourly. At a little distance stood a band of serving-men loaded down with books of exorcism, bells and stoups of holy water. They were looking thoroughly frightened, as if they might take to their heels at any moment.

The first thought that came into Fursey's mind was that the Abbot Marcus had come for him to take him back to Clonmacnoise. He ran down the road and flung himself on his knees at the Abbot's feet. Marcus raised his hand and laid it gently on Fursey's head in blessing. The ex-monk gripped the Abbot's robe and gazed up at the grave face, lined with study. The far-away eyes that were bent on him were kind.

'You're going to take me back?' said Fursey.

The Abbot turned away his face.

'Get up, Fursey,' he said.

Fursey rose to his feet and glanced from one to the other. The big friar was looking at him with great interest, but the Bishop's eyes were as cold as ice, and a sneer was trembling about his mouth. Fursey instinctively knew that in the trio he had only one friend. He turned again to the Abbot Marcus.

'Father Abbot, are you not going to let me go back?'

The Abbot's eyes shifted uncomfortably. 'No,' he said at last.

Fursey stood an abject figure, looking from one to the other. Then he looked at the road and up at the wide sky. He saw everything blurred and dim through a film of tears.

'Come now, my man,' said the Bishop bitingly. 'Weeping won't help you. I am too good a judge of human nature not to know reality from fake.'

'Please, my lord bishop,' interposed the Abbot. 'I've already explained to you the circumstances under which Fursey left Clonmacnoise. I made it clear that he was in no way to blame.'

'Where are the demons he was consorting with yesterday?' snapped the Bishop. 'Let him tell us that.'

'They're gone,' said Fursey.

'Gone where?' asked the Bishop quickly, as if to startle Fursey into an admission.

'I don't know. They just disappeared.'

There was a moment's silence, then Father Furiosus interposed.

'They're certainly not here now,' he said mildly. 'We've rung bells and sprinkled holy water over an area of two square miles. No demon could stand up to that.'

'Did you see any sign of an old woman?' asked the Bishop.

'Yes,' replied Fursey surprised. 'I pulled an old woman out of the river, and brought her up here to the house. She's in there now.'

He turned and pointed to the little cabin behind him.

'What did you do that for?' asked the Bishop sharply. 'Why did you have to meddle?'

'Because,' interjected the Abbot with some heat in his voice, 'it was what any Christian would be expected to do.'

'Even if the object of his misplaced charity was a witch?' queried the Bishop.

'She's not a witch,' said Father Furiosus with some exasperation. 'God clearly demonstrated that she was innocent.'

The Bishop was silent, but he continued to watch Fursey with baleful eyes.

'Father Abbot,' pleaded Fursey, 'let me go back with you to the monastery.'

'That is impossible,' said the Abbot with finality. 'You must understand, my poor Fursey, that the gates of Clonmacnoise and every other religious settlement are closed against you. Be reasonable, Fursey. For nearly two weeks you have consorted with demons. For all we know you may have even formed friendships. No abbot could risk taking you in. These goblins that you know would be likely to return to renew the acquaintance. The fact that you appear to have recovered the free use of your speech and are in a position to challenge them, is no safeguard. That would be a small impediment to imps and demons of the wilier sort. In any case, if I took you back to Clonmacnoise, it's very likely that the whole community would leave in a body.'

'I see,' said Fursey, hanging his head.

A sudden thought seemed to strike Bishop Flanagan.

'Where did you spend the night?' he asked sharply.

'In the cottage,' replied Fursey.

'With The Gray Mare?'

'With the old woman,' answered Fursey innocently.

A sharp intake of breath was heard from Father Furiosus. The thunderclouds gathered on the Bishop's forehead.

'The two of you were alone?' he asked in tones of doom.

'Yes,' said Fursey haltingly.

'In my diocese!' said the Bishop in a horrified whisper. 'An unmarried man and woman spend the night together in the one house without chaperon, and he stands there and has the effrontery to tell me so to my face! Do you know, my man,' he continued, his voice rising to a shout, 'that what you have done is a reserved sin in this diocese? What do you think of such conduct, Father Furiosus?'

Furiosus had tightened his grip on his blackthorn, and he was looking at Fursey menacingly from beneath his ginger eyebrows.

'He must marry the woman,' said Furiosus.

'Of course he must,' replied the Bishop. 'There's no other way to avert the scandal.'

'Marry?' said Fursey faintly.

'And if he doesn't,' continued the Bishop, 'I'll put a penance on him that will cripple him in this life and in the next.'

'Let us discuss this new turn of events,' said the Abbot. 'Oblige us, Fursey, by stepping aside for a few moments.'

Fursey walked some paces down the road and leaned against a tree for support. Meanwhile the three ecclesiastics approached more closely to one another and conversed in grave whispers.

'It mightn't be a bad idea at all,' said Abbot Marcus. 'The plight of this wretched man weighs somewhat on my conscience, and I should like to see him fixed in life. No monastery will admit him, and as he hasn't the wit to earn a living, he will certainly starve on the roadside unless something is done for him. Moreover,' he added thoughtfully, 'you tell me that this woman, tho' not a witch, is nevertheless a great sinner who never goes to Mass. Union with such a godly man as Fursey cannot but have a profound effect on her character. By good example he is very likely to win her back to God and Holy Church.'

Father Furiosus seemed impressed.

'Yes,' he said, 'and you have told us that this Brother Fursey is a man of notable piety. He can, therefore, be trusted to report to the authorities should she at any time be tempted to engage in the black art.'

'This is all irrelevant,' said the Bishop hotly. 'I would remind you that I am in authority in this diocese. The point is simply this — that the unfortunate woman has been compromised by this black-guard, and that wrong can only be righted by marriage. He must marry her. I insist.'

'There is no need to raise your voice,' said the Abbot coldly. 'We are all agreed, tho' perhaps for different reasons.'

He turned to where Fursey was leaning against the tree gaping vacantly out over the countryside, and called him by name, but

Fursey did not appear to hear. He had been trying to assemble his thoughts so as to understand what was about to happen to him, but his mind insisted on remaining an obstinate and tumultuous blank. Father Furiosus went down the road and taking Fursey by the arm, led him back to where the others were standing.

'Now listen carefully, Fursey,' began the Abbot kindly. 'We are all agreed that you must marry this lady. It is your duty, because by your incautious behaviour you have cast a reflection on her honour. From a material point of view you will be making a good match. She appears to have a tidy little property, and you will enjoy economic security for the rest of your life.'

'She has only a broken-down cabin and a goat,' replied Fursey bleakly.

The Abbot looked at him severely.

'I didn't expect to find in one of my monks a sordid greed for material goods,' he replied.

'But I'm a monk,' said Fursey, his voice rising in an hysterical squeal. 'I can't marry.'

'Your vows are simple vows,' said the Abbot smoothly, 'and it's in my power to release you. I shall immediately do so; it would be most unfair to hold you to them.'

'But she is far from comely,' objected Fursey feebly.

'I'm surprised at you,' said the Abbot. 'There will be all the less temptation to desires of the flesh.'

'It's better to marry than to burn,' said the Bishop.

'But I don't feel myself burning,' said Fursey.

'Don't be impertinent,' said the Bishop. 'It's all settled.'

Fursey looked up appealingly at Abbot Marcus.

'What will I do?' he asked.

'Do as I say, marry her,' replied the Abbot, 'and may God bless you both.'

Fursey bowed his head.

'Whatever you say, Father Abbot,' he muttered brokenly. 'I suppose it's for the best.'

'Now we must tell the woman,' said Furiosus.

There was a moment's hesitation as none of the ecclesiastics was anxious to approach a cottage which had been held in such abominable repute. At last Father Furiosus went and called on The Gray Mare to come out. She had been watching the proceedings from the dark interior of her cottage inasfar as her defective eyesight would permit, and she now emerged hesitantly. She glanced to left and right as if considering flight, but Father Furiosus took her gently by the arm and began to lead her down the road, assuring her with a rough kindness that she had nothing to be afraid of. As she came hobbling towards them, the Bishop retreated a pace and made the sign of the cross in the dust of the road with the point of his pastoral staff. She stood before them, a frail bowed figure, making a smacking sound as she sucked at her toothless gums. She looked down at the cross traced in the dust, then up at the Bishop malevolently.

'Haven't youse done enough to me?' she asked bitterly.

Father Furiosus hastened to explain that byegones were bye-gones and that they were all meeting on a friendly footing. He propounded the proposition to her. At first she was incredulous; but when she realised that he was in earnest, she was overcome by a fit of cackling. She threw a gamey eye across at the blushing Fursey.

'So the rascal wants to marry me,' she croaked. 'He's not a bad-looking fellow, with his white head and his young face.'

'I'm forty,' said Fursey, hoping dimly to dam her rising enthusiasm.

'Sure that's only young,' she replied. 'You'd be useful around the house, milking the goat and the like.'

'Well, what do you say?' enquired Abbot Marcus.

'It's not what I'd call a romantic wooing,' she replied, 'but I suppose we could do our courting afterwards. It will always keep.'

She gave Fursey a girlish nudge with her elbow. A wintry smile flickered across her face.

'Well, are you agreed?' asked the Bishop impatiently.

'Yes,' said The Gray Mare. 'I'll try anything once.'

'Well, go down on your knees,' said the Bishop.

The Gray Mare was helped into the required position by Father Furiosus. She complained of her rheumatics, and requested him to stand by to help her up again. Two serving-men were summoned to act as witnesses. The Gray Mare delayed the ceremony for some minutes by her insistence on combing her hair with her long, skinny fingers, and by her efforts to get it to curl over each ear. The Abbot formally released Fursey from his vows, stumbling occasionally over the words, for he was embarrassed by Fursey's dumb, dog-like gaze that was riveted all the time on his face. Then the Bishop approached and placing The Gray Mare's lank claw in Fursey's plump fist, he read through the marriage ceremony in clipped and hurried Latin. The little band of serving-men had drawn near to watch the proceedings. A bird yelped an occasional note from the single rowan tree standing before The Gray Mare's cabin; and the red sun, half below the distant slate-grey mountains, rolled his last laughing beams on the happy couple.

Chapter IV

Fursey and The Gray Mare stood on the road until the ecclesiastics and their followers were out of sight. As the beating of the horses' hooves died away into the grey of the evening, Fursey shuddered, suddenly conscious of his desolation and loneliness. The Gray Mare was pensive as she took his arm and hobbled back with him to her cabin. When they entered the kitchen she wheezed once or twice like an old cat whose day is nearly done.

'There'll be no time for love-making this evening,' she croaked.

Very much relieved, Fursey took a stool and seated himself as far away as possible from his bride. He wished he were alone and had time to think. In the monk's habit he was still wearing, he had discovered a square hole from which a piece of cloth had been neatly cut, a piece of cloth very similar to the scrap of material he had seen earlier in the evening wrapped around the wax image on the table.

Her voice grated in on his thoughts.

'That fellow Cuthbert will be down on top of us in no time,' she said. 'We must prepare to defend ourselves.'

'Who's Cuthbert?' asked Fursey.

'Didn't I tell you already?' snapped The Gray Mare. 'Cuthbert is the sexton of Kilcock Churchyard: his house is not three hundred yards away; you can see it from the door.'

'Is he not friendly disposed?' queried Fursey anxiously.

The Gray Mare was busy stirring the seething contents of the cauldron, but she turned to glance malevolently at her husband.

'Friendly disposed!' she snarled. 'What class of a fool am I wedded to? Didn't I tell you how he denounced me to the Bishop and tried to have me massacred? Do you imagine he's going to give up just because he failed the first time? I tell you there'll be dirty work to-night.'

'Maybe if it were suggested to him to let byegones be byegones,' said Fursey faintly, 'brotherly love and all that.'

'Yah!' replied the old woman. 'Cuthbert's a spry lad at weaving the spells. I tell you he's the crookedest sorcerer in the whole territory. Jealousy, that's what's at the bottom of it. He has an unfair advantage,' she muttered half to herself, 'with that graveyard under his control, full of unbaptised babes and murderers' bones, to draw on just as he pleases. Where are you going?'

'I thought I'd like a breath of fresh air,' replied Fursey feebly.

'Go along inside and tidy up the room beyond,' ordered The Gray Mare. 'You're a distraction to me here.'

Fursey obeyed without a word. There wasn't much tidying to be done, the only furniture being the pallet on which he had slept, and a stool. He began tidying these without much enthusiasm, while all the time the one thought kept grinding around and around in his head. Could it be that the churchmen were wrong, and that she was a witch after all? He had often heard that witches made wax images of people, either to cure or destroy them. The piece cut from his habit, in conjunction with the miraculous cure of his lameness, most disagreeably affected his imagination. Moreover, he didn't like the general trend of her conversation, nor did he like the look of that cauldron over the fire, which spat and foamed every time you went near it. His long experience in the kitchen at Clonmacnoise made him doubt whether the brew was fit for human consumption; it certainly did not look like soup. His apprehension increased a few minutes later, when in the course of his tidying, he discovered a box of toads under his bed. He sat down on the stool to think, but his thoughts were interrupted by the sound of conversation from the outer room. His heart bounded at the thought of perhaps seeing and talking to another normal human being like himself, and he arose and stepped quickly across to the door; but when he entered the other room he stood petrified. The Gray Mare was frantically stirring the cauldron with what appeared to be a human thigh bone, and there was a dim shape, a large black object, very ill-defined, squatting on the hearth. As Fursey came into the room it was in process of vanishing. He stared where it had been, but he could see nothing; so that he speedily doubted if the uncertain light had not deceived his eyes. Then it occurred to him that maybe it was one of the Clonmacnoise demons dogging his footsteps to spy on him. He stood with a beating heart until The Gray Mare caught sight of him.

'Make yourself useful,' she shrilled. 'Go out and milk the goat before it gets dark.'

Fursey hastily picked up the wooden pail which she indicated with a sweep of her arm. He hurried through the doorway, relieved to be out of the cottage in the fresh cool air of the evening. He looked to left and right, but could see no sign of a goat. He proceeded cautiously around the side of the house, and found her at the back tied to a length of rope which enabled her to walk around in a wide semi-circle eating the grass or the thorns in the hedge according to her inclination. At the moment she was apparently not interested in either, but stood with her forelegs against the wall of the cabin eating the thatch off the roof. She had a roving eye, and when she saw Fursey coming around the corner on tiptoe with the pail, she paused in her meal to contemplate him. As he approached she took her forelegs from the wall and stood stockstill watching him. She had a pair of protuberant brown eyes and a long dun beard, so long that Fursey wondered whether she ever fell over it. She held a generous bundle of thatch sideways across her mouth, which created the illusion that she had a military moustache. They stood looking at one another in silence. Fursey did not like the look of her at all, but he approached, gently patting the milk-pail with his free hand to indicate what was expected of her.

'There's a good goat,' he said. 'Come and be milked.'

The goat's moustache suddenly disappeared as she swallowed the thatch with no apparent effort. Fursey squatted on his hunkers and placed the pail in position to commence the operation. The goat immediately took a step sideways, presenting her hindquarters to Fursey. Again and again he placed the pail, but each time she repeated the manoeuvre. He was squatting there contemplating her tufted stern despairingly, when all at once the pail fell from his fingers. He had suddenly remembered the grisly stories that were whispered in Clonmacnoise, of witches and covens, and of the Horned God whom the witches worshipped. What if this were the Horned God in person exacting from him the homage of the posterior kiss? He remained in a squatting position grown languid with horror, until the increasing consciousness that he was being watched made him turn his head.

There was a man on the far side of the hedge looking in at him, a tall man with sloping shoulders and a wipe of black hair hanging down over his forehead. He was dressed in rusty black, and there was a knowing grin on his face. He turned away at once and made off with a queer sloping stride in the direction of a distant clump of trees. Fursey rose to his feet and ran around the house into the kitchen.

The Gray Mare had a broomstick up on the table and was anointing it with a white ointment.

'What's wrong?' she said sharply, as Fursey stumbled into the kitchen.

'A queer-looking man,' began Fursey, 'with a fringe of hair along his forehead, and a big black lock falling over it —'

'That's Cuthbert,' interrupted The Gray Mare. 'He must know I'm back. There's not a moment to lose. Come on and help me.'

She led the way out through the door, and with the handle of the broom on the ground ran around the cottage making a wide circle. Fursey ran behind her, not knowing the moment he might be called upon to assist. When they came around to the door again, the circle completed, she began carefully to trace a pentagram around the house, muttering an incantation as she went. It was borne in powerfully on Fursey that this was witchcraft beyond all question. Any doubts he may have retained were dispelled a few moments later when they returned to the kitchen. He saw her reaching up and taking down a box from the shelf. She took out a handful of newts' eyes and human knuckle-bones, and cast them into the brew. The cauldron moaned hideously.

'Where are you going?' she asked sharply.

'I'm getting out of this while there's still time,' answered Fursey. 'Goodbye, and thank you very much for your hospitality.'

'You're too late,' replied the witch. 'Listen.'

Fursey's blood grew chill as he became aware of a low drumming, growing louder and louder as it approached. He heard a yelping and baying coming nearer and nearer, until before his horrified eyes a score of monstrous hounds with flaming eyes and lolling tongues came bounding over the hedge. He watched from the doorway as the ghastly pack began coursing in a circle around and around the house. When he tried to move, his knees gave way; and The Gray Mare had to help him across the room and on to a stool, where he sat filled with dismal foreboding.

'It was a good thing we made that circle and pentagram,' said the witch, 'we were just in time.'

Fursey was too depressed to take more than a gloomy interest in her further preparations. Above the howling and clamour of the hell-pack that circled the house, he was conscious of a scrambling sound on the roof, where the goat had taken refuge. A few moments later he saw her bearded visage looking down at him through the smoke-hole.

'It's too late to make a wax image of him,' muttered the old woman. 'I should have thought of that before. I'll have to trust to the lightning and the enchanted fleas.'

Fursey had just come to the conclusion that it was time for him to address himself to prayer and so provide for his own safety, when he observed a severed hand holding a knife come floating through the wall. As it drifted across the room towards The Gray Mare, Fursey bounded to his feet and shouted a warning. She turned in a flash and seizing the broom, struck at the horrid apparition. She missed, but the sweep of the broom deflected its course. The broom struck Fursey on the side of the head and sent him sprawling. From the floor he watched the hand and the knife floating out through the far wall.

'Are you hurt, love?' asked The Gray Mare as she helped him to his feet. Before he could answer a wild scrambling was heard on the roof. The goat seemed to have lost her head, and the reason became apparent a moment later when a skeleton threw its legs over the smoke-hole with the evident intention of descending into the kitchen. Fursey seized a box of moles' feet which lay to hand, and flung it, striking the skeleton somewhere about the middle. It immediately fell to pieces, and its constituent bones descended with a clatter on to the kitchen floor. It recovered at once, formed itself into a skeleton again, and threw itself into a fighting attitude facing Fursey. The Gray Mare came quickly to the rescue. She drew a hasty circle with her broom on the floor around the skeleton, and uttered a word unknown to Fursey. The skeleton once more fell to pieces, this time for good and all; and by direction of the witch Fursey collected the constituent bones and threw them into the fire.

'Counter-offensive!' shouted The Gray Mare. 'Open the door wide!'

Fursey flung open the door and ran back into a corner. The witch struck the cauldron three times with the thigh bone, each time uttering a shrill cry. Immediately a swarm of fleas as big as mice sprang out. In two hops they were across the kitchen and had flung themselves on the coursing hellhounds. At first the giant dogs merely stopped occasionally in their career to scratch themselves, but when the fleas had warmed to their work, the hounds retreated precipitately, many attempting the pitiable impossibility of scratching and running at the same time.

'Further counter-offensive action!' roared the witch. 'Stand back!'

Fursey crawled under the table as she beat on the cauldron. She shrieked a jumble of words. There was a blinding flash as a stream of forked lightning streaked across the kitchen and precipitated itself into the sky in the direction of the sexton's house. The quaking Fursey could see through the doorway a similar bar of lightning arising from the house among the trees. The two streaks of lightning forked around one another for a moment as if manoeuvring for position, then they met, wound into a corkscrew, and disappeared in a deafening explosion.

'They've negatived one another,' commented the witch bitterly.

In the unearthly silence that followed, nothing was to be heard but a slight stirring overhead as the goat, thinking it was all over, began peacefully to crop her way through the roof.

The Gray Mare threw an angry glance at the ceiling.

'That one will fall in on us yet,' she said. 'Drat her!'

'Do you know,' said Fursey, 'if you don't mind, I think it was time I was going.'

'You can't go,' said the witch savagely. 'You're my husband. You can't leave me, a bride, on my wedding night.'

'I think all the same,' said Fursey feebly, 'I'll take a little walk. A breath of fresh air would be welcome before I turn in.'

'Are you mad?' screamed the witch. 'If you as much as put your nose outside the pentagram, Cuthbert will shrivel you.'

Fursey ignored her and staggered towards the doorway; but the sight of a bloody head dancing up and down in the air a couple of paces beyond the door made him change his mind, and he turned back.

'Maybe if we said a prayer —' he suggested in a weak whisper.

'What's wrong with you?' barked the witch. 'Are you losing your courage?'

'I never had any,' said Fursey as he went down on his knees.

The witch kicked him on to his feet again.

'If you're not going to help me, at least get out of the way. Along with you into the far room, you half-man, you.'

Fursey crept into the other room and on to the bed, where he lay for a long time with his face turned to the wall. Everything was very still except for the tearing and champing of the goat on the roof. Several times The Gray Mare came into the room searching for the ingredients for new infusions and distillations; one time it was the entrails of a sacrificed cock she was looking for, and she turned Fursey out of the bed to see if they were under the pillow: then she was in enquiring whether he had seen a box of dead men's fingernails which she particularly prized. It was eerie lying alone in the darkened room. He fancied that he could hear a muttering and a moaning about the house, and his imagination pictured hideous beings of dreadful aspect and fantastic shape hovering overhead, grinning and gnashing at him horribly. He could stand it no longer: even the Gray Mare's company was preferable to his own, so he crawled off the bed and noiselessly made his way back into the outer room. She was standing at the table muttering The Lord's Prayer backwards as she extracted the venom from a pair of toads. All around her was the horrid paraphernalia of her art, baneful herbs and cauldrons of hell-broth.

'How are things going?' he enquired with an attempt at friendliness. She looked at him not unkindly.

'So you got lonely in there by yourself,' she said.

'Yes,' he answered shyly. 'Do you hear something?'

She paused in her work and listened.

'Yes,' she said, 'the rain.'

Fursey listened too. It was pleasant to hear the friendly, familiar rain. He listened until he could distinguish the patter of the individual raindrops softly falling on the roof and around the house.

'I'm preparing to send out a spell,' she said, 'that will glue Cuthbert to his chair; but before I send it, I want you to do something for me.'

Fursey's heart sank.

'What is it?' he quavered.

'I'll turn you into a hare,' she said, 'and you can course around and spy out Cuthbert's dispositions.'

Fursey made a move as if he contemplated returning to his bed.

'Well,' said the witch shortly, 'at least you can creep up to the churchyard and bring me back some clay from a freshly-dug grave. That will help me to twist Cuthbert's magic backwards.'

Before Fursey could answer he became sensible of a dreadful sound high up in the air above his head. It was an evil sound, as if the sky was humming with the approach of unholy legions. A look of maniacal menace and fury suddenly distorted The Gray Mare's face. She sprang to her feet.

'The rain!' she screeched. 'He sent the shower of rain to wash out the circle and pentagram.'

She ran to the door, but it was too late. The roof was suddenly swept from the house, and as Fursey threw a terrified glance upwards, he saw a cyclopean claw that seemed to fill the whole sky. It paused for a moment, then it struck. The Gray Mare uttered a hoarse wail as the claw seized her, lifted her high above the house, and flung her back, mangled and broken, into a corner of the kitchen.

Fursey cowered in a corner. It was a long time before he ventured out, to pick his way over the debris of the kitchen to where the old woman lay in a crumpled heap. She was all but dead. Her eyes were still open and showed signs of recognising him, but she could move neither hand nor foot. He put his arm around her bony shoulders and raised her. Her breath came out in a whisper, which he bent his head to hear.

'Oh, the pain!' she whispered. 'I can't die. I wish I could die.'

The generous tears flooded into Fursey's eyes.

'Kiss me once,' came the feeble, throaty voice. 'You've never kissed me. Kiss me once, please.'

Fursey was embarrassed, but he knew his duty in the presence of death. He bent and placed his lips gently upon hers. The Gray Mare, with a superhuman effort, wrapped her skinny arm around his neck, and pressing her mouth to his, blew violently down his throat. A ball of fire seemed to roll through Fursey's veins, he gasped and shuddered. The Gray Mare fell backwards and lay, an old sack of bones, dead upon the floor. For a few moments Fursey crouched beside her while the fire in his body abated, his apprehension that something further had happened to him mingling disagreeably with his regret for the wretched old woman. At last he arose with a sigh and leaning against the table, contemplated the ruin of the kitchen. He had no further fear of the sexton-sorcerer of Kilcock Churchyard: somehow he knew that Cuthbert had been intent on The Gray Mare's destruction, and not on his; but he knew that he had nowhere to go, that no one wanted him, and that the sooner he too was dead, the better it would be for himself and for everyone else.

From these gloomy reflections he was awakened by something that was happening beside the fireplace. A large dark mass was slowly taking shape. Fursey watched aghast, and then he gave vent to a loud groan. There was no doubt about it: an animal like a large dog was sitting on the hearth. It had paws like a bear and was covered all over with rusty black hair. There was a red foggy light in its eyes; and it was apparently a creature unknown to natural history. It did not show its teeth nor exhibit any sign of irritation; but on the contrary gazed at Fursey with benevolence.

'Hello,' said the apparition. 'I'm Albert.'

Fursey averted his eyes, but when he looked back again, it was still there.

'I better explain myself,' continued the shaggy stranger, 'I was The Gray Mare's familiar. Every witch, as you know, has a familiar; and it's a strange fact that a witch cannot die until she has bequeathed her powers and her familiar to someone else. That's why the poor old lady was tossing about in such agony until she contrived to breathe her spirit into you. My lord Fursey, you have succeeded to her powers and incidentally to me.'

Fursey made an attempt to speak, but no words came.

'I beg your pardon,' said Albert.

After a struggle Fursey managed to gasp out the words.

'Do you mean to say that I have become a sorcerer?'

'I do,' said Albert. 'You are now a wizard and I'm your familiar, always at your service whenever you call upon me.'

'But I don't want to be a wizard,' protested Fursey.

'I'm afraid you can't help yourself,' said Albert. 'You have inherited the old lady's powers whether you like it or not. Of course you'll require a good deal of practice before you acquire in the exercises of those powers a proficiency similar to hers.'

'What am I to do?' moaned the hapless Fursey.

'If you take my advice,' said Albert, 'the first thing you'll do is make friends with Cuthbert. It's better to have him as a friend than as an enemy. The Gray Mare fell out with him, and you've seen what happened to her. Besides, he's a man from whom you can learn a great deal, and if I may say so without offence, you have a great deal to learn. It's not much use having the powers of a sorcerer unless you know how to use them.'

'And do I have to have you following me around everywhere?'

A look of surprise came into Albert's red foggy eyes.

'Not at all,' he answered. 'I'll take shape when you call on me for advice or for the performance of some task. You have only to utter one word of dismissal, and I automatically disappear. While I am bound to carry out your commands to the best of my ability, I would, however, point out the advisability of your deferring, at least at first, to my judgment in matters affecting the exercise of your craft. After all, I am a familiar of considerable experience.'

Fursey passed his tongue over his parched lips and regarded his bestial companion with strong distaste.

'Furthermore,' continued the shaggy creature, 'if you desire efficient service from me, it's of the highest importance that you keep me well-fed and in good condition. I shall require, at least every second day, a feed of your blood.'

'What!' said Fursey, considerably startled.

'Somewhere about your person,' continued Albert smoothly, 'you will find that you have acquired a supernumerary nipple. It may look like a wart or excrescence of some sort. That is the point at which you must suckle me with your blood.'

'I'll do nothing of the sort,' asserted Fursey.

'You will perhaps change your mind,' said Albert huffily, 'when you discover the extent to which niggardliness in the matter affects my usefulness and efficiency. Lastly, it is my duty to inform you that if you have the misfortune to fall foul of the law, you will, while you're in custody, be automatically bereft of my assistance and the solace of my companionship.'

'Why?' asked Fursey dully.

Albert looked surprised.

'I don't know,' he said. 'That's the nature of familiars. That's just the way things are.'

Deep in Fursey's consciousness thoughts tumbled and elbowed one another, trying vainly to sort themselves out; but he was too tired, and he felt too broken and helpless to grapple with the situation. He realised that he was in a proper quagmire, but he had neither the heart nor the will to think about the matter further. He leaned against the table gazing dully before him.

'You ought to go down and make the sexton's acquaintance,' suggested Albert.

'All right,' muttered Fursey, rousing himself.

Albert glanced around the kitchen.

'Bring the broom,' he said, 'it may turn in useful. She anointed it and prepared it just before the end.'

Fursey put the broom under his arm and stood in a half-stupor while Albert's red eye ran critically around the remaining poor possessions of the cottage.

'Nothing else of value,' he said. 'Oh yes, put this in your pocket, if you have a pocket in that long skirt you're wearing.'

'What is it?' asked Fursey, looking down at the small box which Albert had placed in his hand.

'It's the ointment she prepared for anointing the broom,' replied the familiar. 'Brooms need anointing from time to time or they lose their virtue. I won't tell you what the ingredients are, as you seem as yet somewhat squeamish about these matters.'

As they left the cottage and walked slowly down the road towards the clump of trees where the sexton's house stood buried in shadow, Fursey cast up his eyes to the wide star-shattered sky. The huge night was all about him. Houseless, friendless he knew himself to be; and nature, seen through the peculiar opalescent atmosphere of night, appeared not only indifferent, but harsh and estranged. Even the shred of moon that leaned drunkenly overhead seemed to him to be curved in a sneer. Was there anyone in the whole wide world who cared what became of Brother Fursey, late monk at Clonmacnoise? He told himself bitterly that there was not. He glanced at the ungainly monster shambling along by his side, grunting and belching in appreciation of the fine night air. There was no doubt about it, thought Fursey miserably, he was deeply in it: he had plumbed the lowest depths, and nothing worse could happen to him. He didn't care, his heart was dead: let come what would.

As they passed along by the wall of the churchyard, Fursey glanced indifferently at the headstones among the weeds. If all the dead who had ever been buried there, were out in the moonlight playing leapfrog over the tombstones, Fursey felt that he wouldn't have experienced either interest or alarm. He was past caring about anything.

They went on to where the shadows of the trees were deepest, and Fursey suddenly found that they were standing before a low thatched cottage. Albert rose on to his hindlegs and knocked discreetly at the door. Shuffling steps became audible within, and the door was opened by the lanky man in rusty black whom Fursey had seen gazing at him over the hedge earlier in the evening.

The sexton bowed, and with a graceful wave of his hand invited them to enter.

'Welcome to my house,' he said courteously as Fursey stepped into the kitchen. The sexton nodded familiarly to Albert as to an old acquaintance, and politely relieving Fursey of the broom, he propped it carefully in a corner.

'Pray, be seated,' he said.

Fursey sat down by the table and took a good look at the sexton. He was a lank, weedy man with sloping shoulders. His mouth was puckered, accentuating the general resemblance his countenance bore to that of a rabbit. A wipe of moist black hair hung down over his forehead. He wore rusty black clothes that had seen better days. He stood opposite Fursey cracking each of his fingers in turn, and regarding his visitor with a scarcely perceptible smile stirring the corners of his rabbit's mouth. Fursey with an effort withdrew his eyes from those of his host and looked around the room. Hanging in a neat row from the wall were wheelbarrows, spades, lengths of rope and the varied paraphernalia of the sexton's profession. There were shelves containing food and cooking utensils. A cheery fire blazed in one corner, and the smoke slithered gracefully up the wall and made its exit through an efficient smoke-hole in the roof. Everywhere was neatness and prosperity. The only evidence that the occupant was other than a highly respectable sexton was a manuscript with cabalistic signs which lay on the table between two rushlights, and a huge brindled cat sitting on the hearth who, when Fursey caught her eye, grinned at him furiously.

The sexton pulled a stool up to the table and seated himself opposite Fursey. He folded the manuscript carefully and put it aside.

'Very fine weather we're having for this time of the year,' he remarked affably.

Fursey agreed that it was.

'Forgive me,' said the sexton, 'I have neglected to make the usual introductions. This is Tibbikins, my familiar.'

'I'm pleased to make your acquaintance,' muttered Fursey hoarsely.

The cat nodded cheerily and favoured Fursey with another grin. Albert lumbered over to the hearth, and the two familiars began a conversation in low tones.

'I judge from the fact that you have Albert attached to you, that you are now of the profession,' continued the sexton, 'but I am unaware of the name by which you are called.'

'My name is Fursey.'

'You are a monk?'

'No. A widower.'

'Ah yes,' the sexton nodded sympathetically. 'I watched the marriage ceremony on the road below this afternoon. Very unfortunate business, your wife's demise; but, if I may say so, she had become a little high in herself recently. There was a goat also who, not content with eating a gatepost and a wire fence, consumed several of my trees and half the produce of my garden. I never knew an animal with such a prodigious appetite. No sooner had I some rare and valuable herbs planted, than they disappeared into her stomach. I'm fond of animals myself, but I do think that if one keeps livestock, one should keep them under control. Don't you agree with me?'

Fursey nodded bleakly.

'Oh Tibbikins,' said the sexton turning towards the hearth, 'perhaps you would like to take Albert into the other room and offer him a bowl of blood.'

Albert had no tail, but he wagged his hindquarters to show his appreciation as he shuffled out of the room in the wake of the brindled cat. Cuthbert leaned over towards Fursey and tapped him confidentially on the sleeve.

'You mustn't think I'm a snob,' he said, 'but I do believe in maintaining the distinction of class. They are, after all, the chief bulwark of the social order. In any case, I should deem it a grave discourtesy to a fellow-human to discuss his private affairs in the presence of servants.'

He arose and put the manuscript carefully away on a shelf. Then he stood for a moment warming his back before the fire.

'The Gray Mare,' he said, 'was a foolish woman. She had acquired a certain, I might even say, a considerable proficiency in the darker arts, but her over-weening confidence in herself betrayed her into the belief that she could match her powers with those of a master.'

His eyes glittered as he brushed back the long lock of hair from his forehead. It immediately fell down over his other eye. He came to the table and again seated himself opposite Fursey.

'I hope you bear me no ill-feeling,' he said anxiously. 'I don't know what you did to the old lady; but somehow, this afternoon I got the impression that it was what is called "a forced marriage".'

'It was,' agreed Fursey. 'I'm not conscious of personal loss.'

'Good,' said Cuthbert, rubbing his thin hands. 'Then we can be friends. You now belong to the brotherhood, the oldest priesthood in the world, older than Christianity, druidism or any religion that man has ever thought up for himself.'

Fursey felt that he should contradict these sentiments; but deeming it wise to be discreet, he continued to stare emptily at the smiling sexton.

'But, my dear Fursey, why are you so enveloped in gloom on what should be the happiest day of your life? Think of it, think of the vast inheritance into which you have entered.'

'I'm rather tired,' said Fursey apologetically. 'I have only had one night's rest in several weeks; and I've had a rather trying time to-day.'

'Insomnia!' said the sexton. 'And here I am chattering away and keeping you from your bed. We'll have plenty of time to talk to-morrow. Come, my poor friend.'

The sexton picked up one of the rushlights from the table and led Fursey into the other room. The two familiars were sitting on the floor engaged in desultory conversation.

'That will be all for to-night, Tibbikins,' said the sorcerer. 'You may disappear.'

The brindled cat slowly vanished, beginning with her ears and continuing the process until it reached the tip of her tail.

'I think you might do the same for Albert,' suggested the sexton. 'You won't require him again to-night.'

Albert looked up at Fursey, the light of expectancy in his smoky red eyes. As Fursey gazed at the rusty black coat and the bear's paws, the creature seemed to him to typify all that had made his life a misery in the foregoing weeks.

'Go away,' he said with distaste.

Albert melted gracefully into the air with a final friendly waggle of his hindquarters.

'Now, lie down, my friend,' said the sexton.

Fursey took off his sandals and stretched himself on the bed. He drew his tattered monk's robe about him and pulled up the blanket to his chin. He was conscious of the sexton's hands making weird passes in the air above him as he felt himself drawn into a blissful sleep.

Chapter V

The cock is a sacred bird: no doubt that is why sorcerers seldom keep poultry. Cuthbert shared the prejudices of his class in this respect: his backyard was devoid of bird-life except for four sinister-looking ducks, who spent their day ambling back and forward from the withered hedge to a pool of the blackest and most revolting mud imaginable, where they disported themselves quacking hoarsely. So it came about that in the absence of a brazen-throated cock to awaken him, Fursey lay hour after hour in deep, hypnotic slumber long into the afternoon. When at last he awoke in the grey half-light of the inner room, he was reluctant to leave his bed, so appalled was he at the thought of having to face another day in the strange and terrible world beyond the blankets. His long sleep had rid him not only of bodily fatigue, but of the dumb, hopeless misery of the previous night, when indifferent to anything that might befall, he had allowed himself to be led into the house of a frantic and atrocious murderer, apparently competent in every kind of sorcery and enchantment. Fursey's mental agony became acute as he let pass before his mind the happenings of the previous day. He did not doubt but that his immortal soul was lost: he could not believe that a wizard would ever be allowed to enter Heaven; and that he had become a wizard seemed beyond doubt. And, he reflected bitterly, even in this life he was fated to be dogged everywhere he went by a hideous creature with long, black, rusty hair, bear's paws and smoky red eyes, clamouring for his blood and pestering him with offers of services of doubtful value in return. It was a black look-out.

Thought after thought turned painfully in Fursey's head. The most urgent need, he told himself, was to escape from this house, which was a hotbed of magic and necromancy. Once away he would be beyond the power of Cuthbert; and could worry about his other troubles in his own good time. But as long as he was within Cuthbert's reach anything might happen; and anything that did happen was sure to be unpleasant and deplorable. If only there was someone to advise him! A sudden thought struck him. There was one creature bound to his service, the hideous Albert. He shrank from the thought of summoning the familiar, for to do so would be a positive exercise of the damnable powers with which he was vested, and he hoped that by neglecting to use those powers he might the more readily obtain divine forgiveness for possessing them. He even cherished a hope that it might be within the competence of skilful leeches and surgeons to cure him of being a wizard, though he had an uneasy feeling that the only way to cure a wizard is to burn him. He saw himself once more on his knees at the Abbot's feet blurting out the whole pitiful story, and the Abbot Marcus, who had never been unkind to him, raising him up gently and telling him not to worry, that all would be well.

A sob shook him as he realised his predicament, and he buried his face in the pillow. He was convinced that his only chance of avoiding utter destruction at the hands of the sexton was to summon Albert to help him; yet by summoning Albert he would be accepting The Gray Mare's hateful legacy and admitting himself a practising sorcerer. He tossed on his bed in a sweat of indecision, but the issue was not long in doubt, for his fear of Cuthbert outweighed all other considerations. 'The end justifies the means,' he told himself. 'Anyway, I can seek forgiveness afterwards.' Besides, in the back of his mind swayed the vague hope that some, at least, of yesterday's happenings were just a bad dream or attributable to a heated and prepossessed imagination. Perhaps he wasn't a sorcerer at all. If Albert failed to appear when summoned, that would prove it.

Fursey sat up in bed and peered into the half-darkness.

'Albert!' he called in a hoarse whisper, 'Albert!'

For a moment nothing happened. Then Fursey discerned on the floor near the bed what appeared to be a small area of black mist.

As he stared at it with peculiar foreboding, it quickly resolved itself into a shaggy hindquarters. Fursey groaned aloud as a pair of bear's paws came into view, followed by the rest of Albert's anatomy. The familiar fixed his red eyes on Fursey expectantly.

'Breakfast?' he asked hopefully. A broad pink tongue emerged from the creature's mouth, made a circuit of his snout, and disappeared again from view.

'No,' replied Fursey with distaste. 'Not yet.'

'I see,' said Albert, his voice betraying his disappointment.

'Tell me,' queried Fursey, 'are you bound absolutely to my service?'

'Of course I am,' replied Albert. 'That is the nature of familiars.'

'Even if what I command you to do seems to you absurd and unreasonable?'

'Even so,' answered Albert. 'Your will is my will. Of course you would be wise to defer to my judgment, at least at first —'

'I know all that,' interrupted Fursey. 'Tell me, is it possible for you to betray me to someone whom I deem an enemy, to Cuthbert, the sexton, for instance?'

Albert looked surprised. 'It's not possible,' he responded. 'I'm bound by my nature to your service, save only if you fall into the hands of the law. But with regard to Cuthbert, I assure you that you're mistaken in thinking him an enemy —'

'Stop talking,' commanded Fursey.

Albert immediately ceased to speak. Fursey was conscious of a pleasant sense of power. For the first time in his life he had given an order, and he had been obeyed. He regarded the shaggy creature benevolently and noticed the hurt in its eyes.

'Come here,' he said kindly.

Albert shambled over to the edge of the bed. Fursey put out his hand and patted him on the head. Albert wagged his hindquarters delightedly, and his smoky red eyes lit up with expectancy.

'Breakfast?' he repeated hopefully.

'No,' reiterated Fursey.

Albert looked aggrieved. 'If you expect nimble and courteous service from me,' he asserted plaintively, 'you'll have to keep me fed. I'm that thirsty, the tongue is fair hanging out of my mouth for a drop of blood.'

'That's enough of that,' rejoined Fursey.

'You'll find that you have acquired a supplementary nipple,' pleaded Albert.

'I have not,' replied Fursey.

'At least have a look,' begged Albert coaxingly.

Fursey ignored the creature's request. 'Where's Cuthbert?' he asked.

'I don't know,' answered Albert.

'Well, put your head around the door and see if he's in sight.'

Albert did as he was told. 'He's not in the kitchen,' he said over his shoulder.

'Well, look outside.'

Albert disappeared from view into the outer room. In a few moments he was back.

'Cuthbert's up at the end of the garden,' he reported. 'He has a stick in his hand and a sort of skipping rope. He's putting a gargoyle through its tricks.'

Fursey concluded that the sexton was at a safe distance, so he slipped out of bed and pulled on his sandals.

'Listen, Albert,' he said, 'I want to get out of this place as quickly as possible. Can't you take me on your back and fly out through the far door and across the hills without Cuthbert knowing anything about it?'

'I cannot,' retorted Albert shortly. 'What do you think I am, a bloody bird?'

Fursey gazed at his familiar with exceeding distaste.

'Well, how am I to get away?' he asked at last.

'There are only two ways,' replied Albert, 'either by walking or by flying on your broom.'

'If I walk, Cuthbert will see me.'

'He most certainly will,' agreed Albert.

'And he probably doesn't want me to leave.'

'You can rest assured that he does not. For one thing, you know too much about the demise of my late mistress, The Gray Mare. What's to prevent you going to the authorities and denouncing him as a sorcerer?'

'What would he do if he caught me trying to escape?'

'That's hard to say,' replied Albert judiciously. 'He might turn you into a toad and keep you indefinitely in a jar in a half-pickled state, or he might compound your ingredients with the white juice of a sea-lettuce and keep you for making love philtres. On the other hand, your bones, if ground to powder and mixed with pulverised flints —'

'Stop it,' commanded Fursey as he seated himself on the edge of the bed and wiped the sweat from his face with the ragged sleeve of his habit. 'It'll have to be the broom. You had better start teaching me how to fly on a broom.'

'I can't,' rejoined Albert. 'I don't know how. You don't seem to have quite grasped our relationship. You're the master-brain, I'm only your servant.'

'It seems to me,' said Fursey shrilly, 'that as a familiar you're pretty well useless. Here, in the first crisis in my affairs since I became a sorcerer, you're not able to afford me the slightest assistance.'

'I'm doing my best,' replied Albert sulkily. 'What exactly do you want?'

'I want to get away from here without Cuthbert knowing it.'

'Well, get Cuthbert himself to teach you how to ride on a broom, and then when he's not looking, you can make your getaway.'

'Do you think it would work?' asked Fursey hopefully.

'It'll probably end by him turning you into an asp or a hyaena; but if you exercise enough guile, you may manage it.'

'Guile?' repeated Fursey.

'Yes,' said Albert shortly. 'Doesn't your own Christian teaching urge you to be not only as innocent as a dove, but as wise as a serpent?'

'So it does,' confessed Fursey, astonished at the possibility of the practical application of Christian principles to the matter in hand. He sat for a long time in thought, wondering whether he could squeeze up enough guile to deceive the wily sexton. Albert's voice broke in on his reflections.

'I hope I'm not being unreasonable,' said the familiar. 'About a quarter-pint of blood would do for to-day, just enough to keep my coat in condition.'

'Disappear,' ordered Fursey.

Albert opened his mouth to protest, but he melted away before he had time to express his resentment. Still seated on the bed Fursey calculated with a coolness of mind that astonished himself. He must win the sexton's confidence; he must convince Cuthbert that he was a genuine apprentice sorcerer eager to learn the craft and excel in wickedness. He must impress the sexton and gain his admiration and respect by pretending to be a character of more than ordinary depravity. The events that had led up to his expulsion from Clonmacnoise would be a great help. Cuthbert was sure to enquire as to his history, and a little alteration here and there in the Clonmacnoise story would make him appear a very evil fellow indeed. No need, for instance, to mention the one-time impediment in his speech; he would pretend that he had willingly harboured the demons in his cell because they were friends of his. That was sure to impress the sexton.

Fursey rose to his feet marvelling at his own ingenuity. Before leaving the room he practised a couple of evil laughs, which were so effective that he found himself shuddering at the hideous sounds which he was able to produce. Then he tiptoed out into the kitchen. There was a pleasant smell of cooking from a cauldron which was suspended over the peat fire. He observed with gratification that the broom which he had brought from The Gray Mare's cottage, was still propped in its place in the corner; and he remembered that he had a box of ointment in his pocket for use, should it be necessary to anoint it further. He hesitated for a moment in the doorway; then with a beating heart he stepped out into the open air and went round the corner of the house to meet the sexton.

It was a day of shifting sunshine and shadow. Fursey was surprised to observe that the sun had long passed its zenith and was leaning down towards the west. It was therefore late in the afternoon; no wonder he felt hungry. At the back of the house was a yard across which four ducks waddled determinedly in single file on their way to a small quagmire of filth and ooze. They crossed his path, making no attempt to get out of his way. In fact, as he approached, they quacked alarmingly and cast malevolent eyes in his direction. Fursey gave them a wide berth: you never knew in a place like this what was going to happen next — in one moment one of those ducks might have him by the throat.

At the other side of the yard was a blasted oak. Fursey carefully avoided its shadow and found himself at the edge of a small orchard. He shuddered and hesitated, for he remembered that orchards were peculiarly connected with sorcery due to the Devil's well-known interest in apples. Before he had summoned up courage to enter and walk down the avenue of fatal trees, he observed Cuthbert at the far end. The sexton waved to him cheerily and began at once to approach, not seeming to walk, but to glide with a curious smooth motion about a foot off the ground. As he alighted beside Fursey the latter put down his hand in an attempt to stay the knocking of his knees beneath his habit. To the sexton's polite enquiry as to how he had slept, Fursey replied hoarsely that he had slept very well indeed. The ex-monk had by now fallen into so languid a state that when Cuthbert invited him to walk through the orchard with him and view his domain, Fursey experienced considerable difficulty in putting one foot before the other without falling on the ground. As they slowly paced the patterned sunlight and shadow beneath the trees, Cuthbert emitted a deep, long-drawn, unearthly sigh.

'How I envy you,' he said. 'There's something beautiful about a man at the threshold of his career. And what a career! By magic felicity can be conferred on one's friends and destruction wrought on one's enemies. The skies will be yours to command, you will ride the winds and the hurricane. It will be in your power to bring madness, and to countenance or thwart fertility. You will pass through the gates of midnight to the caverns of the dead, there to learn the awful secrets of existence. Ah, Fursey, my friend, forgive me if I repeat myself; but my heart is full of joy for you. I cannot understand why, with this immense heritage in your grasp, you still remain languid and apparently reluctant. It is that you are a man with a natural super-abundance of melancholy?'

Fursey's reply came from his throat in a husky whistle: 'I think I have not yet fully realised my good fortune.'

Cuthbert nodded understandingly, and when he spoke again his voice was heightened with enthusiasm.

'You will have intercourse with sylphs and salamanders,' he declared. 'You will learn the virtue of herb, wood and stone. You will learn to raise spirits by conjured circles. Circles, you must understand, are made round, triangular, quadrangular, single, double, or treble according to the form of apparition that you crave. Much you will learn by studying the entrails of beasts, by the singing of fowls and by their actions in the air.'

'It sounds very interesting,' quavered Fursey.

'Interesting!' shouted Cuthbert. 'Do you realise the fierce joy of hidden knowledge and secret power? To the magician nothing is impossible. He knows the language of the stars and directs the planetary courses. The elements obey him. When he speaks, the moon falls blood-red from heaven, the dead arise in their shrouds and mutter ominous words as the night wind whistles through their skulls. The wizard at his pleasure can dispense joy or misery to mankind. He is the master of past, present and future. And this you speak of as "interesting"!'

Fursey passed his tongue over his parched lips.

'Is it not the case,' he enquired feebly, 'that sorcerers usually end their lives in a violent and dishonourable manner?'

'No,' thundered Cuthbert. 'Given ordinary guile and cunning, the sorcerer is master of his own safety. With the exercise of reasonable care he can be neither surprised by misfortune nor overwhelmed by disaster.'

'I see,' said Fursey.

'Well,' asked Cuthbert more affably. 'What kind of a sorcerer do you think you'll make?'

'I'm afraid I'll need a good deal of practice and instruction,' replied Fursey. 'I must get you to teach me how to fly on a broom to begin with.'

'All in good time,' answered Cuthbert. 'You will certainly need practice and careful instruction, but what you require most of all is courage. Neither skill nor courage must fail you; if they do, there will be disaster. A sorcerer who is afraid of water, will never command the Undines; one who is timid of fire, will never impress his will on salamanders. If one is liable to giddiness, one must leave the sylphs alone and forbear from irritating gnomes; for you must know that inferior spirits will only obey a power that has overcome them in their own element.'

'Have no fear that you will find me lacking in courage,' squeaked Fursey.

Cuthbert threw a quick look at him, but did not reply. Fursey's heart began to hammer beneath his habit, and he plunged into a halting account of his adventures in Clonmacnoise. They had reached the further end of the orchard and stood at the fence gazing out over the sexton's garden, which stretched from where they stood to the hedge that bounded The Gray Mare's property. There were a few hazel trees and chestnuts and neat rows of deadly nightshade, wild parsley and sage. Fursey observed peaches and bitter almonds, and against the graveyard wall fungi noted for their deadly and narcotic properties. As he related the dark and mysterious tale of the invasion of Clonmacnoise, he noted with gratification that the sexton seemed impressed. Fursey's courage grew with his narration, and he talked glibly of his acquaintance with incubi, hydras and gryphons; and boasted that when the legions of Hell had been all but defeated, he was the one who had saved them from expulsion from the monastery.

'You acted very well,' said Cuthbert at last. 'It's true that demons are inferior spiritual intelligences, with whom I have little to do. They are a creation of Christianity, while I am the servant of a more venerable religion; still, demons are all right in their own place. I have more liking for them than for monks and religious jugglers. You tell me that you are acquainted with Satan himself?'

'Acquainted!' echoed Fursey indignantly. 'He's a very dear friend of mine.'

'Good,' said Cuthbert with a tinge of respect in his voice.

Fursey realised that now was the moment to win the master sorcerer's full confidence. He emitted an evil laugh and leered wickedly at the sexton.

'Well, what's doing to-day?' he asked throatily.

Cuthbert's eyes expressed well-bred surprise.

'I beg your pardon,' he replied.

'What's doing in the way of iniquity?' demanded Fursey, rubbing his hands in his best sinister fashion.

'Oh,' responded Cuthbert. 'Perhaps to-night we'll sacrifice a live cock at the crossroads by way of initiating you.'

Fursey's eyes expressed his disappointment. He stuck out his underlip.

'Aren't there any women around?' he asked harshly. 'I'd like to make the acquaintance of a lively and engaging female vampire. Couldn't you conjure up one for me?'

Cuthbert became very grave. Fursey's heart missed a beat as he thought for a moment that his request was going to be granted. The sexton took him by the arm.

'My dear Fursey,' he said, 'you must learn to walk before you can fly. I must warn you that the activities of vampires are very destructive of the health of their acquaintances. In fact, visits from the tribe are fraught with danger.'

'Ah, who minds danger?' retorted Fursey lustily. 'We must have courage.'

Cuthbert shook his head gravely.

'If you take my advice,' he said, 'you'll lay off the vampires. I had one staying with me here once for the week-end, a rather cadaverous gentleman. I distinctly recollect that when he took his departure on the Monday morning, he left me somewhat debilitated as a result of his attentions. I never invited one since. After all, that was no way to repay hospitality.'

'I suppose you're right,' admitted Fursey.

They moved away from the fence and started to walk slowly back along a path that bordered the orchard.

'Strange thing,' said Cuthbert. 'When you were telling me just now of the demons in the shape of fabulous beasts with whom you are acquainted, your story recalled to my mind an incident that happened to me when I was a young man. I had forgotten it these many years.'

'Yes,' said Fursey politely.

'I suppose you've never met a basilisk?' asked Cuthbert.

Fursey thought rapidly and decided that it was safer to say 'no'.

'Just as well for you,' observed Cuthbert. 'You'd scarcely be here if you had. Instead there would be a fine stone statue to you in Clonmacnoise. This story of mine has a moral, so you might as well hear it. The moral is: "Keep your wits about you and always act with expedition in a crisis".'

'Act with expedition in a crisis,' repeated Fursey. 'I'll make a note of it.'

'When I was quite a young man,' began Cuthbert, 'I was out walking one evening along a country road, when on turning a corner I came suddenly on a basilisk rambling along by himself enjoying, I suppose, the mild evening air. Fortunately I recognised him at once for what he was, and knowing that the gaze of a basilisk turns one to stone if one is so foolish as to meet it, I immediately dropped my eyes and fixed them on a spot on the road midway between his front two hooves. At the same time I bent rapidly and picked up from the ground a piece of straight stick which was lying to hand.'

'And did you feel no ill-effect from his gaze?' asked Fursey breathlessly.

'I felt a certain chill,' conceded Cuthbert, 'and I cannot say but that an occasional twinge of rheumatism which I get to the present day is not the result of his survey. However, my whole being told me that I must act with the utmost despatch; so, holding the piece of stick vertically at arm's length, I advanced it rapidly to the tip of his nose. I did not dare look up, but I judged accurately where the tip of his nose must be, by keeping my eyes directed on a spot on the road midway between his front hooves. As you know, the instinct of both animal and human is to keep the eyes fixed on any object that is rapidly approaching. A basilisk's eyes are protuberant, so that by the time the vertical stick had reached his nose, his two protuberant eyes were looking inward at one another, and he effectively turned himself into stone. When I ventured to look up, there was a very fine specimen of a young bull basilisk in stone with his eyes crossed.'

'Dear me,' ejaculated Fursey.

'He remained there for many years, much admired by the besotted peasantry, and an object of great interest to visitors. Finally he was discovered by an archaeologist who had lost his way one night. A learned paper was written, and a whole school of archaeologists descended on the neighbourhood from the monastery of Cong. They took measurements and drew pictures of him, and wrote several shelves of learned volumes. I understand that they argued his presence proved the early inhabitants of this island to have come from the land of Egypt, where such monuments abound. The fact that his eyes were looking into one another interested them greatly; and they deduced from that fact that the religion of our Egyptian forefathers laid great stress on the virtues of introspection.'

'Is he there still?' asked Fursey.

'Unfortunately,' replied Cuthbert, 'some years later the local authority broke him up for road metal. As you are no doubt aware, material considerations in this country always outweigh considerations of antiquarian interest. I thought it was a pity myself. He was an interesting and unusual monument of our past and was of considerable importance to the local tourist industry.'

'Well,' averred Fursey, 'I'll know what to do if I ever meet a basilisk.'

Their path had brought them to a small grotto in the shade of an oak tree that seemed to Fursey to have a particularly haunted look. Cuthbert paused.

'I want to show you my latest acquisition,' he remarked, 'a young gargoyle which I purchased from a seafaring man from the country of the Franks.'

He whistled sharply, and an ungainly creature lurched into view from the dark interior of the grotto. It was swarthy in hue and had two sharply pointed ears. Its mouth hung open in a permanent grin, and from the tip of its tongue there was a steady drip of yellowish liquid. Fursey, who felt himself afraid of nothing as long as he had Cuthbert on his side, cautiously ventured out his hand to pet the creature.

'Be careful,' warned the sexton. 'That drip from its tongue is venom. Every drop wounds.'

Fursey hastily withdrew his hand and stepped back a pace.

'It's nearly an obsolete form,' explained Cuthbert, 'although the creatures were at one time common in the country of the Franks. Of late the people in those territories have been making images of them in stone and affixing them to the exterior of their churches.

There's a perverse strain in the master builders of that country, which finds expression from time to time in such freakish behaviour.'

'What are you going to do with him?' asked Fursey.

'Well,' said Cuthbert, 'it's a little experiment of mine. I'm trying to make him half-human. I hope to pass him off as a minor man of letters. He has many of the qualities. Observe the cute narrowly-spaced eyes and the steady dribble of venom from the tongue. He will make a very passable man of letters, or rather one who imagines himself to be a man of letters.'

'He doesn't look very human to me,' observed Fursey.

'He's not supposed to be very human,' rejoined Cuthbert. 'Didn't I tell you he's to be a minor literary man? Wait.'

Cuthbert put his hand into his pocket and took out a handful of horse's teeth, which he spaced carefully across the gargoyle's mouth, beneath the upper lip. 'How's that?' he asked.

'I suppose it's an improvement,' muttered Fursey, without much conviction.

Cuthbert nodded to the gargoyle, which shambled back into the depths of its cave. The sexton glanced up at the sun, which was very round and red, and just above the horizon. 'Time for something to eat,' he remarked, and started to lead the way back to the cottage. As the two sorcerers crossed the orchard, the shadows of the trees lay like long grasping arms across the grass. With the advent of evening Fursey felt that something more than eerie had begun to pervade the neighbourhood of the sexton's house. As they left the orchard and passed the blasted oak at the end of the yard, something in its woody depths sighed heartbrokenly.

'What was that?' enquired Fursey with a tremor of fear in his voice.

Cuthbert smiled slightly. 'A tax-collector whom I embedded there many years ago,' he replied. 'A very forward fellow.'

As they made their way across the yard, the four ducks buried their heads in their inky pool, so that as Fursey and Cuthbert passed, only four sinister sterns were visible pointing heavenwards. Whether they were eating mud off the bottom or whether it was an act of homage to their master, Fursey was unable to say. Cuthbert pushed in the door of the cottage, and Fursey, with growing apprehension, followed him into the kitchen. The sexton took the lid off the cauldron, which was simmering over fire, and smelt its contents.

'Done to a turn,' he remarked brightly. He removed the meat with a pair of tongs and placing it on the table, deftly hacked it into two portions with a hatchet. He pushed one portion in front of Fursey.

'I think I can produce food too,' announced Fursey, who thought it was time to give a further demonstration of his wickedness. 'You haven't got a rope, have you?'

Cuthbert pointed to a coil of rope on the wall, and watched approvingly while Fursey took the rope down and with trembling hands cast one end of it over the crossbeam that supported the roof.

'What will we require?' asked Fursey.

'Butter, bread, ale and condiments,' replied Cuthbert, beaming at his pupil.

Fursey fixed his mind on butter and pulled the rope gently. A lump of choice butter slid half-way down the rope, stopped, and travelled back into the rafters again, where it disappeared.

'You must pull harder,' said Cuthbert encouragingly.

Fursey flung all his weight on the rope and was immediately deluged in a shower of foodstuffs. Rather breathlessly he retrieved them from the door and placed them in a neat pile on the table.

'My soul is lost,' he told himself; but he didn't allow his mind to dwell on such a painful subject. As he seated himself at the table he found himself wishing that he knew how to imprison Cuthbert in a tin canister, so that he might make his escape. The two ate in silence, Fursey tearing greedily at the meat, for he was very hungry. At length they sat back and contemplated with satisfaction the heap of bones that lay piled between them.

'Do you know,' began Cuthbert, 'I never saw a goodlier man than yourself, nor one so well of eating. It's hard to believe that you're a monk at large.'

'I'm no longer a monk,' responded Fursey. 'They relieved me of my vows. That was good meat,' he added by way of changing the subject.

'Very succulent,' agreed the sexton. 'I'm very addicted to goat's flesh myself.'

A sudden feeling of nausea clutched at Fursey's stomach.

'Was that a goat?' he asked faintly.

'Yes,' replied Cuthbert, his eyes glinting viciously, 'that was The Gray Mare's goat. She died last night in the course of certain operations of a magical character which I was forced to conduct in self-defence. I think you were present at the time.'

Generous tears came into Fursey's eyes as he gazed down at the neat heap of bones which represented the last mortal remains of his late acquaintance. 'I'm not only a sorcerer,' he told himself, 'I'm a cannibal.'

The sexton noticed his distress.

'Come now,' he said soothingly, 'a mug of ale.'

He filled two beakers, and a long draught of the heady brew served to clear Fursey's depression of spirit.

'To give that goat her due,' said Cuthbert, 'she was a most remarkable animal. One afternoon in the course of one of her incursions into my garden she ate a row and a half of belladonna — enough poison to lay every man, woman and child in the territory on their backs frothing at the mouth, but did she show any sign of it? Not a bit, except for a gamey light in her eye. She finished off with a dessert of mandrakes, hemlock and hazelnuts, and walked back to The Gray Mare's cottage without a stagger.'

Fursey contemplated the heap of bones and shook his head sadly.

'You know,' continued Cuthbert reminiscently, 'The Gray Mare was a bit of a snob — she liked to show off, and she always rode that goat to a sabbath instead of coming on a broom like the other warlocks and witches of the countryside. I remember once as she was flying by the steeple of Kilpuggin Church, nothing would do the goat but to turn aside to eat the weather vane and some of the lead off the spire. It was a most comical sight — the other witches careering by on their brooms enjoying to the full The Gray Mare's embarrassment; while the poor old lady, red in the face and half mad with chagrin, belaboured the goat and tried to drag her away from the weather vane, and all the while the goat held on to the lead of the spire with her teeth.'

Cuthbert was silent as memory after memory chased across his forehead. At length Fursey ventured to speak.

'I don't wish to interrupt your contemplations,' he said, 'but I have resolved to let no day pass without learning something of value to me in my new profession. I should deem it a great favour if you would instruct me as to how to ride on a broom. I have my late wife's besom with me, and it wants still a couple of hours to darkness. I could do a couple of practice flights up and down the orchard.'

'Certainly,' replied Cuthbert, 'but first I must show you my store-room.'

Fursey chafed at the prolongation of his stay in the cottage, but he was careful to avoid arousing the sexton's suspicions. It was evident that Cuthbert was rather vain of his possessions. The sexton led the way across the room to what seemed to Fursey to be a blank wall.

'You see,' remarked Cuthbert, 'the magician also controls visibility.'

He clapped his hands and uttered a string of evil-sounding jargon. Immediately there appeared in the wall a green door engraved with the mystical number seven. Cuthbert opened it, and they went in.

The store-room was not large, but its contents were so neatly packed on shelving which reached from floor to ceiling, that advantage had been taken of every inch of available space. Fursey realised with horror that he was in a veritable arsenal of witchcraft. There was a shelf of witches' poisons: aconite, deadly nightshade and hemlock. Neat trays contained the ingredients for vicious brews and enchantments: hazelnuts, chestnuts, mandrakes, mallows, metals, poplar leaves, salt, wild parsley and vervain. There was a plentiful supply of mandragora, which is potent in death spells. In a corner was a keg of powder suitable for the manufacture of love philtres. There were cages containing snakes, toads, frogs, beetles, hornets, ferrets, owls, vipers and asps; and a neat row of bats hung upside down from a rack on the wall. In carefully labelled boxes there were moles' feet, murderers' knucklebones, hogs' bristles, sage, powdered flints and loadstone. Nothing was wanting that might be required in the black ceremonies of the night. Fursey realised with horror how well Cuthbert was supplied so as promptly to execute whatever iniquity his mind might suggest.

'It's fascinating,' he muttered as he followed Cuthbert out again into the kitchen, and the green door effaced itself from the wall behind them.

'Fascinating,' said Cuthbert, 'but rather frightening. Isn't that what you really mean?'

'Yes,' agreed Fursey.

Cuthbert seemed pleased at this attitude of mind in his pupil, and as they made their way once more to the orchard, he chatted wickedly, giving Fursey many abominable counsels. Fursey scarcely heard him, his mind was too taken up with the necessity of making his departure with the utmost despatch. He kept a tight grip on the broom, which he had taken from its corner behind the door. When they reached the orchard, they took their stand on the grass between the trees.

'You'll have a clear run,' remarked Cuthbert, 'down the avenue between the trees, and then you can fly back. Don't try for altitude at first. Keep about a yard and a half off the ground.'

'What do I do?' asked Fursey.

'Throw your leg across, and sit on it,' replied Cuthbert. 'It's only a matter of balance.'

'But how do I make it go?' enquired Fursey.

'Just wish it to go,' answered Cuthbert. 'You can give your directions aloud if you like.'

'But is it not the case,' queried Fursey anxiously, 'that once unknown forces have been unloosed, not even the sorcerer himself can always control them?'

'Nonsense,' retorted Cuthbert. 'I don't know where you got these odd scraps of information. They're certainly not applicable in the circumstances. Try it now.'

Fursey gripped the broom frantically with his hands and knees. He closed his eyes.

'Fly,' he lisped in a thin, quavering voice.

He was conscious of being suddenly yanked into the air and found himself a moment later in a tree. Cuthbert was standing underneath with set lips contemplating the broken branches and the pink apple blossom which was still fluttering to the ground.

'What did you do that for?' asked the sexton crossly. 'Come down.'

'How did I get here?' asked Fursey in amazement.

'You flew straight into it,' replied Cuthbert shortly. 'Come down before you do any more damage.'

Fursey descended amid a further shower of apple blossom.

'Now be careful,' admonished Cuthbert. 'Look where you're going.'

Fursey threw his leg over the broom once more. 'Fly,' he repeated desperately.

The broom shot over the hedge, across the yard and made straight for the wall of the cottage.

'Stop!' howled Fursey.

The broom reared in mid-air, and fell, together with Fursey, into the ducks' pool.

'You appear to have an impetuous and fatal tendency to do the wrong thing,' asserted Cuthbert a moment later, as he helped Fursey out of the quagmire. 'You're very black; you better come in and wash yourself. I wonder where my ducks are.'

'I'll try it once more,' declared Fursey desperately. He pointed the handle of the broom at the gap between the cottage and the clump of neighbouring trees.

'Fly,' he shouted, 'as quick as you can.'

The broom sprang forward. It just missed the gable of the cottage, and in a moment was careering down the road borne at a height of about two yards above the ground.

'Come back!' he heard the sexton shouting, but he bent his head over the handle of the broom and whispered agonisingly, 'Quicker!'

His habit flapped madly in the breeze as he careered around the bend of the road and over a bridge. It was difficult to steer the broom around the many corners of the road without disaster, but Fursey clung on grimly, a great feeling of exultation in his heart. 'I'm away,' he kept telling himself. 'I've escaped.'

A mongrel dog came tearing out of a farmhouse and followed the broom for half a mile barking furiously, but the pace was too much for him, and he had to give up the chase exhausted. A band of pilgrims which was coming along the road intoning a doleful hymn, dropped their staves when they saw Fursey approaching, and precipitated themselves over the hedges. One foolish fellow who kept running back and forward, unable to make up his mind as to whether the left- or right-hand ditch promised the greater safety, had reason to repent his indecision, for he was struck on the forehead by Fursey's sandal and stretched senseless as the broom careered past. Fursey held on like grim death, not presuming to move a muscle for fear he would fall off. The cattle in the fields stared at him with unbelieving eyes before turning to scamper in all directions. A hen who seemed to imagine that he was chasing her, ran in front of him for at least a mile before flinging herself in desperation through a hole in the hedge.

Fursey had been so intent on escaping from Cuthbert's cottage that he had given no thought at all to the question of where he was to go. This problem began now to insinuate itself into his mind. The only place he could think of was the monastery. It was the only home he knew, and the Abbot Marcus was the only person who had ever been really kind to him. So he bent towards the broom handle and whispered: 'Take me to Clonmacnoise.'

No sooner were the words uttered than the broom forsook the road and made across country towards the line of mountains. Most alarming of all, it started to rise steadily, and the terrified Fursey observed the fields beneath him shrinking in size and the roads becoming thin wavering threads. It seemed to him that his plight was desperate, alone in the upper air, with only a slippery shaft of wood between him and destruction. Suppose he ran into a cloud and was suffocated!

'Albert!' he called hoarsely. 'Albert!'

Slowly the familiar took shape, seated on the broom handle facing Fursey. His fur was all blown backwards by the wind, and he clung desperately to the slippery handle with his bear's paws. He glared at Fursey with angry resentment.

'Nice time to summon me,' he snarled. 'Do you want to break my neck as well as your own?'

'Albert,' whimpered Fursey, 'stop it from going so high. Bring it down nearer the earth.'

'Why did you get on to the bloody yoke,' screamed Albert, 'when you didn't know how to manage it?'

'Albert, please. How will I get it to go down?'

'You've only to tell it to stop,' shouted Albert above the screaming of the wind. 'Not now, you nincompoop! We're flying over a lake.'

Fursey ventured to look down and saw a stretch of water far below. He shuddered and closed his eyes.

'Albert, don't go away.'

'Open your eyes and look where you're going,' howled Albert. 'Do you want us to crash into a mountain at this speed?'

'Albert, I'm sorry if I was ever unkind to you —'

Albert bared his teeth in a hideous grin.

'Order me to disappear,' he screeched. 'I'm only upsetting the balance of the broom.'

'Don't go, Albert. I like your company.'

Albert glared at his master with his eyes full of bale.

'We're crossing the mountain ridge,' gasped Fursey.

Albert made an effort and swallowed his ire. 'Tell the broom to go down to within a few yards of the ground and not to hit anything,' he said huskily.

Fursey managed to enunciate the command and added the injunction that speed should be slackened. The broom descended and swooped gracefully over a mountain top. Fursey drew his breath and looked around him. They were descending a green, swampy glen that cut deep into the hills. Lower in the valley were scattered cottages and in the distance a glittering river winding through the plain. He recognised the curve of the River Shannon.

'It won't be far now,' he announced joyfully.

'If you're making for Clonmacnoise, as I judge from the look of the countryside,' responded Albert, 'I'd advise you to dismiss me. I don't imagine I'll be popular with the monks.'

'That's true,' admitted Fursey. 'You may vanish.'

Albert thoughtlessly permitted his paws to disappear first, with the result that he fell off the broom before the process was complete. Fursey looked over his shoulder and saw the familiar rolling among the rocks and vanishing as he rolled. But Fursey had no time to feel concern for Albert's safety. The broom had crossed a small stream on the floor of the valley and was ascending a low ridge of grassy hill. As it topped the rise Fursey saw the broad, sluggish Shannon before him meandering between its lines of golden reeds. Between him and the river was the Pilgrims' Way and a mile away on his left the two round towers and the cluttered huts of Clonmacnoise. As he came sailing down the hillside and turned into the Pilgrims' Way he saw monks who had been working in scattered groups in the fields, suddenly dropping their spades and running hell-for-leather for the monastery. As he approached flying at a height of six feet above the roadway, he saw the great gates being slammed, and a moment later a discordant clamour of bells smote the air. The broom reared sharply and flung Fursey on to the road, where he rolled over and over in the dust.

When he scrambled to his feet he found he was only twenty paces from the gates. A sea of horrified white faces stared out at him from between the wickerwork. The din of the bells was deafening, for the monks were ringing everything that they had got. As they watched the ragged, entirely black figure picking itself up off the road and come staggering towards the gates, they retreated precipitately, ringing their handbells like so many maniacs. Brother Patrick's horror was such that he lost the use of his legs, and on the approach of the ooze- and slime-covered stranger, he pitched forward senseless. Father Crustaceous began a hymn in a thin, cracked treble; and those of the monks who were able to produce a sound from their throats, followed him in shrill falsettos. Quavering, the hymn rose and fell.

Fursey reached the gates and gripping the wickerwork desperately with his hands, he stared in, half-blinded with tears at the wide semi-circle of retreating monks and the prone body of Brother Patrick in the foreground.

'Let me in,' he cried. 'I'm Fursey. Brother Fursey.'

The hymn stopped dead on a high note, but was immediately taken up with renewed vigour. If anything, the clangour of the handbells increased, and it was swollen by the pealing of the great bell of the monastery which Father Sampson had reached and was dragging at, as if he wanted to pull down the steeple. Again and again Fursey cried aloud for admittance, but on the semi-circle of white faces he could see only horror and hatred. Still holding fast to the wickerwork, he sank in a heap on the ground and buried his head, sobbing bitterly.

The singing and the rattling of the bells ceased suddenly as the Abbot Marcus strode out of the great church and forced his way through the crowd of monks.

'What's the matter?' he demanded sternly.

'Fursey!' shouted a dozen voices.

The Abbot looked towards the gate; then his eyes fell on Brother Patrick, who had recovered consciousness, but had not enough strength in his arms to raise himself from the ground. In his efforts to rise the wretched lay brother was scratching at the ground like a dog digging a hole.

'What's wrong with Brother Patrick?' demanded the Abbot.

'Fright,' replied Father Leo.

'Some of you go and help him,' commanded the Abbot.

The monks looked at one another uncertainly, but under the Abbot's fixed gaze two of the fathers stepped forward and advanced gingerly towards the gate. They lifted the prostrate lay brother under the armpits and ran back quickly with him to the others, his feet trailing along the ground behind him. Father Sampson was with difficulty detached from the monastery bell-rope and instructed to practice his first aid on Brother Patrick.

The Abbot stood motionless gazing across the short intervening space to where Fursey lay slumped before the gate. A few of the older monks had crowded around the Abbot and were talking to him in urgent whispers.

'We all saw him! He flew over the hill and down the road on a broom. There it is, about twenty paces down the road, can't you see it?'

For a long time the Abbot Marcus stood silent and like a statue, while the semi-circle of monks watched breathlessly. Then the Abbot moved. Brother Cook immediately burst from the crowd and flung himself at the Abbot's feet.

'Don't let him back,' he wailed. 'Father Abbot, don't let him back. If you let him back, there'll be demons grinning at me from every corner of the kitchen.'

The Abbot paid no heed, but advancing slowly towards the gate, he began to pull back the wooden bolts. A murmur of horror arose from the monks. Marcus dragged the gate open and stepped out into the road. Fursey turned up a grimy, tear-stained face.

'Get up, Fursey,' commanded the Abbot.

Fursey struggled uncertainly to his feet.

'Come with me,' said the Abbot, and he led the way down the road to a grassy bank, on which he seated himself.

'You may sit down too, Fursey,' he said.

Fursey seated himself on a stone. Within the gates the horrified monks had fallen on their knees, and Father Crustaceous was leading the prayers 'for the safety of our beloved father, the Abbot'.

'Now tell me everything,' commanded the Abbot. 'Why have you left your wife?'

Fursey's story took a long time. The shadow of approaching night deepened on the Pilgrims' Way; a chill breeze moved among the rushes at the river's edge and came stirring the long grasses by the roadside. From within the monastery gates the murmur of prayer arose and fell, and all the time the Abbot sat motionless looking into Fursey's face as the story was slowly unfolded. Occasionally his eyes widened with surprise, but he spoke no word until Fursey had finished. Then he sighed.

'So it's true,' he said, 'that you flew over the hill on a broom. You admit that you're a sorcerer?'

'Yes,' agreed Fursey. 'I'm a sorcerer.'

For a long time nothing more was said. A rabbit emerged on the far side of the track, and stared hard at the two motionless figures before bolting again into its burrow.

At length the Abbot arose. He seemed stiff and tired.

'I can't let you into the monastery,' he said, 'but there's a swineherd's hut beside the river. You can sleep there for the night. In the morning we'll talk further.'

Fursey thanked him profusely, and together they walked down to the hut by the river. When the swineherd was informed that Fursey was to pass the night in his hut, he manifested a marked disinclination to remain there himself. He volunteered to sleep out on the mountain if the monastery could not accommodate him, but the Abbot promised him a pallet within the gates, and assisted with his own hands in spreading the straw for Fursey's bed. As he and the swineherd made ready to depart, Fursey from his couch in the straw suddenly seized the Abbot's hand and kissed it. When the door closed behind them, he stretched himself on his warm, rustling bed, his face wet with happy tears.

Chapter VI

In the chill, unfriendly morning when the sky was yellowing in the east, the monk whom the Abbot had despatched to Cashel on his fleetest horse, arrived back at Clonmacnoise, jaded and travel-stained, at the head of a troop of armed men. The door of the swineherd's hut was flung open, and Fursey was dragged out. He was thrown on his face, and his hands fastened behind his back with stout thongs. Fursey whimpered as he was pulled on to his feet and bundled into a high cart. The Abbot stood in the roadway, his face as if carved out of stone. Trembling, Fursey ventured to look at him.

'I must do my duty like every other man,' said the Abbot. 'You have admitted that you are a sorcerer. Goodbye, Fursey.'

He turned and walked slowly back to the monastery while Fursey stood making little whimpering sounds as he watched the retreating figure. A soldier raised the butt of his spear and pushed Fursey on to the floor of the cart, where he lay in abject misery. The soldiers were more diffident about handling the broom. Four of them took it gingerly and quickly tied it to a second cart which had been provided for the purpose. Then the procession moved off rapidly, armed men riding before and behind.

It was a dreary journey, the cart jolting along the rocky road, mile after mile, while the sun arose, became enmeshed in patches of grey cloud and was finally lost in the overcast sky. The thin rain fell, wetting Fursey through and through. He lay prostrate on the floor of the cart, more a suffering animal than a man, more a dumb, lifeless thing than an animal. They paused about mid-day beneath some overhanging trees, the soldiers crouching for shelter from the rain while they ate ravenously their small ration of bread and stopped to drink at a wayside well. No one came to feed Fursey. They moved off again through the thin mist, the horses steaming, their riders cursing and yanking at the bits every time they stumbled. Mile after weary mile was left behind, and it was late in the evening when the exhausted cavalcade arrived at the northern gate of Cashel.

The torchlight shone on the ruddy faces of the guards as the wicker gates were dragged open, and the troop moved slowly between the cabins to draw rein finally before the cluster of monastic huts which occupied a quarter of the area of the city. Fursey was hoisted from the cart; and as he was too stiff to walk, he was carried within the enclosure, down a flight of steps, and into a cave-like cell which had been excavated deep in the earth. He was flung on a crude pallet, where he lay motionless. His captors untied his limbs, and closing the door behind them, left him in darkness. Hour after hour he lay in his wet clothes shivering with cold and misery, until at last sleep came, and he slumbered fitfully.

On the following morning Bishop Flanagan breakfasted heartily on eels' meat and stirabout, washed down by a flagon of black ale. Father Furiosus was early in attendance, and when he had kissed the Bishop's ring, he wryly sipped the dregs of ale which the hospitable prelate poured into a cup for him. A slave was despatched to the Royal House with a message that the Bishop desired the presence of the King. Cormac lost no time, but came galloping in his chariot down the hill from his own house and up the hill to the Bishop's Palace. Stable boys ran to hold the restive steeds and assist the monarch to alight. Cormac entered the Palace and the Bishop's presence with all the dignity possible to a man only five feet in height. After the usual courtesies the three seated themselves, and the Bishop broached the matter in hand.

'I have given the affair much thought,' began the prelate, 'and I have no doubt whatever but that we have in custody a wizard of the most subtle character imaginable. Father Furiosus and I have met this man before, and his seeming innocence is in the highest degree deceptive. For twenty years he has succeeded in deceiving the worthy monks at Clonmacnoise and in convincing them that he is a man of exemplary virtue. When I presided at his nuptials a few days ago, having a quick capacity I did vehemently suspect him, for I felt that such innocence and simplicity as he manifested were altogether out of the course of nature; but I allowed myself to be persuaded by the Abbot Marcus, whom this odious sorcerer appears to have thoroughly befooled. We have had ample evidence that the countryside is abounding fearfully in witches and wizards. They will have us all properly bedevilled unless we take immediate steps to thwart their direful and insupportable activities. I believe this man, Fursey, to be the Master and Prince of the satanic coven which operates in this neighbourhood. The good God has delivered him into our hands. Nothing remains but to torment him as grievously as can be devised, prior to burning him alive and scattering his ashes to the wind.'

King Cormac nodded sagaciously, but deemed it wise to say nothing until a question was addressed to him. Father Furiosus shifted his great bulk on his stool.

'Of course,' he said heavily, 'the wretched man is entitled to a fair trial.'

'He'll get it,' snapped the Bishop. 'A fair trial and a quick burning, but first we must sift him as wheat: he must undergo the question, ordinary and extraordinary.'

'The matter of torture hardly arises,' observed the friar, 'if he admits his guilt, as I understand he does.'

The Bishop's underlip began to vibrate with a curious jerking motion as he sensed opposition.

'What about his accomplices in the monstrous and detestable art?' he asked with acrimony. 'Only by the most prolonged and excruciating torments can we hope to wring from him the names of the members of his coven, so that we may utterly destroy the infernal regiment and prevent thousands of innocent people being carried away to their final confusion. Don't you agree with me?' he asked, turning sharply to the King.

'Of course, my lord,' answered Cormac hurriedly.

'It needs thought,' retorted Furiosus obstinately, 'but first of all one of us should visit him in his cell to ascertain from his own lips whether or not he is pleading guilty to the dire charges that are laid against him. Procedure in these matters has been fixed by centuries of traditional practice, and it would ill behove us to depart from what is usual. I know that your lordship would not wish to break with the established tradition of the Church.'

'Of course not,' said the Bishop hastily. 'God forbid!'

'Then no doubt your lordship will wish to undertake the examination personally?'

The Bishop stirred uncomfortably. 'Is it not the case,' he asked hesitantly, 'that sorcerers, even when they are in custody, are sometimes dangerous to those that approach them?'

'Sorcerers are always dangerous,' replied Furiosus smoothly.

The Bishop's eyes shifted nervously from the placid face of the friar to that of King Cormac.

'I imagine,' he said, 'that the King, as representative of the civil arm, should undertake the holy duty of interviewing and questioning the prisoner.'

'I plead to be excused,' exclaimed the King. 'I know nothing of witchcraft, or of how these people should be examined. Father Furiosus is experienced in these matters. He is licensed by the Synod of Kells to search for necromancers and conjurors. Surely it is but commonsense to let him conduct the proceedings, seeing that he has conducted many such examinations without hurt to himself.'

'Well, Furiosus?' said the Bishop.

'I will conduct the preliminary examination if your lordship wishes it,' replied the friar, 'but only on one condition.'

'You presume to make conditions with me?' asked the Bishop hotly.

'I do,' rejoined Furiosus, pushing out his red, stubbly jowl determinedly. 'I beg respectfully to remind you that I am licensed for this work by a Synod of the Church, and that I'm merely a visitor in your lordship's diocese, and as such not subject to your lordship's jurisdiction. If your lordship does not wish to make use of my services, I shall betake myself to another diocese where perhaps my work will be accorded greater appreciation.'

The Bishop bent a sour gaze on the sturdy friar.

'What is the condition on which you insist?' he enquired at last.

'I'm a man,' said Furiosus, 'who is not accustomed to do things by halves. If I'm to conduct the preliminary examination of this man, I must have charge of the entire proceedings — his trial, torture and execution.'

For some moments the Bishop hesitated.

'Very well,' he agreed grudgingly.

'Order the prisoner to be conveyed here,' said Furiosus. 'I'll examine him in your presence and in the presence of the King.'

'But is not the proximity of a sorcerer dangerous in the extreme?' began the Bishop.

'Not when one knows how to handle him,' retorted the friar. 'He should be led here with his hands tied and with an adequate armed guard.'

When Fursey was dragged out of his dank cell, he stood at first blinking in the light of day while the soldiers pinioned his hands behind his back. As they led him between the huts and up the incline to the Bishop's Palace, he began to notice the motley groups of people in the streets and the unusual hubbub. A many-coloured stream of life was pouring into the settlement, for it had been noised far abroad that a master-sorcerer had been taken. As Fursey was led past, the crowds withdrew hastily into the shadows between the cabins, from which they watched him with livid faces. With sick apprehension he observed a file of men sedulously toiling up the incline bowed beneath bundles of brushwood, which they cast on a great pyre in the open space in front of the Bishop's dwelling.

In the audience chamber King Cormac had taken a seat in that corner of the room furthest from the door through which the odious sorcerer was to be led, while Furiosus stood boldly in the centre with his hands on his hips. The Bishop sat on his gilded throne and fixed on Fursey a penetrating and animated eye. Cramp seized both of Fursey's legs as he encountered the Bishop's gaze, and he had to be supported by a soldier on either side.

'We have a repertoire of the most exquisite tortures,' began the Bishop in a hard metallic voice. 'If you fail to answer our questions to our satisfaction, I'll have you most strangely tormented until your blood and marrow spout forth in great abundance.'

The hinges of Fursey's knees gave way, and he fell on the floor.

The two soldiers dragged him to his feet and held him in an upright position facing his lordship.

'Have you ever heard of the torture of the Pilliwinckes upon the fingers,' asked the prelate, 'or the binding and wrenching of the head with cord?'

'My lord bishop,' remonstrated Father Furiosus. The Bishop was silent as the friar stepped up to the quaking Fursey.

'Wretched man,' thundered Furiosus, 'you are accused of being one of a swarm of wizards and witches that infest this territory and hover abroad at night in the foul and murky air. You are accused of being a man of wonderfully evil and pernicious example, guilty of deeds foul, unheard of, and productive of ill. What have you to say to these accusations?'

Fursey returned the gaze of his questioner, but was unable to speak. He was experiencing an intense weakness in all his limbs, and a swooning sensation came over him. Father Furiosus retired a few paces to consult with the Bishop.

'It's remarkable that he attempts no answer to these grave charges,' he said. 'Most sorcerers are hot in denial. I do remember that the Abbot Marcus told us that this man was afflicted at one time with an impediment in his speech. Could that be the reason for this strange silence?'

'No,' replied the Bishop. 'It's perversity, or a ruse to defeat the ends of justice.'

King Cormac, who was becoming frightened in his corner of the room, crept forward to the foot of the Bishop's throne so as to be near the others.

'Did you ever see such a grim and ill-favoured fellow?' whispered the King in awestricken tones, as he gazed at the unfortunate Fursey's moonlike face. 'He has a fierce and horrid visage. I can smell the brimstone off him.'

'Indeed, he is ill-looking, dark and hideous,' answered the Bishop, 'but I wouldn't expect anything else. Please continue your examination, Father Furiosus.'

The friar turned to confront Fursey once more, but it was obvious that the latter had lost consciousness. The friar seemed puzzled, and he contemplated the sorcerer for some time without speaking while the two soldiers, with beads of sweat on their foreheads, supported Fursey by the armpits. His head hung forward on his chest, and his legs were stretched out left and right with the heels resting on the floor.

'Has he had food since he was brought to Cashel?' asked Furiosus suddenly.

'No,' replied one of the soldiers.

'Return him to his cell,' commanded the friar, 'and keep him fed until he's wanted again.'

The two soldiers dragged Fursey out, his heels rattling across the floor. When the door had been closed, the Bishop could no longer contain his exasperation.

'Is he not to be tortured?' he burst out. 'Not even a taste of the *Peine Forte et Dure?*'

'No,' answered the friar shortly.

'Why not?' snarled the Bishop.

'Because I'm in charge,' replied Furiosus fiercely.

The Bishop from his high throne watched venomously as the friar strode thoughtfully up and down the floor. At length the prelate spoke again, this time mildly and in carefully modulated tones.

'But is there to be no torture at all, not even a turn on the wheel? After all, we have to find his accomplices.'

Father Furiosus stopped in his walk.

'My lord bishop,' he said, 'forgive me if I have been short in my answers, but this is a case of considerable complexity and one that requires judicious consideration. I suspect that the trial will show Fursey's sorcery to have been of a very subtle quality. I admit that I don't yet quite understand his style of villainy. We cannot proceed with the trial until the arrival from Clonmacnoise of the Abbot Marcus and of any other witnesses who may wish to testify. When Fursey has been found guilty, then will be the time for the application of the best available tortures with the object of securing the names of his confederates. If he pleads guilty and penitently names his accomplices in the Black Art, there will be no need for torture at all: we may proceed straight to the burning. If, however, he should obstinately insist on his innocence, torture will of course be necessary until he admits himself guilty of those crimes with which he is charged. So contain yourself in patience; and please trust my experience in these matters, which is considerable.'

Bishop Flanagan made no answer, but gathering his robes about him, left the room.

Meanwhile Fursey had been revived by the action of the fresh air and by a bucket of water emptied over him by the soldiers, who had grown tired of carrying him; and he was proceeding feebly back to his cell. His guards untied his hands, and leaving him a pitcher of water and a crust they withdrew, fastening the door behind them. Fursey groped in the darkness until he found the pitcher. He raised it shakily and took a long draught. Then, cupping the crust in his hand he succeeded in smashing it against the stone that served him as bolster, and for some time the cell echoed to the grinding of the pieces between his teeth. When he had finished his meal he rolled himself on to his pallet and lay with his face pressed against the wall, listening dolefully to the scampering of the rats across the floor.

A few days later a distinguished stranger arrived at the southern gate of Cashel. He was dark in complexion and was dressed in an expensive sable robe, which proclaimed him a person to whom every consideration was due. When asked his name and condition, he replied that he was Apollyon, a prince of the Byzantine Empire, and that as a traveller in these parts he had been commissioned by the Emperor at Constantinople to convey the Emperor's greetings to his noble brothers, the King and Bishop of Cashel, together with sundry gifts. The dark stranger was attended by a numerous retinue, all heavily veiled, as was apparently the custom in the distant country from which they had come. The stranger's courtliness and affability won for him the good opinion of all, and this was by no means diminished when it was learned that the ox-cart in his train was loaded with boxes of gold and precious stones, the gifts of the Emperor to his good friends in Cashel. What a pity, everyone said, that such a noble and gracious gentleman should have that slight limp.

Father Furiosus watched with disapproval as two lines of porters carried the boxes of gold into the houses of the beaming King and the delighted Bishop, but a moment later the courtly stranger approached him leading on a leash a high-stepping dog of very superior pedigree.

'The special gift of the Emperor to Father Furiosus,' said Apollyon with a courtly bow. 'The Emperor is very well acquainted with the noble work you are doing in suppressing the hateful passion of love in this land, and he bade me present you with this sagacious animal to assist you in your labours. He is called a "pointer" and is trained by huntsmen to spot game. With a little further direction from you he will be an invaluable ally to you in your rambles along the roads of Ireland. He will "point" the lovers in the ditches and doorways from a distance of thirty paces, and enable you to deal with many whom you would otherwise have missed. No, do not thank me. The Emperor graciously added that when you have cleaned up the holy land of Ireland, he would be pleased to welcome you to the Byzantine Empire, where the relations between the sexes are not all that His Imperial Majesty would wish.'

The friar's ill-humour immediately vanished and, having thanked the stranger profusely, he led the graceful hound around to the back of the palace, where he secured for it a comfortable habitation and a bed of clean straw. After a sumptuous dinner in the stranger's honour the Bishop conducted his guests to the sun-room, where reclining gracefully in intricately carved chairs, they engaged in genteel conversation. It was not long until the capture of the notorious sorcerer, Fursey, came to be mentioned.

'The trial is fixed for tomorrow,' said Bishop Flanagan, 'and will be conducted before the Canons of the Chapter, who will be his judges.'

The Prince of the Byzantine Empire immediately smote his forehead and apologised for his forgetfulness. The Emperor had especially charged him with the duty of conveying valuable gifts to the Canons of the Chapter of Cashel, who, the Emperor had been informed, were the finest and stoutest body of ecclesiastics in Christendom. Further boxes of gold were unloaded from the ox-cart and carried to the apartments of the joyful churchmen. Meanwhile in the sun-room of the Bishop's Palace the mead and ale flowed freely. Furiosus regaled the company with story after story of mighty tussles with the forces of evil, of shifty demons battered into submission, and of noonday devils encountered by the roadside sitting on stiles, and wrestled with during an entire afternoon.

The Bishop made from the corner of his mouth subtle ecclesiastical jokes with a strong dogmatic flavour. King Cormac plunged into a rambling account of one of his campaigns, but fell asleep in his chair before he had it finished, his head drooping forward on his chest and his beard covering his knees like a white apron. But the Byzantine prince outshone everyone with the brilliance of his wit and the charm of his conversation, so that at times his hearers were filled with a dazed delight. It was when the joyousness and good-feeling of the company were at their height, that the dark stranger made his strange request.

'When I was a younger man,' he said, 'I practised law, and I have appeared in cases which resulted in the happy burning of as many as twenty sorcerers at a time on the banks of the Bosphorus. It would intrigue me greatly if you would allow me to enter this case and conduct the defence of this wretched man Fursey. It can do no harm: from what you tell me he is as good as ashes and cinders already; but the clash of two legal systems and methods of procedure, that of your mighty Kingdom of Cashel and that of the Byzantine Empire, cannot but be in the highest degree instructive to us both.'

The Bishop put down his ale mug suddenly and regarded Apollyon with narrowing eyes.

'The man is capable of conducting his own defence,' he asserted suspiciously. 'He is the slyest sorcerer imaginable.'

'I don't for a moment presume to think,' replied Apollyon, 'that I shall be able to influence the verdict of your court. The Canons of your Chapter are obviously estimable men who are determined to see justice done, but a legal tussle with the famous Father Furiosus would afford me the greatest intellectual pleasure, as well as providing me with something of which I can boast at some future date to my children's children. What do you say, Father?'

The friar met the stranger's eye gladly.

'I think it's an excellent idea,' he said. 'There's nothing I like better than a fight, mental or physical. And I have every confidence in my ability to bend back the sophistries practised in Byzantine argument and tie them into knots.'

'I must withhold my approval —' began the Bishop.

'I don't care who approves,' roared the friar, banging his ale-mug on the arm of his chair. 'I'm in charge of this case. I appoint Prince Apollyon counsel for the defence.'

The Bishop did not reply, but sat vulpine in his great chair. He drank no more that night.

On the following morning Apollyon craved permission to pay a visit to his client before the trial began. Permission was courteously accorded, and the guards conducted him to the cell, and rolled Fursey off his pallet on to the floor, so that the foreign gentleman could see him with convenience. At Apollyon's request they closed the door and left lawyer and client alone.

'Don't you know me?' queried the Prince eagerly.

Fursey had been so many days in darkness that he could see as well as a cat. He took one look at the stranger's face and emitted a hollow groan.

'So you've come for me,' he said. 'Aren't you a little premature? I'm not burnt yet.'

'Come now, Fursey,' answered the Devil, 'get up off the floor before the rats eat you.'

Fursey struggled up and sat on the edge of his pallet, sunk in the profoundest melancholy. He thought of the flames of Hell and of the flames of the pyre that was shortly to consume him, and he couldn't make up his mind which he disliked most. The Devil took his limp hand and shook it warmly.

'How are you, my dear friend?' he asked.

'You find me in a deep despair,' answered Fursey.

'Come now, where's your courage?'

'Please don't make jokes,' replied Fursey. 'I'm shortly to be incinerated, and I cannot truthfully say that I regard the prospect with equanimity.'

'But while there's life there's hope,' urged the Devil.

'I'm glad you think so,' replied Fursey gloomily. 'Will you please go away and leave me to be burnt in peace.'

The Devil appeared to be deeply moved. He seated himself on the pallet and took Fursey's arm impulsively.

'Have confidence in me,' he said earnestly. 'I will never desert you.'

Fursey glanced up at him, and seemed to become even more depressed.

'It looks as if that's the way it's going to be,' he answered huskily.

The Devil shook his head reprovingly. 'I don't know how a man of your intelligence allowed himself to be caught,' he said. 'Why didn't you order your familiar to thicken and obscure the air about you? By his familiar's workmanship upon the atmosphere a wizard may remain unespied.'

'It's a long story,' answered Fursey. 'Anyway, my familiar is no good. He's always thinking of himself. He suffers from a raging thirst.'

'Hm!' said the Devil. He was silent for a while; then he cocked a sympathetic eye at Fursey's honest visage. 'I suppose you know,' he said, 'that your trial is due to commence at noon.'

'What!' ejaculated Fursey, 'as soon as that!'

'They have assembled an imposing battery of witnesses,' continued the Prince of Darkness, 'not that it makes much difference. I never knew a man or a woman tried for sorcery who didn't end by going up in smoke.'

'You needn't keep harping on it,' replied Fursey irritably.

'Trust me,' said the Devil, 'I have been commissioned with your defence.'

'Oh my God!' said Fursey, and he spoke no more.

'You may wonder,' continued Satan, 'why I concern myself on your behalf at all. Well, firstly, I feel myself in your debt for the hospitality, unwilling though it was, which you extended to myself and the boys in your cell at Clonmacnoise. Secondly, I have a strong personal affection for yourself. Thirdly, I have every hope that now that you have become a wizard, you will view in a more favourable light that little business proposition of mine relative to the sale of your soul. Fourthly and lastly, I'm determined to get the better of these clerical jugglers. I'm particularly down on his lordship the

Bishop Flanagan. I'm going to harry that man exceedingly before I leave this city. Mark my words,' added the Devil darkly, 'when that man finishes his career in this world and gets to Hell, the first thing he'll do is found a Vigilance Society. He'll have us all properly pestered with complaints about the nudity of the damned and the like, as if anyone could expect clothing to survive in that temperature. He'll still be trying to alter the machinery of creation, like he does in this world.'

The Devil brooded darkly for a few moments. 'As if Hell wasn't bad enough already,' he muttered. 'As it is, I'm bored stiff most of the time. But come, Fursey, why are you so sunk in gloom? Be not moved to fear. The hour of battle is at hand; and the victory is not to the strong, but to the crafty.'

Fursey did not answer, so the Devil arose with a sigh, patted him kindly on the shoulder and took his leave.

It was high noon. In the Chapter House the Canons had assembled, rotund men with placid, proud faces. The Civil Service sat on their two little stools, their filing cabinets of wax tablets piled about them, the younger Civil Service looking demure and shabby, the older pompous and self-important. King Cormac sat in his chair, his beard freshly brushed and powdered, and his chubby face screwed up into an expression of extreme sagacity. To one side stood Prince Apollyon, unassuming, courtly and civilised; while over against him the stalwart Furiosus had taken his stand, clutching his blackthorn stick as if he suspected that someone present might presume to contradict him. On a bench against the wall amongst those who were to testify, sat the Abbot Marcus, his face gentle and meditative. Beside him sat Cuthbert, the sexton of Kilcock Churchyard, his eyes turned up to Heaven and his lips moving in silent prayer to the great edification of all. Three monks were present from Clonmacnoise, Father Crustaceous, Father Placidus and Father Sampson, their folded arms expressing their determination to do their duty. The broom on which Fursey had made his ill-fated journey was clamped to a table in the centre of the hall. Beside it lay a goat's horns and a long dun beard, while at the other end of the table was a board on which were stretched the bedraggled corpses of four ducks. At the far end of the room there was an interesting display of wheels, thumbscrews, charcoal braziers and other instruments which might be required by the counsel for the prosecution; and alongside was a comfortable couch for the convenience of the prisoner and his questioners. Two sallow gentlemen in holy orders presided over that part of the arrangements. Bishop Flanagan sat remote from everyone, high up on his great mauve, gold and purple throne, his chin resting on his hand, his gaunt, ascetic face intent.

A shudder of expectancy passed through the assembly as the doors were thrown open, and the entire armed forces of Cashel in a solid phalanx marched into the room. In obedience to a ringing command four soldiers stepped smartly to one side, and it was seen that Fursey was in the midst loaded down to the ground with chains. Two blacksmiths came forward and riveted the hanging pieces of chain to the floor with iron spikes. Although it was generally believed that a sorcerer was bereft of his powers while in the hands of lawful authority, it was thought wise in the present instance, in view of the fearsome reputation of the prisoner, to forestall any attempt on his part to escape by flying through the smoke-hole in the roof.

The moment he entered the hall Fursey's eyes fastened themselves on the array of peculiar instruments at the far end of the room. The two hard-featured clerics who presided there, returned his gaze impassively.

'How do you feel?' whispered the Prince of the Byzantine Empire.

'I wish I was elsewhere,' muttered Fursey, without turning his head.

The reading of the indictment passed unheard by Fursey, and it was only when he was ordered to plead guilty or not guilty that he managed to tear away his eyes from the array of instruments and look at his questioner. His gaze wandered from the full-blooded face of the friar across to the smug faces of the Canons, then up to the lean visage of the Bishop. He shuddered; then his eye fell on the row of witnesses, and he recognised Abbot Marcus. The Abbot had his face averted and was looking at the floor.

'Guilty,' said Fursey.

Father Furiosus shot out a huge fist covered with ginger down.

His forefinger snapped out and pointed straight at Fursey.

'You admit that you are a sorcerer?'

'Yes. I'm a sorcerer.'

'I object,' interjected the Byzantine Prince.

'Sit down,' said the friar, 'you can't object at this stage.'

'Why not?' queried Apollyon determinedly.

'Because the prosecution does not accept the prisoner's plea,' replied the friar. 'His guilt must be proved. Witnesses have come here at great trouble and expense, and they can't be sent home again after a trial lasting only six minutes. Anyway, the accused is entitled to a fair trial.'

Apollyon appeared to meditate for some moments, then he sat down without a word.

'If the accused should be found not guilty after the evidence has been considered,' conceded the friar, 'we will start again at the beginning and accept his plea of guilty. First witness.'

The first witness proved to be a shepherd clad inadequately in a yard-and-a-half of sacking. He testified to happenings of a diabolical character in the neighbourhood of The Gray Mare's cabin, sundry lightnings, and barbarous and discordant screams. He was followed by Cuthbert, who left his coat open so that the court might appreciate the fact that he was wearing a hair-shirt. Cuthbert, it appeared, had been startled from his prayers by the hubbub at the old woman's cottage, and on coming out into his yard to investigate, he had been nearly knocked down by the sudden descent of Fursey on a broom. When he had sought refuge in his cottage and bolted the door, the baffled Fursey had cast a malignant spell and slain everything within its ambit. The sexton burst into tears as he contemplated the four stricken ducks. A murmur of sympathy ran around the hall.

'How precious to him are a poor man's possessions,' muttered Canon Pomponius.

Other witnesses testified to finding the murdered body of The Gray Mare. The three monks from Clonmacnoise swore to having seen Fursey capering and ambling through the air on a broomstick up to the very gates of the settlement. Lastly, the Abbot Marcus arose and in dry, colourless words answered the questions that were put to him by Father Furiosus. Yes, the prisoner had told him a long, rambling story, in the course of which he had freely admitted that he was a sorcerer and had practised sorcery. The Abbot's voice sounded through the room like a dull bell, cold and toneless. Not once did he glance at Fursey. At the other end of the hall the two grim-visaged clerics, who had been listening intently to all that was said, began to lay out additional instruments and to test their machinery, watched by Fursey with a disturbed and unquiet eye. Suddenly Bishop Flanagan's voice inserted itself between the friar's questions and the Abbot's mechanical answers.

'We have heard enough,' he announced, his words falling like metallic drops. 'The wretched man is a very synthesis of deformities. Let us proceed at once to break him on the wheel and tear his flesh from his bones with hooks of iron.'

A murmur of approval passed along the benches. When Fursey recovered his breath, he glanced agonisingly at his lawyer. Apollyon shook his head dolefully.

'You're in a tight corner,' he whispered, 'but I have a card up my sleeve yet.'

Abbot Marcus did not resume his seat. 'My lord bishop,' he said, 'I have not finished. It is but proper that I should relate to you the story that this poor man, your prisoner, told me when he admitted his sorcery.'

Cuthbert stirred uneasily on his seat and threw a covert look at Apollyon who immediately glanced away. From the moment he had first espied the Byzantine Prince in the court, Cuthbert had manifested a slight uneasiness and the appearance of being puzzled. The two had glanced at one another frequently during the proceedings, but had not once met one another's eyes. It was as if two armed, but mutually neutral, powers had for the first time discovered that there was a point at which their interests clashed, and each seemed to feel embarrassment.

The court listened spellbound while the Abbot Marcus repeated Fursey's story in simple, telling words. Cuthbert's face expressed bewildered indignation as the tale of his sorceries was unfolded. Father Furiosus was the only one who manifested impatience. When the Abbot had finished he could contain himself no longer.

'Of all the absurd stories,' he burst out. 'It was clearly demonstrated at the water-trial which I myself conducted a week ago, that this much-maligned woman, The Gray Mare, was innocent of the charge of witchcraft. Anyone who doubts it, flies in the face of the whole body of canon law and sacred tradition, and is little better than a heretic.'

The friar glanced fiercely from face to face as if to challenge anyone to contradict him, but no one seemed interested in The Gray Mare; all eyes were bent on Cuthbert. The Bishop's nostrils had widened, and when he spoke, his voice was as smooth as silk.

'What has our honest friend Cuthbert to say to these charges which the prisoner has levelled against him?'

The sexton fell upon his knees and, throwing his eyes to Heaven, called on all the saints in the calendar as witnesses of his innocence. He tore open his coat to show that he was the wearer of a hair-shirt; and struggling to his feet, he raised his robe so that all might see the horniness of his knees from frequent praying. Never had such a wicked charge, he said, been preferred against a good man. Was further proof needed of the execrable Fursey's guilt?

Not a muscle moved in the rows of white faces that were bent upon the sexton. At length Father Furiosus spoke.

'Was not this the man who laid the charge of witchcraft against the saintly Gray Mare?'

There was a nodding of bald heads.

'And was not this the man against whom the saintly Gray Mare laid a countercharge of sorcery?'

There was a further nodding of heads.

'And that charge is now corroborated by the story of the prisoner. My lord bishop,' said the friar with finality, turning to the great gilt throne, 'this matter requires further investigation.'

'Why?' asked the Bishop mildly. 'Is it not an accepted principle in witchcraft proceedings that where doubt exists, one should convict? The Church's point of view is happily summed up in the well-known phrase: "Burn all; God will distinguish His own."'

'That is true,' agreed the friar.

'There is an excellent pyre erected outside my palace,' continued the Bishop. 'It can easily accommodate two.'

Cuthbert emitted a forlorn groan as if to express his opinion of human depravity, and once more cast up his eyes to Heaven; but this time he was careful to note the exact position of the smoke-hole in the roof. Help came, however, from an unexpected quarter. The Byzantine Prince was once more on his feet.

'I object,' he said.

'Sit down,' commanded the friar.

'I won't sit down,' replied Apollyon hotly. 'I object.'

'You can't object,' retorted Furiosus.

'What about the defence?' asked Apollyon shrilly.

'What defence? Your client has been proved guilty.'

Apollyon swung away from Furiosus and faced the Bishop and the assembled clergy.

'My lord and very reverend fathers,' he cried, 'my client is not a sorcerer. The unfortunate Fursey has had an experience which few of us would wish to undergo, he has become possessed by a devil. And this devil, intent on the innocent Fursey's destruction, speaks through his mouth and proclaims him a sorcerer, just as he pours forth hideous lies damaging to the character of this good man, the sexton Cuthbert.'

A wavelet of excitement stirred in the hall. The Abbot Marcus rose to his feet and for the first time looked across at Fursey. Then he turned to the Bishop and spoke with agitation.

'This may well be,' he said. 'It would explain much. I can vouch that Fursey has been all his life an exemplary monk. A man does not all at once turn to wickedness.'

Cuthbert was quick to see his advantage. 'It's very likely true,' he cried. 'When Fursey came careering into my yard on the broom-stick, he swayed uncertainly as if the control did not rest in his own will, but in some force hidden in the dark depths within. And this extraordinary fabrication of lies about me is surely not the invention of a simple monk, but of a demon of more than ordinary wickedness and wile.'

Father Furiosus seemed momentarily thrown off his balance by the quick turn of events and by the change in mood of those present. While he hesitated, Apollyon addressed the assembly in ringing tones.

'During the recent haunting of Clonmacnoise,' he cried, 'when devils abounded in every hole and corner, my client had the misfortune to inhale a demon of a particularly mischievous and mendacious character, who now possesses him utterly. In Fursey himself there is no guile. He is deserving of your tears, not your reprobation.'

'Have you known of such cases?' queried the Bishop, turning to Furiosus.

'They're quite common,' replied the friar shortly. 'I knew an Archdeacon once who swallowed a demon in a lettuce. But if this man is possessed, I'll soon rid him of his tormentor.'

'What are they going to do to me now?' quavered Fursey, as he saw the friar rolling up his sleeves.

'It's all right,' hissed Apollyon in his ear. 'It'll hurt, but it's far better than being burnt.'

The Bishop did not seem to like the turn of events, but he said nothing as the friar ordered the two blacksmiths to unloosen Fursey from the floor. Furiosus then took Fursey by the arm and led him gently but firmly to the end of the room where the two hard-featured clerics were sorting out their instruments.

'Don't worry,' he said kindly, as he gripped Fursey firmly by the shoulders. 'I'll have that noisome devil out in no time.'

'You won't hurt me?' whimpered Fursey.

'No,' replied Furiosus, surprised. 'I won't hurt *you*. I'll only hurt the devil that possesses you. Open your mouth wide, and keep it open.'

The friar shouted a litany of prayers down Fursey's throat, and then three times adjured the devil to come forth. Nothing happened. All present had crowded around and gave sundry advice, which the friar shook off impatiently. He commanded that the doors be left wide open so that the devil might find a ready exit; and he advised that all should keep their mouths tightly closed lest the demon discover a refuge, and he would have to go through the whole exorcism again. The onlookers needed no second warning, but stood with their lips tightly compressed. King Cormac made doubly certain by covering his mouth with both hands. Prince Apollyon followed the proceedings with the greatest interest. In fact, everyone was pleasantly thrilled except Fursey.

'The essence of the operation,' explained Father Furiosus, 'is to make the body of the possessed person such an uncomfortable habitation that even the most obstinate demon does not care to remain in it.'

Fursey heard this speech with dismay, and he was further disquieted when he saw the two sallow clerics come forward and take their places on either side of the friar.

'I want to give warning,' continued Furiosus, 'that there will be much fracas when I draw forth the foul and unclean spirit. He will be in the highest degree evil-smelling and may box the ears of some of those present, but no matter what buffets you must endure, stand your ground and do not withdraw. The strength of the possessed person may well exceed the strength of the weightiest Canons of the Chapter, so you must all be ready to fling yourselves on this unfortunate man and hold him down while I draw forth the confused demon. The first method I shall attempt is that of fumigation.'

One of the lantern-jawed assistants handed the friar a salver of white powder. Furiosus applied a taper and held the burning material under Fursey's nose. Fursey sneezed several times, and the tears ran down his cheeks while the friar with much muttering and murmuring attempted to draw the demon from his nostrils. This method proved unsuccessful, and on the friar's instructions a tub was filled with water. Fursey showed exemplary patience as he was deftly stripped and immersed.

'We may get the demon out by the fear of drowning,' explained Furiosus, 'but the subject must be held completely under the surface lest the demon seek refuge in his hair.'

Several of the bystanders ventured to open their lips to mutter from the corners of their mouths that it was all most interesting, and that there could be no doubt but that Father Furiosus was a most well-informed and experienced man. When a few minutes later Fursey was lifted from the tub and laid on the couch in a half-drowned condition, they crowded around, anxious to miss nothing. Furiosus expanded his chest and addressed his audience once more.

'Indeed, this is a most stubborn demon,' he said. 'We must apply fire to the subject's feet.'

When a moment later Fursey emitted a bloodcurdling, sub-human howl, a thrill of excitement passed through the onlookers.

'At last,' said the friar with satisfaction, 'we have made contact with the demon, and it is evident that he does not like our attentions,' and he distributed cudgels to six of the sturdiest present. Between them they gave Fursey many sore strokes, but in spite of his screams and harrowing contortions, the demon would not come forth. They ceased their good work at last through pure weariness, and Fursey's cries died away in a whine of despair.

'Indeed, he is troubling you sorely,' said the friar, bending over Fursey sympathetically. Fursey returned his gaze with eyes dull and glazed.

'Carry him to his cell,' commanded the friar. 'It is grown late in the afternoon. Let his wounds be searched in the best manner. Tomorrow we will try breaking him on the wheel.'

Fursey was carried out by four soldiers, and the company broke up, congratulating each other on their interesting and informative day.

Chapter VII

It is usual to complete a day of arduous religious duties with a solemn banquet. When the foods and wines had been transferred from the sweating tables to the capacious ecclesiastical stomachs, and the guests were reclining on the rush-strewn floor about the great fire in the Bishop's dining hall, Apollyon announced that it was incumbent on him to leave Cashel on the morrow and continue his journey. The other guests were too replete to argue with him, so they contented themselves with murmuring their regrets and continued dreamily cracking walnuts between their teeth. Apollyon obtained permission to pay a last visit to his client, and left the fire-lit room alone. When he reached the street, he summoned one of his veiled attendants, who was on duty at the ox-cart.

'Be prepared to vanish, ox-cart and all,' he told the rest of his entourage, 'immediately on my return.'

He then made his way between the huts closely attended by his cloaked and veiled companion. When he reached the flight of steps that led underground to Fursey's cell, the soldiers on guard, who had already experienced the foreign gentleman's generosity, hurried forward to open the gates. Apollyon paused to congratulate them on the care they were taking of their prisoner, and distributed a few chunks of gold which he withdrew from the depths of his pocket. When he reached the noisome cell in which Fursey was confined, he found the demoniac sitting on the edge of his pallet dolefully examining the blackened skin and blisters on the soles of his feet. He greeted Fursey heartily.

'Well,' he said, 'we can congratulate ourselves on our resounding victory.'

'Ay,' replied Fursey colourlessly.

'Why are you so morose?' asked the Devil warmly. 'You're alive, aren't you, unburnt?'

'Yes,' replied Fursey, 'but I think that most of my bones are broken.'

'Tut, tut,' said the Devil. 'I never knew such a complaining fellow. It's nothing to what they propose to do to you to-morrow.'

Fursey looked at him, but said nothing.

'They're determined to get that devil out of you. They're going to break you on the wheel to begin with, and then they'll proceed to tear you in all parts of your body with red-hot pincers. If the demon still obstinately refuses to quit your body in spite of the dire tortures to which he is subjected, they will have to dig for him.'

'What do you mean, "dig for him"?'

'Disembowelling,' replied the Devil.

'But can't you explain to them,' suggested Fursey anxiously, 'that all this vast expenditure of labour will avail them nought, as I haven't got a devil.'

'If they can't find a devil after thoroughly searching you, they'll conclude that their first diagnosis must have been correct, and they'll burn you as a wizard.'

'I see,' said Fursey.

'I'm told,' remarked the Devil, 'that a sorcerer in the fire feels only the calm ecstasy of purification and deliverance as the flames devour his body.'

'I hope you're right,' responded Fursey, without much conviction.

'Don't worry,' declared the Devil. 'I have a plan.'

'No, thank you,' rejoined Fursey. 'I'd rather be disembowelled. I don't think you're a man whose judgment can be trusted.'

'Don't be silly,' replied Satan, 'I can effect your escape.'

'That's all very well,' replied Fursey, 'but will I survive the project?'

'Of course,' asserted the Devil, stepping aside. 'Look.'

'Who's that behind you?' asked Fursey suspiciously, as he peered at the cloaked figure in the shadows.

'One of my faithful servants, who will now exchange clothes with you and so enable you, in the guise of my attendant, to effect your departure from this melancholy abode.'

'It's very nice of your faithful servant,' replied Fursey, 'but what happens when they find him in the morning? Has he no objection to being disembowelled in my stead?'

'Your substitute, who by the way is a lady, will vanish shortly after you and I gain the street, and in the morning when they come to look for you, the cell will be empty.'

'Oh, so she's a demon,' observed Fursey with distaste.

A shrill feminine voice came from behind the veil.

'I'm not a demon,' it said testily. 'I'm an elemental.'

'That's all right, Gertie,' said the Devil soothingly. 'He didn't mean any offence.'

Satan seated himself beside Fursey and rubbed his hands with satisfaction.

'I'd better explain,' he said. 'Take off your cloak and veil, Gertie, and let the gentleman see you.'

Gertie did as she was bid and disclosed an attractive young woman of considerable embonpoint, daintily clad in the prevailing fashion.

'The stench in this place is something awful,' she remarked acidly.

'To the best of my recollection,' said the Devil, turning to Fursey, 'I've already informed you that certain of the ecclesiastics known to us both fill me with a strong distaste. In particular I don't relish that vulpine bishop at all. I think he's about due for a very thorough harrowing, and I'm going to set the matter in train to-night. Now, it's not easy for a demon to harrow an ecclesiastic who is quick with the holy water and the Latin adjurations. Many of my nimblest demons have been worsted in such an encounter and bear the marks of the struggle to the present day. So I've borrowed four frisky elementals, who, as they are many thousand years older than Christianity, are quite unaffected by holy water, adjuration or exorcism; and I've instructed them carefully in the principles of infestation and temptation. Gertie here is a specimen. Isn't she lovely?'

'Don't judge all sylphs by me,' interjected Gertie bitterly. 'I had a figure once, but what he's done to the four of us in the way of exaggerating our curves passes all belief. I always said the Devil had no taste.'

'Now Gertie, don't start complaining again,' retorted the Prince of Darkness. 'You'll all get your figures back when the job is done. I've explained to you till I'm worn out that the clergy's conception of women, both physically and mentally, is a conception of something which doesn't exist in this world. To tempt them properly and efficiently you must appear to them as they conceive women to be. The moment the operation is complete I'll restore your figures to the four of you, and you can wander off to your woods and streams, the sweet, slender creatures that you always were.'

'I hope there'll be no mistakes when you're turning us back,' was Gertie's acid retort as she looked down in disgust at her plump hips.

'Come on,' said the Devil, 'we've wasted enough time already. Strip off, Fursey, and exchange clothes with the lady. You can turn your face to the wall and throw your clothes over your shoulder if you're bothered by the virtue of modesty.'

'I don't think I like the plan,' said Fursey.

'So you'd prefer to be disembowelled and burnt?'

'No,' responded Fursey glumly, and he turned his face to the wall. As he took off his habit he felt in the pocket the little box of ointment which he had taken from The Gray Mare's cabin. Reflecting that it was his only possession, he pulled it out and laid it on the bed.

'Here,' said the Devil, 'put these on.'

'I don't know how women's clothes go on.'

'I'll help you,' said Satan impatiently.

In a few moments Fursey was dressed, the Devil hooking him dexterously down the back and helping him into the sylph's cloak and veil. Fursey picked up the box of ointment and after some struggling with the unaccustomed clothes, found a small pocket into which it fitted nicely. Meanwhile, Gertie, wearing his tattered habit and sandals, had stretched herself on the pallet. The Devil shouted for the guard, and when the door was opened, the two conspirators passed out and up the narrow steps into the open air.

'What are you walking like that for?' hissed the Devil. 'Do you want to attract everyone's attention?'

'I can't help limping,' replied Fursey indignantly, 'with the soles nearly burnt off my feet.'

'There's no need for you to limp with both feet at the same time,' retorted the Archfiend. 'It looks awful. I never saw anything like it. It looks as if both your knees were broken.'

'I'll try walking on my toes,' replied Fursey miserably.

It was dark in the street at first, but a round, jolly-faced moon came sailing from behind a cloud, flooding the open space with mellow light.

'Come into the shadow,' whispered the Devil.

Fursey stood shivering against the gable of a cottage while the Devil gave him his final directions.

'Go up the hill past the King's House. You'll meet less people that way. Keep in the shadow of the houses. The palisade of the city runs along by the King's House. You must get over it somehow.'

'How?' interjected Fursey.

'By ingenuity,' answered the Fiend impatiently. 'Once you're across it, you're out of the city. If you turn to the left, you will come to the northern road; if you turn to the right, you will soon reach the road that leads to the south.'

'Which way will I go?' asked Fursey.

'How do I know which way you'll go?' replied the Devil irritably. 'That's your affair. Go now, and go quickly; for you've one thing to remember. The moment Gertie decides to vanish from your cell, her clothes which you're wearing will vanish too. And let me tell you, it'll be no joke for you if they catch you in a Christian city like this scampering around in your pelt. You'll have to face a charge of indecent exposure as well as charges of murder and witchcraft, and I don't know that the authorities don't look on it as worse. Goodbye now, and go quickly.'

As the Devil vanished in a delicate thread of smoke, Fursey glanced around fearfully. The moonlight lay on the roofs of the huts and the cabins, giving the entire settlement a ghostly character. The shadows of the houses lay squat and square across the silvery road. Fursey gulped and set off, hobbling rapidly in the direction that the Devil had indicated, pausing hesitantly before he ventured to cross each patch of moonlit street. He stopped once to crouch in a doorway as a drunken townsman passed him singing heartbrokenly about the beauty of love. Otherwise the streets seemed deserted: the hour was late; good people, no doubt, were at home and in bed. As the moon drifted coyly behind a downy cloud, Fursey uttered a sigh of thankfulness and limped quickly up the incline towards the King's House. He was skirting the King's backyard when the sound of someone humming a gay, little air made him press himself back against the wall, where he stood, not daring to breathe. He heard footsteps slowly approaching, and a moment later a small figure turned the corner. It was King Cormac, back from the Bishop's banquet, full to the gills with wine, out for a saunter up and down his yard before going to bed. Fursey uttered a prayer that he would not be seen, but it must be that a wizard's prayers are obnoxious to Heaven, for at that moment the moon began to come out again smilingly from behind her cloud, as if she and Fursey were playing a game. As the shadows crept back before the light, Fursey glanced around him desperately. In a moment the moonlight would reach him. He made out the outline of a doorway behind him, and quickly lifting the latch, he disappeared into the interior, closing the door gently behind him. Breathlessly he watched through a crevice as Cormac sauntered unsteadily up and down the yard in the best of good humour, stroking his beard and telling himself jokes, but a moment later Fursey was startled by a rustling of wings in his rear. He threw a frightened glance in the direction from which the sound had come, and realised with a sinking heart that he was in the Royal poultry house. A monotonous clucking began in the darkness, and in a moment every hen and fowl had awakened and was clucking and cackling indignantly at the intruder. Fursey pressed his face against the door and gazed out in terror through the crevice to see whether the King had heard. Yes, Cormac had heard, and evidently believing that some dishonourable fellow was stealing his hens, had drawn his sword and was creeping towards the poultry house on tiptoe.

The door was flung open, and Cormac stood with his sword at

the ready, the fire of battle in his eyes.

'Come out,' he commanded.

Fursey emerged without a word.

'Ha!' said the King. 'A wench. Exactly what was needed to finish a perfect day.'

He returned his sword to its sheath and stood beaming at Fursey. Then he laid his hand on Fursey's arm. 'Come around the corner of the house,' he whispered, 'there's a seat there.'

'What for?' asked Fursey.

The King nudged him playfully. 'As if you didn't know,' he said.

Fursey followed the King apprehensively around the corner of the house and seated himself on the edge of the bench.

'You seem to be bad on the feet,' remarked Cormac as he sat down in close proximity. 'Have you been drinking too?'

He went off into a fit of convulsive laughter at this jest, and Fursey managed to conjure up a feeble grin with the object of keeping the King in good humour. Then Cormac plunged into a rambling account of the evening's festivities, every sentence borne on a wave of wine fumes, which he exhaled as a dragon does its fiery breath; but Fursey scarcely listened. He was too worried at the possibility of being seduced. At last the King was silent, and Fursey cautiously turning his head, observed that Cormac was watching him roguishly. A moment later the monarch had slipped an arm around his waist. Fursey withdrew as far as it was possible to do so, without falling off the bench.

'A high-born gentleman like you wouldn't take advantage of a poor girl,' pleaded Fursey, pitching his voice to a shrill falsetto in keeping with his character as a lady.

'Wouldn't I now?' rejoined Cormac, stroking his moustaches in a very dashing fashion. 'You don't know the sort of fellow I am.'

'If you don't behave yourself, I'll scream,' declared Fursey in a cracked treble.

'What are you afraid of?' asked the King. 'There are none of the clergy around.'

'I'm a decent girl,' asserted Fursey.

'That's what they all say,' grinned the King, 'but I know better.'

Fursey's brain simmered as he laboured to find a solution to his present predicament, but almost before he realised it, the situation resolved itself.

'You've a lovely face,' murmured the King, bending forward, a tremor of emotion in his voice. He raised a bejewelled hand and gently drew back Fursey's hood, advancing at the same time his white bewhiskered visage with the evident intention of planting on Fursey's cheek a chaste kiss, but at the sight of Fursey's close-cropped head of white, stubbly hair he stopped petrified. The arm encircling Fursey's waist stiffened with terror. For a moment he stared at Fursey, then his voice came out of his throat in a horrified hiccough.

'The sorcerer! The demoniac! Maybe both!'

It was borne in powerfully on Fursey that it was time to betake himself elsewhere. He arose quickly and ran around the corner of the building, pulling his hood over his ears as he ran. The fascinated King came staggering after him. In front was the palisade, but against it leaned a man-at-arms, idly sharpening the head of his spear. He glanced up quickly as Fursey approached; then his eyes fell on the King, who had reached the corner, but whose legs would take him no further. For once Fursey's little share of wit stood by him. He walked coolly up to the soldier.

'Here, fellow,' he pronounced in ringing, feminine tones. 'Help me over the stockade.'

The surprised soldier glanced from Fursey to the frozen figure of King Cormac in the shadow of the building. Fursey turned and waved his plump hand daintily in the King's direction.

'Goodbye, my love,' he shrilled.

Cormac staggered and leaned unsteadily against the wall, still incapable of speech; but the guard appeared to notice nothing untoward. A sly smile spread slowly over his honest visage.

'I understand, my lady,' he said knowingly. 'You don't want to be seen leaving by the front.'

The soldier bent his shoulder and in a moment had hoisted Fursey on to the top of the palisade. Fursey squirmed uncomfortably on the tips of the sharpened stakes, but the soldier lent a willing hand to disentangle his dress, which was caught in the thorns and spikes. It was at this moment that Fursey's clothing suddenly vanished, leaving him struggling on the top of the stockade completely naked. The sudden disappearance of a charming, well-dressed lady and the unaccountable substitution of a small, plump, white-headed man in the buff was too much for the soldier. He immediately took to his heels, and King Cormac, who saw no reason for remaining, joined him in his flight. The two of them ran hell-for-leather around the building, and Fursey, who had fallen on the far side of the palisade, only paused to pick up his box of ointment before making off as fast as his legs could carry him in the opposite direction. He had run down the incline and half-way up the opposite hill before he paused to consider in which direction he should go. He stood trying to recover his breath as he stared at the settlement below him and at the two white roads that led north and south. The northern road led to Clonmacnoise. For a long time he stood uncertain. He thought of the peace which he had once known in the cloister, and he remembered the gates closed in his face. Still he hesitated. Then he remembered the Abbot Marcus as he had stood in the roadway in the cold, early-morning light when Fursey had been pinioned by the soldiers and thrown into the high cart. He saw the Abbot's face again, hard, as if carved out of stone; and a cold flood of water seemed to flow over Fursey's heart. He turned his back to Clonmacnoise and slowly made his way to the moonlit road that crept away over the hills towards the south.

It was late in the night when the Bishop's serving-men helped the last guest into his cloak and persuaded him to go home. Bishop Flanagan stood in the doorway of his dining hall and eyed with distaste the overturned goblets and the scattered remnants of food that lay on the tables and floor. Father Furiosus, who was in residence at the Palace, was the only one left. He sat crouched over the fire, his wine-flushed face reflecting the leaping flames, whistling meditatively the notes of one of the more popular hymns.

'The worst of these banquets,' declared the Bishop, 'is that there are always some few of the fathers who manifest a marked disinclination to go home. I thought I'd never get rid of Canon Pomponius. He attempted to sing his way through the entire Seven Penitential Psalms in the hall. I had to send two of my house boys home with him lest he be an occasion of scandal to the neighbourhood.'

The friar interrupted his whistling for a moment.

'I never saw a man with a goodlier appetite for wine,' he averred.

'I am not myself a wine-bibber, as you have no doubt observed,' remarked the Bishop frigidly. 'It disagrees with my stomach.'

'You might be a better man if you were,' replied the friar mildly, and he re-commenced his whistling.

'I think it's time for bed,' said the Bishop, lifting a torch from its bracket. Father Furiosus arose and stretched his huge frame until the joints cracked.

'It was a massive feast,' he remarked regretfully as he followed the prelate to the door, the nutshells that littered the floor cracking pleasantly beneath their feet. They made their way along the dim corridor to the sleeping apartments. The Bishop's room adjoined, but was beyond that which Father Furiosus occupied. In fact, the only entrance to the prelate's chamber was through the room in which the friar slept. When they entered the first room, Father Furiosus wandered across to his bed and stretching himself again, opened his mouth to emit a yawn like the roar of a young lion. When Bishop Flanagan had lit the rushlight by the friar's bed from the torch which he carried, he paused at his own door and stood watching the friar's tonsils vibrating in the torchlight. When the yawn was finished, and the friar had closed his mouth, the Bishop addressed him.

'Do you remember during the trial this afternoon,' he asked, 'it was asserted that a witch could only die if she succeeded in breathing her unholy powers into someone else? Can that be altogether true? After all, a witch is successfully disposed of at the stake.'

'Cases vary,' replied the friar, 'but it has been proved to be true in many instances. Witches, however, may always be destroyed by fire or by drowning. That's why the Church and the secular authority always insist on execution by fire, so as to make certain of the witch's destruction.'

'Yes, of course,' agreed the Bishop. 'The assertion of the demoniac Fursey, that detestable powers were breathed into him by the old woman so that she might find relief from her pains in death, has been exercising my mind ever since. That's why I asked you.'

Father Furiosus had drawn his habit over his head preparatory to retiring, and his voice came out muffled by its folds.

'The story told by the devil who possesses Fursey, was logical and correct,' he answered, 'but fortunately we know that The Gray Mare was not a witch.'

The Bishop remembered that The Gray Mare's innocence was a point on which Father Furiosus felt strongly, so he did not pursue the matter further.

'Good night,' he said.

'Good night, my lord,' replied the friar, hanging his habit on the back of the door.

In his own room Bishop Flanagan lit the rushlight on the table beside his bed and extinguished the torch by pressing it against the earthen floor. Then he knelt to say his prayers, which were tedious and protracted. He had not been praying for very long before he heard the friar's snores reverberating in the neighbouring room. He shook his head disapprovingly. The fact that Father Furiosus was already asleep meant that the friar's prayers had been brief, even if fervent. Bishop Flanagan continued on his knees for an hour, ending with a stern petition for a recall to their duty of those of his flock who were in arrears with their contributions to their pastors. At length he arose and turning down the bedclothes, drew back the undersheet. He took from the table by his bedside a small shovel, and from a corner of the room he shovelled up a heap of smooth stones that were neatly piled there. These he distributed judiciously beneath the sheet on which he was to lie. Such was the nightly practice of this godly man so as to mortify the flesh, lest unawares he should fall into the sin of luxury. When this pious operation was completed, he undressed himself and assumed a long nightshirt composed of crude linen and horsehair, which modestly covered his person from his ears to his heels. Then he clambered gingerly on to his hard couch and drawing the blankets over him, composed himself for sleep.

With his long, lank neck stretched on the pillow the Bishop had passed into the happy, dreamy state between waking and sleeping, when from ever so far away the sound of soft music came seeping into his consciousness. The music was sweet, and the Bishop's thin lips jerked with sleepy satisfaction and appreciation. The soft, insidious air increased in volume, the melody swaying from something that was very near to heartbreak, back through tones that came falling prettily, little golden notes that dropped one by one. The prelate moved his head restlessly on the pillow, and the corners of his mouth came apart in a happy grin as the memory of Prince Apollyon's gift of gold now in his cellar came creeping in upon his mind. The music swelled in a voluptuous curve, and fell; and from nowhere there crept in on the harp notes a woman's singing voice, laden with sweetness.

Bishop Flanagan sat up in bed suddenly, his heart pounding with terror. There could be no doubt about it: the music and the cloying voice filled the room. Could it be that there was a woman in his palace? He stretched out his arm and taking the flint from the table by his bedside, struck it and lit the rushlight with a shaky hand. The flame threw grotesque shadows on the walls as he moved the taper to left and right, and peered around the room and up at the ceiling. The music had ceased. He listened for a long time, but he could hear nothing other than the surge and ebb of the friar's snoring in the neighbouring room.

'Most remarkable,' he said aloud, as he extinguished the rushlight and laid his head back on the pillow, but he had no sooner decided that his experience belonged to the deceptive borderland of dreams, than he was once more startled into a sitting position by a sound which he immediately identified as the insidious rustling of a comb. His ears followed in horror the sensuous sweep and the little crackling sound of a comb moving through hair that was long and luxurious. There could be no doubt about it, there *was* a woman in his room. Before the affrighted prelate could decide what action to take in this unprecedented situation, a sweet, winning voice spoke close to his ear.

'What a lovely man!'

Surrendering himself to the wild impulse of the moment the Bishop precipitated himself on to the floor. He scrambled hastily to his feet and retained enough presence of mind to seize the rushlight and flint before dashing into the friar's room. He closed the door behind him and, after several attempts, succeeded in lighting the taper. He glanced fearfully at the wavering shadows on the walls, and then hurried over to the friar's bed. Father Furiosus was slumbering fitfully, but when Bishop Flanagan shook him, a tousled red head rose suddenly from the pillow.

'There's an evil and sportful female in my room,' whispered the Bishop urgently. 'She's trying to entice me to licentiousness!'

'What's that?' exclaimed Furiosus, sitting bolt upright in bed and disclosing a chest covered with matted ginger hair.

The Bishop repeated his alarming intelligence. Father Furiosus stared at him incredulously, but the prelate's estranged face and his eyes, fiery and hollow, carried conviction.

'Did you see her?' demanded the friar.

'No,' replied the Bishop, 'but I heard her combing her hair, and I heard her voice when she tried to entice me, a voice sweet and evil like the sound of flutes.'

'I'll soon fix her,' exclaimed the friar, stretching a muscular arm under the bed for his blackthorn stick. 'Do not let the matter flurry or excite you. I can see that your nerves are all unstrung.'

'Be careful,' begged the Bishop as Furiosus clambered out of bed. 'She can sing. Take heed lest she lewdly excite you by trolling filthy songs.'

'I can withstand the most alluring nymphs,' affirmed the friar, brushing him aside. 'Before I've done with the trollop,' he added fiercely as he tightened his grip on the blackthorn, 'I'll give her many sad strokes.'

He snatched the rushlight from Bishop Flanagan and striding across the floor, flung open the door of the other room.

'There's no one here,' he exclaimed.

Bishop Flanagan peered nervously over the friar's shoulder.

'She was here,' he asserted. 'Look under the bed.'

There was no one under the bed. Father Furiosus held up the

rushlight and examined the ceiling, then he turned and eyed Bishop Flanagan suspiciously.

'Are you quite certain that you didn't consume more wine this evening than you admit?' he asked roughly.

All the Bishop's dignity and habits of command came back to him as he heard this insult.

'Certainly not,' he retorted frigidly, and he drew himself up to his full height, an imposing figure in his horsehair nightshirt. 'I tell you I was not mistaken. If there is no one here of flesh and blood, then what I heard was by the contrivance of a demon.'

Furiosus expanded his nostrils judiciously.

'It may be,' he said at last. 'I myself have been much troubled this night by persistent dreams of a very lewd character. The Devil may be attempting to excite us to bad thoughts. But it's cold here, so I'm going back to bed; and I advise you to do the same. Address yourself to prayer, and if there's a further manifestation, call me.'

The friar strode out of the room banging the door behind him, and the Bishop heard the bed in the far room creaking painfully as Furiosus climbed into it. Bishop Flanagan crept back into his own bed too, more chagrined at the ease with which the friar had taken charge of the situation than fearful for his own safety. He left the taper lighting on the table so that he might be the better able to grapple with any situation that might present itself, and he saw to it that his bowl of holy water and his book of exorcisms were close to hand. What an overbearing fellow Furiosus was, always ready to push himself forward and take charge, making everyone feel like a small boy in his presence! Bishop Flanagan made up his mind firmly to deal himself with any further lascivious sleight-of-hand on the part of visiting sprites or imps, and on no account to summon the help of the masterful friar. He was sitting in bed propped up by the pillows, meditating thus, when he became aware of a well-shaped damsel slowly assuming shape in the far corner of the room. In spite of his determination to remain cool, sweat broke out on the Bishop's forehead and, trickling down his face, disappeared drop by drop inside the collar of his nightshirt. Still he refrained from stretching out his hand for the holy water. He told himself that he must wait until the impudent vision had taken full shape; the target would be bigger and there would be less chance of missing with the holy water.

At last she was entirely there in all her evil comeliness, an enchanting vision, her form elastic and light, with flexible limbs and a juvenile grace in her every movement. As she moved towards the alarmed prelate, her expressive features and eloquent action harmonised blandly with each other. A sound indicative of his anguish burst from Bishop Flanagan's throat, and seizing the bowl of holy water he flung it desperately at the approaching vision. To his horror it passed right through her and was shivered in atoms against the wall. As she continued to approach he sprang out the far side of the bed and, clutching the book of exorcisms, he swamped her in a deluge from the Vulgate. He did not dare raise his eyes from the page until he was out of breath. When he glanced up fearfully she was still there, scarcely three paces from him, evidently experiencing the greatest difficulty in restraining her merriment.

'Begone!' quavered the Bishop. 'I know you to be nought but a vain impression in the air.'

She regarded him for a moment roguishly; and when she spoke, her voice modulated itself with natural and winning ease.

'I'm thousands of years old,' she said in dulcet tones. 'You'll never get rid of me with that modern Christian stuff.'

Bishop Flanagan's mouth fell open, but no sound came forth. He cowered against the wall as she opened her lips again, and sweet, amatory words came out.

'Why are you so difficult?' she asked. 'You will never find a woman so passionate, so loving or so submissive.'

It is likely that the Bishop would have lost his life through sheer horror at these plausible words, only that he was suddenly recalled to the consciousness that the friar was in the neighbouring room by a series of bull-like roars which proceeded therefrom. Bishop Flanagan was immediately galvanised into action, and seizing the rushlight, he tore open the door and dashed into Furiosus' bed-room. Great as was the Bishop's alarm, he stopped petrified at the sight that met his eyes. The friar was tumbling around on the floor fighting madly to escape from the obscene advances and abandoned caresses of three females of the most luscious character imaginable. But Bishop Flanagan did not forget his own peril for long. He ran to the struggling mass on the floor.

'Nice time,' he snarled, 'to be slaking your lusts, when I'm half-slaughtered by the most hideous apparition that was ever seen!'

With a mighty heave Father Furiosus was on his feet, flinging the three sportful damsels against the far wall. He seized Bishop Flanagan by the throat and pressed him back against the bed-post.

'Let me go,' gasped the Bishop, 'or you will incur the penalty of excommunication.'

'What do you mean by that accusation,' howled the friar, 'and I locked in deadly combat with the forces of Hell? Take it back before I tear the skinny throat out of you.'

'I'm sorry,' panted the Bishop, 'I take it back. I didn't know they were demons too. There's one in my room, the most terrible vision that eye has ever seen.'

Father Furiosus released the Bishop and stood looking around the room breathing heavily. The three high-stepping females had disappeared. The friar tiptoed over to the door and looked into the Bishop's room. It was likewise empty. Then he returned to Bishop Flanagan, and the two of them conversed in whispers.

'She had a singularly evil countenance,' said Bishop Flanagan, his voice still trembling with fear. 'There was a hot, unholy fire in her eye. Neither holy water nor exorcism availed ought against her.'

'That's bad,' replied Furiosus, shaking his head gravely. 'It would appear from what you tell me that these painful phenomena are female elementals, probably sylphides — most difficult to get rid of. However, I will sprinkle my stoup of holy water on the walls and ceiling. While I am so engaged, do you turn up your most powerful exorcism, and we will read it aloud together.'

'What will we do if all four renew the assault in unison?' asked the Bishop shakily.

'It will be a triste and ominous affair,' replied the friar gloomily, 'and may well spell damnation for us both.'

'Not if we continue heroically to resist their unhallowed designs,' asserted the Bishop hysterically.

'The flesh is weak,' muttered the friar darkly. 'I will thoroughly besprinkle the walls. Then we will pray.'

When the last drop of sanctified water was exhausted, and the pair had read in tremulous tones the most powerful exorcisms available, they took their seats back to back in the doorway between the two rooms, so that between them they had the whole field of battle under surveillance.

'I fear me,' said the Bishop in a tremulous voice, 'that if they renew the onset, they will have some new artifices and stratagems at their command.'

'Whatever they contrive or whatever manoeuvres they indulge in, we will give them a good fight,' responded Father Furiosus.

'What avails a good fight, if one loses it?' said the despondent Bishop.

Father Furiosus did not answer. Though he did not care to admit it even to himself, he was considerably shaken by the night's happenings. It was the first time in his career as a thwarter and scarifier of demons that he was faced with the probability of the usual spiritual weapons breaking in his hands. Moreover, he was a man who never before had failed in such work, and the possibility of being this time unsuccessful was galling to his spirit in the extreme. He had never before been faced by forces as old as the world itself, and he did not like the new experience. Further, he was a man of simple mind, who became annoyed when confronted with something which he did not understand. And he could not understand what had got into the elementals to make them behave as they did. He understood them to be ordinarily a people who amused themselves playing hide-and-seek in forests and rivers, or disporting themselves in flame or in the upper air — a more or less useless people who had at least the virtue that they left human beings alone. But if what Bishop Flanagan asserted was true, if both holy water and exorcism had failed, then things looked black indeed. He hardly cared to think what might be the outcome of the affair.

He was sunk in gloomy contemplation when the Bishop's sharp elbow stabbed him in the ribs.

'Listen,' squealed the Bishop hoarsely.

Furiosus listened. He heard music, at first faint, then swelling in volume and coming nearer, soft, sensual cadences, with little runs of semiquavers of a particularly suggestive character. The friar raised the sleeve of his nightshirt and wiped his eye into which the sweat was running, half-blinding him. He could feel the Bishop's bony back pressed against his own, stiff as a board with fright. In a few moments the air about them was throbbing with curious songs and music. The friar turned, and putting out his hand, took his companion by the arm. The Bishop immediately fell on the floor.

'What did you do that for?' demanded the friar in a testy whisper.

Bishop Flanagan seemed incapable of movement, but his eyes held a world of pathos.

'Don't leave me,' he managed to gasp.

Father Furiosus helped him to his feet.

'The holy water has let us down,' said the friar hoarsely. 'It must indeed be elementals. Be prepared for a manifestation any moment.'

It had begun. In the wavering glimmer cast by the rushlight, gossamer shapes swayed and slowly took on the form of four highly agreeable females. They lounged gracefully in a corner of the room, smiling engagingly at the paralysed ecclesiastics. Father Furiosus essayed an exorcism in a cracked voice, but his heart was not in it, for he felt a certain premonition that his efforts would be unavailing. His voice trailed off and stopped. Just as he had feared, the four sylphs, far from disappearing in a sulphur flash and a foul smoke, started putting the finishing touches to their coiffures and adding a last dab of rouge to their lips and cheeks.

'Hurry up, Gertie,' said one of them. 'Let's get them.'

'It's my considered opinion,' muttered the friar, 'that it's high time for both of us to take evasive action. The best moral theologians have only one recommendation to make in cases of acute temptation — *Fuga*, which is translated "Flight".'

'But suppose,' quavered the Bishop, 'that they surround us?'

'I wish you wouldn't keep clinging to me,' exclaimed Father Furiosus irritably. 'Please let go my nightshirt. Now, listen. By "Flight" the Fathers do not mean merely that one should remove oneself physically from the location and occasion of the temptation:

that would avail us little, as I doubt not but that these harpies can run as fast as we; but it is implied also that one should forcibly occupy one's mind with other things, and on no account venture to reason or argue the temptation out of existence. That way lies failure, the death of the soul and the pit of Hell. Nothing is so salubrious in temptation as the mortification of the flesh which is tempted, so let us betake ourselves with all speed to some refuge where we can proceed at once to the practice of the counsels of the Fathers in the matter.'

'There's a fine bed of nettles against the wall of my stockyard,' said the Bishop eagerly.

'Come on,' said the friar, and the two of them made off through the far door. The Bishop, who was lithe and nimble, soon outdistanced the friar, and he had the backdoor of the Palace unbolted before Furiosus caught up with him. They raced across the yard barefoot, the Bishop pattering far ahead. The prelate, who felt that the situation was critical, did not hesitate to pull his nightshirt over his head as he ran, so that he was stark naked when he reached the nettles, of which there was a particularly luxurious bed. Father Furiosus saw him stretch his skinny frame at the head of the slight incline where the nettles grew, and roll himself over and over down through the nettles until he reached the bottom. Then he picked himself up, scampered up again over the broken stems and repeated the operation.

'There'll be a nice scandal,' muttered the friar, 'if any of the parishioners see his lordship running around in the buff.'

But Father Furiosus did not delay in following the Bishop's example. He stripped off his nightshirt and with tightset lips selected a corner where the nettles were five feet high. The ground shook as his brawny frame tumbled over and over down the incline.

Some time later the moon, which had modestly hidden her head, emerged sailing from behind a cloud. She saw two naked men squatting uncomfortably in the centre of a completely flattened nettlebed, watched from beyond its fringes by four pensive sylphs.

'I fear we have ground all the venom out of the nettles,' whispered Furiosus, 'and the bad women are still there. I fear that unholy desires may yet arise in me.'

'Sh!' said the Bishop, 'lest they hear. There's a small pond beyond the stockade. Let's make a run for it.'

All the long night through, the sylphs, once more in their native element, danced beneath the trees by the side of the pond, while from the centre, immersed to their necks in freezing water, the Bishop and the friar watched them glumly.

Chapter VIII

The road that goes south from Cashel winds crazily; taking little runs over ridges, and curving so as to skirt the irregular boundaries of the farmlands. It is an absurd, switchbacking Irish road, never straight for more than a hundred paces, encouraging the wayfarer with the hope that there may be something unusual and peculiar around the bend or over the brow of the hill. The roadway is hemmed in on either side by hedges of blackthorn, brambles, gorse and sallies. Through gaps, ineffectively blocked by old buckets and pieces of bedsteads, the traveller catches glimpses of the endless green fields and the contented cattle scattered over the plain. From behind a gate an occasional cow, having nothing better to do, will stare with gloomy insolence at the passer-by; or on turning a corner you may suddenly come upon a donkey who to all appearances has been standing in the middle of the roadway for weeks sunk in inutterable boredom. There are not many human habitations, and such few as there are, are built in the wrong places — on low ground, so that the rainwater gathers on the surrounding hillocks and flows with ease in through the front door. When evening comes and the beginning of twilight, the road and countryside become charged with a peculiar opalescent atmosphere as if a faery world had been superimposed upon our own, so that one almost doubts the reality of tree and field; and, according as temperament dictates, either hurries on in terror of what one may meet, or else lingers filled with a sense of wonder and a content that seems to belong to another existence.

But as the traveller by daylight winds his way further, he will come nearer and nearer to the great mountain wall that bounds the Tipperary plain on the south. When he has passed through a brief stretch of woodland and stream, he will find to his astonishment that the road, instead of going around the mountains in a civilised manner, is intent on running straight at them and trying to jump. More amazing still is the road's success. It is true that its progress up the precipitous hillside is drunken in the extreme, but a thousand feet up it finds a great cleft which local people call 'The Gap'; and in there, a little out of breath, the road knowingly worms its way.

At this point, twenty miles south of Cashel and a thousand feet above the Tipperary plain, on a grassy bank by the roadside sat Fursey thinking of his sins. Below him lay the rich plain, an astonishing checkerboard of green and golden fields in neat squares, the opulent domain of the men of affairs and of the priests. Above him arose the cliffs and shoulders of the Knockmealdown Mountains, windswept and torn by storms. Over on his left he could see among the bogs and the rocks the shimmer of a small mountain lake, and near it a white dot which was a cottage.

'I seem to be a desperate character,' was Fursey's sad summing-up of the situation. 'To begin with, I'm a genuine sorcerer. It would be useless to deny that I've meddled with very dark powers and practised the blacker forms of magic. Then, in one afternoon I told Cuthbert more lies than most men tell in a lifetime. I'm a notorious hobnobber with demons, and I encouraged King Cormac to lechery, at least I did not repel his advances as a decent girl should. I have probably been an occasion of sin to the innocent in that for a day and a half I roamed about the countryside undraped (someone is sure to have seen me), and lastly I'm a thief. I had no moral right to rob that scarecrow of his rags — he was possibly the property of a poor man, and now the birds will eat all the seed so laboriously sown. There's no doubt about it but that I'm a most abandoned ruffian,' he concluded gloomily. 'Probably my like for villainy has never been seen in the world before.'

Fursey sighed and grew tired of thinking of his iniquities. Instead he began to remember that he was very hungry. If only he had a rope —! Even the tiniest bit of cord would do. If he had a little bit of cord, he would throw it over a thorn bush, and by pulling hard enough he could probably produce at least a couple of hard-boiled eggs. He sighed a second time and told himself that the practice of sorcery was a sin; still he wished he had a small piece of cord. His soul was by now so deformed and hideous that one extra little sin wouldn't make much difference.

However, sitting still wasn't going to produce food, so he got wearily to his feet and continued his way along the rocky road. From time to time he glanced across at the distant whitewashed cottage beside the mountain tarn. There would be food there, but would they give him any? Would they even lend him a rope for a few minutes if he promised to bring it back? They'd probably conclude, he reflected gloomily, that he wanted to hang himself, and indignantly refuse.

He came to a point where a pathway joined his road. He paused and looked down the crooked track. That would be the path that led to the cottage. He felt that if he went down the track and approached the dwelling, the owner would probably set the dogs on him. Hospitality would scarcely be extended to a man of the tramp class so inadequately clad in a scarecrow's cloak and kilt, as to be almost an offence against decency. Yet he hated to continue further on his way: the mountain road looked as if it led only to menacing and barren lands, and he was sick and tired of nature anyway. He longed to hear human voices and feel the warmth of a peat fire against his knees. Then he remembered again how hungry he was, and he sat down on a stone. He sat there for a long time with his head between his hands thinking of nothing, and then he began to think of Albert. He hesitated for a while, but at last he raised his head.

'Albert!' he called softly. 'Albert!'

There was a movement in the dust of the road, and Albert's bear's paws slowly took shape, and soon the whole of Albert was there, but an Albert jaded and sulky-looking and very much emaciated. His red, foggy eyes observed Fursey steadily.

'Nice mess you got yourself into with the clergy,' he said. 'I thought they'd burn you to a cinder.'

'Well, they didn't,' replied Fursey.

'I suppose you'll tell me that it was your superior intelligence that got you out of it,' remarked Albert sarcastically.

'Please don't nag,' answered Fursey. 'I'm hungry. I want something to eat.'

'*You* want something to eat!' replied Albert shrilly. 'What about me? Look at the state I'm in, with the skin of my belly clinging to my spine. For once and for all, are you, or are you not, going to part with some of your blood? Answer yes or no.'

Fursey looked at his familiar with heavy eyes. Right enough, the creature had shrunk away to mere skin and bone. Fursey felt sorry for him, but he did not see that he could do anything about it. He sighed again.

'I want you to scout around, Albert,' he said, 'and see if you can find me a bit of rope.'

Albert faced him determinedly. 'Once,' he said with a tremor of indignation in his voice, 'I was as frisky a familiar as you'd meet in a day's walk, but your confounded meanness —'

'Don't argue,' commanded Fursey. 'Do as you're told. Scout around and find me a rope.'

Albert threw a venomous look at his master and began a half-hearted sniffing and snuffling up and down the ditch. It was just then that an old man of the farmer class came around the bend of the track. He was carrying a long stick of ashwood to which was tied a piece of cord and a worm. He stopped opposite Fursey.

'That's a queer class of a dog you have, mister,' he said, blinking short-sightedly at Albert. 'What breed would he be, now?'

'Vanish,' commanded Fursey.

'What's that?' asked the old man.

'Nothing,' answered Fursey. 'I haven't got a dog. You're making a mistake.'

The old man peered where Albert had been.

'Dear me,' he said, 'the old eyes are going on me. I would have sworn I saw a dog.'

'Not a dog for miles around,' responded Fursey blithely. 'Are you going fishing, sir?'

'Yes,' replied the old man. 'I'm going down to the lake.'

'Then you're going in the wrong direction,' said Fursey. 'The lake is behind you.'

The old farmer looked bewildered.

'So it is,' he replied at last, and turned back the way he had come. Fursey arose from the stone and fell into step beside him.

'May I ask if you live in the cottage beyond?' he queried.

'Yes,' responded the ancient. 'That's my house.'

'Very convenient having the fishing right at your front door.'

The old man looked surprised.

'The lake is at the back of the house,' he said.

For a few minutes they walked side by side in silence. Then the old man stopped and peered sharply at Fursey.

'What are you accompanying me for?' he asked.

'So that you won't lose your way to the lake.'

'How could I lose my way to the lake?' retorted the old man. 'Don't I live beside it, and haven't I fished it these forty years.'

He continued on his way, and Fursey fell into step with him once more. When they were within a few hundred yards of the cottage, the old man stopped again and turned to Fursey.

'You're still following me,' he asserted. 'You're up to something. If you don't go away, I'll call my daughter.'

Fursey's voice broke. 'It's some days since I've had anything to eat,' he said. 'Maybe you have a slice of bread in the house that's not wanted, and a cup of milk?'

'What are you?' asked the old man, looking down suspiciously at the scarecrow rags that covered Fursey. 'A travelling man?'

'Yes,' lied Fursey.

The ancient regarded him closely for a few moments, then he answered gruffly.

'All right. I'll see what the daughter can do for you.'

Fursey stepped out joyfully beside him.

'Do you do much fishing, sir?' he asked politely.

'Forty years,' responded his companion, 'and I haven't caught one of the little devils yet. I'm beginning to suspect that there aren't any fish in the lake.'

Fursey, who had fished once or twice with a bent nail and the cord of his habit in the Shannon at Clonmacnoise, plunged into a discussion on the relative merits of the lugworm and the lobworm as bait. The old man listened with interest until they came to the fence of the cottage.

'We'll have to find the daughter first,' he said. 'She's probably feeding the hens at the back of the house.'

As they made their way into the yard, the old man sighed and turned to Fursey.

'I'm in a bad way here,' he confided, 'what with the advancing years and the fishing, I don't be able to do much work about the farm. I had a good farmboy, but off he went yesterday to fight in the war.'

Fursey muttered sympathetically. He did not enquire which war, as he knew that among the one hundred and eighty kingdoms of Ireland there were always several wars in progress, and they were usually very confusing. Moreover, he had never understood geography. But he quickly saw his opportunity.

'What about taking on a new boy?' he asked eagerly. 'I'm a willing and hardy worker.'

The old man turned his head and inspected Fursey closely.

'You're a queer-looking boy,' he replied at last, 'with your hair snow-white. How old are you?'

'I'm forty.'

'You look about a hundred.'

'You'd do well to take me,' rejoined Fursey. 'I understand everything about a farm, from paring edible roots to milking a goat. I'm a great hand at feeding hens. To say nothing of my knowledge of fishing.'

The old man seemed impressed.

'I'll have to talk to the daughter,' he replied.

They found her at the back of the house spreading out clothes on the hedge to dry, a fine, wide-eyed girl of about thirty-two, with a large, full-lipped mouth and two sets of the whitest teeth Fursey had ever seen. She watched Fursey curiously while the old man explained the immediate need for a slice of bread and a cup of milk. Under her friendly gaze Fursey stood grinning bashfully, his cheeks and his ears pink with his blushes. When the old man had finished, she immediately led the way into the kitchen and put Fursey on a stool by the fire. She loaded the table with bread, butter, cheese and cold vegetables, and drew a beaker of ale from a cask in the corner. Fursey ate with difficulty, partly because he was embarrassed by such hospitality, and partly because the old man had emptied three canisters of lugworms on to a corner of the table and was earnestly soliciting Fursey's opinion as to their quality and striking power. He was too shortsighted to observe Fursey's efforts to be polite and at the same time to prevent the bait from crawling into his food and up his sleeves. The girl stood leaning against the wall by the hearth smiling at them both.

While the meal was finished and the lugworms had been returned with difficulty into the three canisters, the old man and the girl went into the far corner of the room and conducted a long conversation in whispers, while Fursey sat with his knees to the fire anxiously awaiting the outcome. At length the girl came forward and seated herself at the table.

'My father tells me,' she said, 'that you'd like to be taken on here as farmboy.'

'Yes,' replied Fursey eagerly.

'There's not a great deal of work to be done,' she explained. 'Just to keep the yard and outhouses clean and dry, bring water from the well and milk the cow. We'll give you your food and your bed here by the fire, and an old suit of my father's as well. He thinks it's hardly decent to have you going around the way you are, with a young woman in the house.'

Fursey could find no words to express his thanks, but the tears welled up into his eyes and crept down his face. When the old man observed Fursey's emotion he was powerfully affected himself, and it was with difficulty that his daughter succeeded in shepherding the two of them through the door out into the yard, where she put the ash rod and line into her father's hand. She instructed Fursey that his first duty was to see the old man down to the shore of the lake and into his coracle. Then Fursey was to return and sweep the yard.

Day after day crept by, days of scudding cloud, of rustling showers and defiant sunshine. Never had Fursey been so happy. In the mornings he accompanied Old Declan to the lake and saw him safely into the coracle. The old man browsed around the little tarn all day, and it was one of Fursey's duties to summon him to his meals, otherwise he would have forgotten to come home at all. Fursey swept the house and the yard, milked the cow and carried water from the well. He flapped around in a suit of the old man's clothes, which were far too big for him, chatting amiably to the cow and the hens, amusing Declan and his daughter with his antics, and all the time he felt an elevation of heart that he had never known before. He could scarcely credit his happiness and good fortune. Sometimes in the cool of the day he sat on a rock at the edge of the lake, and as he watched the water come wrinkling in towards his feet, he brooded on his happiness and wondered uneasily how long it would last. He would close his eyes and tell himself that there was no reason why his present blissful state should not continue always. Then he would hug his knees and lose himself listening to the hollow slapping of the water among the stones and the metallic notes of the birds, the long drawn-out twitter of some individual songster that seemed to have an impediment in its speech, mingling with the curling chirps and the tuneful tootings of the others.

Fursey thought it was a most beautiful lake. Its threatening cliffs awed and delighted him. When the sun was high overhead he would stand dazzled by the sparkle of its waters, and many an afternoon he sat hour after hour wondering how it was that the water seemed all the time to be moving in towards him, although there was no breeze and the fringes of the water did no more than rustle among the reeds. When he arose and moved back towards the cottage, it often seemed to him that the whole hollow in the hills where lake and cottage lay was filled with a music of which he was aware but which he could not hear. He would look up at the heights where mountain was piled upon mountain, and his heart would be flooded with humility. As he approached the cottage he would, as often as not, hear the sound of Maeve's singing as she went about her work. 'It's a good thing to hear a woman singing in a house,' Old Declan confided to him. 'It means that the house is a happy one.' Fursey would creep noiselessly into the kitchen, returning diffidently her ready smile; and seated on his stool by the hearth, he would watch her surreptitiously as she kneaded the dough or turned the handle of the churn.

Occasionally he accompanied Declan on his fishing excursions, but the old man had to fish from the shore when Fursey was with him, for nothing would persuade Fursey to trust himself to the frail coracle. Declan did not mind very much where he fished from: he never caught anything anyway. Sitting on a boulder he would explain the philosophy of fishing to Fursey.

'It's not necessary to catch fish,' he would say. 'Men fish because it brings them back to their boyhood. They like scrambling over rocks and crossing streams and endangering their lives on lakes, just as they did when they were children. Moreover, it brings them to pleasant, interesting places which they wouldn't ordinarily have a chance of seeing. All the same,' the old man would add grimly, 'I wish I could catch one of the little devils.'

But it was when the door of the cottage was closed against the freshness of the night, and Declan and Maeve had drawn in about the glowing peat fire, that Fursey really came into his own. They quickly discovered that their unusual farmboy, though he could neither read nor write, had a fund of peculiar information. He seemed to have a wide knowledge of demonology and the un-principled behaviour of witches, and from his stool beside the fire he gravely gave them advice as to the correct procedure in certain unpleasant sets of circumstances; for instance, if one had the misfortune to encounter a basilisk on the highway. He seemed to them a man with a considerable knowledge of the great world beyond 'The Gap'. He had visited Cashel and seen in the flesh the great men of the Kingdom, the Bishop, the King and the great lords and ecclesiastics; he had even visited remote Clonmacnoise and seen the River Shannon. While Fursey told his halting tales, Maeve, from her place on the far side of the fire, kept her big eyes fixed on his face. Declan muttered to himself all during Fursey's recital, and occasionally gave vent to a mournful groan when some act of human or demoniacal depravity came to be told.

There was one thing that puzzled Fursey greatly. Often, on a warm, golden evening as he sat by the lakeside, he asked himself how it was that in his flight from Cashel he had not been pursued. He had been two days on the road, and in that time he could easily have been overtaken by horsemen or by fleet runners. It was true that he had spent most of the daylight hiding in the hedges and had travelled for the greater part by night; still, there had been no evidence whatever of a desire on the part of the authorities to recapture him. Was it that they were afraid to approach him and that they thought they were well rid of him? He could not bring himself to believe it. Father Furiosus and the Bishop, he felt, were not the kind of men to allow a suspected sorcerer to be at large without making every effort to capture him. And even if they were convinced that he was not a sorcerer, but a demoniac, they would be just as inflamed with zeal to catch him and rid him of his malignant guest. Fursey could not understand it; but as day after day passed and he found himself unmolested, he began to think about the matter less, being only too willing to believe himself secure. He took the precaution, however, of surreptitiously anointing the cottage broom with the ointment which he still carried, lest it should be necessary to make a hurried escape; and one evening when Declan and Maeve were absent, he had a practice flight up and down the yard to the considerable alarm of a large body of hens. He had of course taken the further precaution of not telling his name to the old cottager and his daughter. On his first evening when they had asked him how he was called, he had answered on the spur of the moment, giving his dead father's name — Flinthead, and as Flinthead he was known to Declan and Maeve.

Although it was still only July it was time to commence bringing in the winter's supply of peat, and this onerous task was willingly accepted by Fursey. Late one evening as he came to the cottage sweating under the weight of the heavy creel on his back, he saw three horses tethered in the yard. He at once swung the creel to the ground, but before he could properly grapple with his alarm, Declan came to the door and beckoned him reassuringly.

'We have three old friends paying us a visit,' said the old man, taking Fursey by the arm and conducting him into the kitchen. Maeve was clearing the table of the remnants of a meal, and Fursey glanced fearfully at the three strangers. One was a more than middle-aged woman with a gamey eye, who was introduced as 'the Widow Dykes from beyond the mountain'. The second was Phineas the Clerk, a rusty little fellow of indeterminate age, clad in a shabby, black cloak. From the inkhorn and bunch of quills which were slung from a cord over his shoulder, Fursey identified him at once as one of those men who could read and write and who made a living travelling around the country writing letters for people. But it was the third stranger who filled Fursey with instinctive dislike and dread. He was Magnus, a soldier, a big, lusty fellow, who rested his elbows on the table as if he owned it. He was sucking the last succulent morsel of marrow from a bone when Fursey entered, and he nodded contemptuously when the new farmboy, Flinthead, was introduced. The others smiled slightly as they glanced at Fursey's cloak, which was so big for him that it had to be wrapped around him twice, and at his kilt, which was so long that it covered the calves of his legs. Fursey threw a quick glance towards the door to assure himself that his broom was in its accustomed place, before seating himself in the darkest corner of the room. Maeve handed him his bowl of stirabout, for he had not yet had his evening meal.

'Go on with your story, Phineas,' said Magnus, flinging the bone into the fire.

From his place beside the comfortable widow Declan bent towards Fursey.

'Phineas has been telling us,' he explained, 'about the extraordinary happenings at Cashel. It seems that they captured the prince of all sorcerers, a man called Fursey; but he subsequently escaped.'

'Indeed,' replied Fursey, burying his head in the bowl of stirabout.

'There's nothing much more to tell,' said Phineas. 'As I have already related to you, he appeared in the guise of a woman in the Royal courtyard and tried to strangle good King Cormac. On the night on which he disappeared, he took with him by some magic art known only to himself, every bit of gold which the Byzantine prince had so generously bestowed on the clergy and citizens. Every gold bar vanished at the same instant as the monstrous Fursey himself. Chunks of gold disappeared from the soldiers' pockets. They were there one moment, and they were gone the next. Even a valuable dog of superior pedigree, presented by Apollyon to Father Furiosus, disappeared without leaving a trace.'

'But was he not pursued?' asked Declan. 'A sorcerer in woman's clothing, loaded down with gold, and with a pedigree dog under his arm, should be easily identified.'

'No,' replied Phineas. 'Those who were best qualified to direct the pursuit, the Bishop and Father Furiosus, were incapable of doing so. They were found in the early morning in a semi-frozen condition in a pond on the Bishop's estate, having apparently been enmeshed in the spells of this malignant wizard. They were in bed for some days half paralysed and with violent colds in the head and chest; and when they became once more capable of movement, the scent had grown cold. Even yet, good Bishop Flanagan cannot be said to have fully recovered, for he is still much given to involuntary crying, shouting and barking, and other symptoms of hysteria.'

'How terrible,' murmured Maeve. 'Did you see the wizard yourself?'

'Yes,' replied Phineas a trifle pompously. 'I saw him.'

'Oh!' breathed Maeve. 'How old was he? What did he look like?'

'I should say that he was very old,' answered Phineas judiciously, 'perhaps eighty. His hair was snow-white, and he was much bowed both by his years and by the heavy weight of his iniquities.'

'I was told,' interrupted Magnus, who seemed restless because Phineas was monopolising the conversation, 'that the fellow was entirely black in appearance.'

'I saw him myself,' answered Phineas testily. 'It's true that his face was black, as was appropriate considering that all his contrivings against mankind were of a black and deadly nature, but the rest of him was white, particularly his hair. It was snow-white like Flinthead's over there.'

The company glanced involuntarily into the chimney corner from which Fursey's moon-round visage stared back at them from behind his bowl of stirabout.

'He must have been a fearsome sight,' ejaculated Declan.

'He was,' replied Phineas. 'He was a man of singularly evil countenance. His mouth was twisted towards his ear, and from him there came a cadaverous smell which was well-nigh insupportable. When he spoke it was in a muffled voice. You had but to look at him to realise that never was there in any character a more complete concentration of every quality that distinguishes a man of evil and pernicious principles. They say that he was the seventh son of a seventh son, which means that the Devil had marked him as his own from the very day of his birth.'

'He used preside at cannibal feasts,' said Magnus, 'and he put on Cuthbert the Sexton such a malignant spell that after violent retching the unfortunate man brought up pieces of coal, bodkins, stones, brass, eggshells and a variety of other objects.'

'I'll be afraid to go to bed to-night,' shivered Maeve.

'But isn't it a terrible thing,' interjected the Widow, 'that even godly men like Bishop Flanagan and Father Furiosus are not immune from his spells? I heard that his parting gift to them was a murrain, which still afflicts them sorely.'

'God save me and mine from all such legacies!' ejaculated Declan piously.

'It may well be,' replied Phineas. 'It is certainly the case that he caused the unfortunate Cuthbert to vomit stones so big that it was incredible how they could come out of any Christian mouth.'

'What do you think of it, Flinthead?' asked Declan, turning to where Fursey sat quiet as a mouse in his corner. 'Would you not be scared by such horrid manifestations?'

Fursey grinned feebly, but before he could think of an answer Magnus let out a great horse laugh.

'Why do you ask him?' he demanded roughly. 'I wouldn't set any great value on an opinion of his.'

'Oh,' rejoined the old man mildly, 'Flinthead is very learned in the ways of witches and demons.'

Magnus leaned back in his chair and shifted his soldier's belt as if to laugh more comfortably.

'My God!' he said, 'you're not serious. Why, one has only to look at him to see that his brain is naturally moist.'

For a moment the heart of Fursey burned within him at these contemptuous words, but the fire flickered and went out as Maeve leaned across and placed her hand comfortingly on his.

'Now, now,' she said, 'I won't have anyone making fun of Flinthead. He's a friend of mine, and we all like him very much.'

The Widow and Phineas the Clerk smiled tolerantly. Old Declan seemed to be still worried about details of Phineas' story, and he did not appear to notice that the Widow had quietly taken his hand into her plump paw and was gently squeezing his gnarled fingers.

'What about The Gray Mare?' he asked anxiously. 'Was she a witch or not?'

'There are two schools of thought in the matter,' replied Phineas. 'The Bishop and the King are believed to be of opinion that she was a witch; but Father Furiosus urges that she was undoubtedly innocent and was murdered by Fursey, whom he now believes to be possessed by a devil as well as being a sorcerer. Father Furiosus is a man of great force of character, and he has a considerable following among the clergy and the populace. He believes The Gray Mare to have been a martyr, and he has had her remains translated to an expensive tomb in Kilpuggin Church, which has become a place of pilgrimage. Sundry cures have already been reported, and only for the outbreak of war with Thomond, the cause for her canonisation would have been by now well advanced.'

Fursey sat motionless in his corner, his countenance seemingly busied in unceasing converse with his heart. At first he had listened anxiously, but as he became convinced that there was little danger of being recognised, his attention wandered, and he reflected how little he knew of human nature and of the ways of the world. From time to time he gathered in his vagrant thoughts and told himself that he must listen because all this news was of the most immediate concern to him; but his eyes invariably returned to rest on the line of Maeve's temple where the hair was brushed back, and he would feel for a moment as if he were falling into a lunacy, for ever since she had lain her comforting hand on his, his love was so hot that he wist not where he was. Once more he pulled himself together. They were talking of war. War had broken out between Cashel and Thomond. It was very difficult to grasp what it was all about, but it seemed that the King of Thomond was an idealist, who kept reiterating that 'a principle is a principle.' In answer to King Cormac's curt ultimatum, his reply had been: 'Men and matters come and go, but a principle is eternal.' Thereupon the hounds of war had been unleashed, and the whole fighting forces of Cashel had been flung into Thomond territory. No engagement had ensued, for the reason that the army of the King of Thomond was not yet ready — the season had been late, and the hay had not yet been saved. Accordingly, the only casualties that had resulted were two Thomond hermits who, betrayed by wanton curiosity, had put their heads out of their caves to find out what all the noise was about, and had immediately had their heads struck off.

Magnus had now got control of the conversation.

'Cormac is a master strategist,' he said approvingly. 'He is the only king in Ireland who maintains a standing army, and although the upkeep of those twenty-four men is a considerable burden on the State, they are well worth it. Other kings must wait until the agricultural work of the spring and early summer is over before their clansmen are free for warfare; and again and again it has happened that a king has been left alone in the field of battle by reason of his army going home to their farms to gather in the harvest. Cormac's long-sighted policy has ensured that he is never wholly deserted in this fashion. Nine-tenths of his army may go home, but he has always the hard core of twenty-four men left to fight for him. His strategy consists then in this: that he keeps manoeuvring his forces with consummate skill all during the summer; and with the coming of the harvest when the fighting men must go home, the opposing king finds that he and his sons have to face alone the full onset of the standing army of Cashel. Many and many a war has Cormac won by these methods. He is admitted all over the world to be the finest general in the history of warfare.'

'You won't have to go to the war yet awhile?' asked Maeve.

'Well, I've been summoned,' replied Magnus, 'but my hay isn't quite in yet, and I've a cow with a swollen teat; I'll have to fix that first. But in a week or so I expect to be in a position to answer the call.'

'Maybe the war will be over before you're ready to go,' said Declan hopefully.

'I don't think so,' replied Magnus. 'It will be a long and bitter conflict. I estimate that in another week agricultural operations will be completed throughout the territory, and provided the weather remains good Cormac should be able to gather a sufficiency of men to form an army large enough to manoeuvre.'

'It's time for us to go,' announced Phineas, rising to his feet and moving his inkhorn and quills to a more comfortable position in the small of his back. 'We've allowed the night to overtake us.'

There was a moving back of chairs and a stirring of feet as the guests were assisted into their cloaks. Fursey was sent to the yard to untie the horses and lead them around to the door. He stood back in the shadow of the cottage listening to the muffled wailing of the wind through the mountain gap as Phineas, Magnus and the Widow from their saddles bade farewell to Declan and Maeve. Magnus sat astride his horse like a king, his great bulk silhouetted against the night sky, while Maeve stood at the horse's head talking to him. Fursey could hear his hearty laugh as he slapped his sword. Then in a chorus of farewells he rode off jingling, followed by the other two. None of them had remembered to say goodbye to Fursey.

On the following afternoon Fursey and Maeve sat by the edge of the lake breathing in the warm, sweet air. She was seated on a smooth rock while Fursey squatted on the ground facing her. There were clouds overhead and a breeze, and Fursey watched the shadows scampering across the flanks of the hills when he wasn't engaged in watching her face. She seemed to him pensive and sad, and to have lost a little of the freshness of her youth.

'Flinthead,' she said suddenly, 'I'm afraid my father is going to marry the Widow Dykes.'

Fursey grunted to show his astonishment.

'He has formed an unfortunate attachment to her,' continued Maeve sadly.

'But,' remarked Fursey diffidently, 'she is no longer young.'

'Neither is my father,' replied the girl. 'She is a scheming woman, and she wants the house and the little bit of land. She knows how to flatter him, and men are so vain. I fear that he is sore assotted on her.'

An image of Declan doddering around the house and the lake, came into Fursey's mind, and he marvelled exceedingly.

'Well,' he answered at last. 'After all, if your father is seriously and honourably attached to her —'

'Do you know anything about marriage,' interrupted Maeve, 'the kinship of soul that is necessary —?'

'Yes,' replied Fursey with conviction. 'I'm a widower myself.'

'I didn't know you were ever married,' replied Maeve, surprised.

'My wife predeceased me,' explained Fursey.

'That's too bad,' said Maeve, dropping her voice sympathetically. 'How long were you married?'

'About six hours,' replied Fursey gloomily, 'but I know all about marriage. Compatibility of temperament is of the first importance.'

A laugh bubbled up from Maeve's heart. Fursey glanced up at the two rows of pearly teeth and smiled himself. He knew that she was laughing at him, but he did not mind. She arose and began to lead the way back to the house.

'I don't think it will be a good thing,' she said, and Fursey wondered at her gravity. He did not venture to speak for a few moments, and when he did speak, he spoke unevenly with a little break in his voice.

'It may be,' he suggested, 'that he loves her passing well. When I close my eyes, I can picture the two of them walking down the path from the house and around the borders of the lake, having goodly language and lovely behaviour together.'

Maeve seemed annoyed. 'I tell you,' she said, 'that she is after his house and land, and he is too blind and foolish and vain to realise it.'

'Maybe,' said Fursey miserably, 'he so burns in love that he is past himself in his understanding.'

They had reached the door of the cottage. Maeve turned and faced him. 'What you don't appear to realise,' she said with a sudden sob, 'is that there's no room for two women in the one house,' and she turned and hurried into the cottage.

Several times during the ensuing week Phineas the Clerk came and went. He spread his parchments and quills on the table in the kitchen and seemed always on the point of indicting something important. There were conferences between him and Declan and Maeve, but nothing seemed ever to come of them. He would sigh and rolling up his parchments, address himself to the evening meal which they spread before him. He brought news from the great world beyond The Gap. There had been a fierce and bloody encounter at a ford in the Mulkeen River. From sunrise until sunset the conflicting armies had been in death grips. The countryside had echoed to the thunder of chariot wheels, and many a field of promising corn had been trampled into the earth by the manoeuvring legions. At sunset the King of Thomond had withdrawn his defeated forces leaving two men dead on the field. Cashel's losses were a sergeant deprived of an eye by a well-aimed stone. 'The battle was fiercely and evenly contested,' says the Annalist, 'and to this day the place is known in the Gaelic language as "The Ford of Slaughter".'

But later news was not so good. King Cormac, elated by his resounding victory, had withdrawn his army into the hills, where he had commenced manoeuvring with consummate strategy. In his absence the armies of Thomond, swollen now by hundreds of troops released from their agricultural pursuits, had swept across the Tipperary plain, laying fire to the houses of the rich. A trail of flaming residences and billowing white smoke marked their passage. 'Every gentleman's seat in the country is aflame,' said Phineas vehemently to Fursey, who nodded sympathetically and continued for some hours to ponder on the meaning of the strange phrase. When news of these happenings had been conveyed to King Cormac in the hills, he was reported to have remarked philosophically, 'The King of Thomond doesn't understand the art of warfare,' and to have moved his army into the mountains nearer the Thomond border, where he recommenced manoeuvring on a larger scale.

One evening ten days later while Fursey was milking the cow in the kitchen, where he had brought her because of the rain, he was startled by the sudden clatter of a horse's hooves on the cobbles of the yard outside. He went to the door and saw Magnus astride his steaming war-horse, looking very important and terrible with his sword and spear, and his leathern shield upon his arm. He dismounted and ignoring Fursey's feeble welcome, pushed by him into the kitchen with a curt 'Out of my way, farmboy.' Inside he shook the rainwater from his martial cloak.

'Where's Maeve?' he demanded of Fursey, who was trying to persuade the cow to leave the house.

'In the other room,' answered Fursey.

'Tell her I'm here,' commanded Magnus.

With a final heave of his shoulder, which he had placed against the cow's buttock, Fursey succeeded in expelling her through the front door. He turned and knocked at the door of the other room.

'Come in,' came Maeve's voice.

Fursey opened the door and went in. Declan was sitting on the floor trying shortsightedly to disentangle a fishing line. There was a flush in Maeve's cheeks, and Fursey noticed with a sinking heart that she was tying a ribbon in her hair.

'Magnus is here,' reported Fursey.

'Yes, I heard him,' she replied. 'Tell him I'll be out in a moment.'

Fursey conveyed the message, and when he had lifted the pail of milk on to its shelf, he sat down despondently in his corner by the fire. Magnus strode up and down without deigning to speak to him. Maeve emerged a few moments later in a flutter of ribbon and girlish laughter. She gave Magnus her hand.

'So you're off to the wars,' she said gayly.

'Yes,' replied the soldier.

'I'm proud of you, my boy,' said Declan, who had followed his daughter into the room.

Fursey dutifully drew a mug of beer and placed it before Magnus. Then he returned to his corner and, seating himself, fixed his eyes furtively on the soldier's broad, handsome face.

'The situation in which the Kingdom finds itself,' began Magnus, 'is in the highest degree critical. The cowardly King of Thomond, instead of leading his army into the hills and starting to manoeuvre opposite King Cormac, has flung his entire forces into the Cashel plain, and the capital city itself is closely beleaguered.'

'Dear me!' exclaimed Declan. 'And what is King Cormac doing to counter this outrageous behaviour?'

'He is manoeuvring frantically in the hills, trying to attract the King of Thomond's attention and coax him to lead off his forces from the devoted city; but seemingly to no avail. The King of Thomond, who is as cowardly as he is ignorant of the principles of warfare, shows not the slightest inclination to face Cormac in the field. Instead, four hundred of his slingsmen surround the city of Cashel and shower stones on it as big as your fist by day and by night. The unceasing whistling of their artillery is something terrible, and already a most respected citizen of the town has had his brains dashed out as he ventured forth from the door of his dwelling to bring in the morning milk.'

'But,' asked Declan, 'what of good Bishop Flanagan? Can he do nought to abate the murderous rage of Thomond?'

'The Bishop is playing a man's part,' replied Magnus. 'From the door of his palace on the hill he hurls anathemas and maledictions at the enemy. He has pronounced the sentence of excommunication against the first man that damages ecclesiastical property.'

'Is then Thomond so abandoned to wickedness as not to be moved by the representations of his lordship?'

'Unfortunately,' replied Magnus. 'Bishop Flanagan's efforts are largely negatived by the counter-maledictions and anathemas of the Bishop of Thomond, who is urging on his countrymen to raze every church and abbey in Cashel to the ground, having first sequestered the gold ornaments and valuables for the use of the Church in the Thomond diocese.'

'I think war is terrible,' said Maeve.

'It is a pursuit in the highest degree dangerous to the partici-pants,' declared Declan, shaking his head gravely. 'I hope you come through it without any broken limbs, Magnus.'

'I'll be all right,' replied Magnus jovially, 'but God help any man that stands against me!'

'And what of the courageous garrison that defends Cashel?' the old man asked.

'There is a sprinkling of soldiers,' replied Magnus, 'but it is the townspeople themselves, men, women and children, who are manning the palisade. Every stone that falls on the city is flung back in the faces of the encircling enemy.'

'Bravo!' exclaimed Declan enthusiastically.

'It shows fighting spirit,' agreed Magnus, 'but unfortunately it also serves to keep the enemy provided with an endless supply of ammunition. However, the forces of Thomond have been kept at a sufficient distance to prevent their setting fire to the thatch roofs of the city. In this regard the recent rain must also have been a help.'

'The dirty ruffians!' exclaimed the old man. 'I've a good mind to join Magnus and fight in the war myself.'

'You'll do nothing of the sort,' said Maeve. 'Who'd guard the house if you were gone, with broken bands of soldiers roaming the countryside lusting for blood and plunder?'

'That's true,' muttered Declan, sitting back in his chair.

'The siege will be raised to-night,' asserted Magnus with conviction. 'The hay is in, and there'll be a full five hundred of us gathered at the Cow's Head Tavern two hours before sunset. When we march, God help Thomond!'

There was a few moments' silence in the kitchen as the listeners pondered these ominous words. Fursey stirred uneasily and wondered why Magnus gazed so long and so steadfastly at Maeve. At last the soldier arose.

'It is time for me to go,' he said gruffly.

'Run out to the yard, Flinthead,' said Declan, 'and lead Magnus' horse around to the door.'

Fursey did as he was bid, and stood holding the halter until the soldier came and took it from him. Maeve had accompanied Magnus out into the thin rain, and as they came up to Fursey, he heard Magnus say to her, 'It's definitely fixed for Saturday then.'

Fursey retired to the shelter of the doorway with a strange, oppressive feeling in his heart. He stood beside the old man as Declan shouted good wishes and farewells to the soldier. Magnus waved his hand to Declan, and putting his arms around Maeve, kissed her tenderly. Then he sprang into the saddle, waved his hand in a final adieu, and slowly paced his horse out of the farmyard. Maeve walked behind the horse until she came to the head of the track, where she stood waving her hand to the retreating horseman.

'Did you see that?' the question came from Fursey in a breathless gasp. 'He kissed her.'

'Of course he did,' grinned the old man. 'They're being married on Saturday in Kilpuggin Church. It'll be a double wedding. I'm marrying the Widow Dykes myself.'

He doddered off into the far room, emitting little crackles of knowing laughter. Fursey stood stock-still while moment after moment passed. Then he walked across the kitchen to the fireplace and took down a coil of rope that hung there. As he moved back towards the door, Declan emerged from the far room.

'Where are you going?' he asked.

'To Cashel,' replied Fursey.

'Not to fight in the war?' gasped the old man.

'No,' replied Fursey. 'The war will be over by the time I arrive. Didn't you hear the soldier say so?'

'What are you going for then?' asked the old man shrilly.

Fursey turned to him a face that was expressionless and dead.

'To give myself up to the authorities,' he answered. Then he turned and left the house, going round by the back and across the yard, for fear that he would meet Maeve.

Chapter IX

One hour after sunset all the dogs in the neighbourhood of Cashel awoke and began to bark. Battle had been joined in a field within sight of the city, and the irate farmer was running up and down the boundary dyke screaming to the opposing armies that they were ruining his spring wheat. Within half-an-hour the issue was decided. The Cashel legions had the advantage of surprise. The slingsmen of Thomond had been for two days hurling their ammunition at the city, which was a large target impossible to miss; and they experienced considerable difficulty in suddenly shortening their range and hitting individual infantrymen who appeared out of nowhere and ran at them brandishing swords and shouting obscene and blasphemous language. The Thomond swordsmen, who should have taken the first shock of the assault, had been corrupted by two days' inactivity; and they were carousing in a neighbouring ditch when the battle broke upon them. They were immediately overthrown and their ale-kegs seized by the patriot forces. The soldiers of Thomond were in no way lacking in courage and martial ardour, but the surprise was complete in that they understood from their generals that every Cashel fighting man was in the hills manoeuvring with King Cormac; and their once-proud army of five hundred men trailed back, broken and in disorder, towards the frontiers of Thomond, each man with a sense of grievance and feeling that somewhere or other there had been foul play. Forty-two of their generals and many other high officers fell into the hands of the victors, and were immediately put to death by immersion in a neighbouring pond. The gates of the city were flung open, and the excited populace vociferously welcomed the victors and the captured ale-kegs. Bishop Flanagan ordered a solemn *Te Deum* to be sung in the Cathedral, which was attended by those of the army who did not feel it incumbent on them to return to their farms. A fleet runner was despatched to the hills to inform King Cormac of the good news, and to suggest respectfully that the moment was now opportune for him to descend into the plains and wipe out Thomond for ever.

Fursey heard the news from individual soldiers who passed him on the road on their way back to their farms. He nodded indifferently and continued to plod fatalistically towards Cashel. Few thoughts passed through his head as he trod the road, for his mind was cold and dead. When it became dark, he crept into a dry corner of the hedge, but he did not sleep; he lay instead all through the night gazing up at the indifferent stars. At sunrise and at midday he cast his rope over the branch of a tree and procured food; but he ate little; most of the time he squatted on his hunkers gazing dully at the bread and meat. He walked on towards Cashel as if impelled by some force outside himself, but the nearer he approached the settlement, the slower grew his gait, for somewhere inside himself he did not want to die, and least of all by fire. It was on the evening of the next day when he was still about ten miles from the city, that he sat down on a stone by the wayside and began to think. He remembered the trees as they had been in early spring, their skeleton branches sprinkled with green. He remembered the primroses, the dandelions and the wayward daffodils. All yellow, he said to himself dully, all yellow and green. That was before the demons had come to Clonmacnoise. He tried to conjure up a picture of himself as he had been then, a simple, innocent, stuttering lay brother paring edible roots in a corner of the monastery kitchen, while Brother Cook stood by the fire humming grimly to himself as he stirred the soup. He remembered Father Crustaceous, who had only one tooth, and was always complaining that the meat was tough. He remembered Father Sampson, who had been a professional wrestler before he entered the cloister, big Father Sampson with his swinging stride, the only monk who had not been afraid of the demons, but seemed rather to enjoy an encounter with them as it gave him an opportunity of trying out once more his wrestler's grips and holds. He recalled Father Placidus, that testy, purse-lipped man; and the suave, cool Master of Novices, whom everyone feared. He remembered with a lump in his throat little Brother Patrick, a lay brother like himself, and the fun they all had years before when a class had been set up in a half-hearted attempt to teach the lay brothers to read and write. And he remembered the Abbot Marcus — Abbot Marcus as he used to enter the refectory, his robes rustling, to take his seat at the centre of the table on the dais, his scholarly face shadowed by thought. 'I mustn't think of him,' muttered Fursey through his clenched teeth, 'it'll only make me cry.' But in spite of himself he did think of Abbot Marcus, and he did not cry. Something had entered into Fursey; his heart felt like a chunk of the moon, cold, dead and indifferent.

'How happy I was,' he said, 'though I didn't realise it.' But then the year had moved into late spring, the trees had darkened to a deeper green, and the demons had come and the beginning of his tribulations. With the first brazen flowers of summer had come sin. He had practised sorcery, had become an accomplished liar and even a thief.

'There's no going back,' he meditated bitterly. 'Clonmacnoise is closed to me for ever.'

Then he thought sourly of what a weak, frightened creature he himself was, when compared with a broad-shouldered, daring fellow like Magnus. What a contrast! Magnus despised a mean, little fellow like him, a wearer of another man's cast-off clothes. At best Magnus thought him funny and looked at him, when he noticed him at all, with amused contempt. And Magnus was right! Fursey rested his forehead between his two clenched fists, his elbows on his knees, and reflected how much he hated Magnus — a coarse and boastful bully, who had only to put out his hand to get all that he wanted in the world. Success went to the men of action, the men of affairs; as for the dreamers and the gentle, it was enough for them that they were permitted to live.

'That's another sin,' he said, sighing hopelessly. 'Hatred is a great sin. We must hate no one on this earth.' With a painful effort that was like a stone being turned over in his head, he put Magnus out of his mind. He remembered that he had one friend, or rather one creature bound by nature to his service, whatever that creature's real feelings might be — the lugubrious Albert. The moment he remembered Albert, he felt the pressing necessity of opening his heart to someone. He leaned forward and whispered the name gently. He waited for a few moments, his eyes fixed on the dust of the road, but he could note no movement.

'Albert!' he said more loudly. There was still no sign of the bear's paws or the red, foggy eyes. Fursey looked over his shoulder to see whether the creature was behind him, but there was no trace of his familiar. Very astonished, he rose to his feet and taking his stand in the middle of the roadway he called a third time in a loud voice: 'Albert!'

Nothing happened. The full significance of his familiar's failure to appear came to Fursey in a rush. Could it be that he was no longer a sorcerer, or at least that his damnable powers were wearing off? With a beating heart he hurried to the nearest tree. He uncoiled his rope with trembling fingers and flung it over a branch.

'Bread!' he shouted exultantly, and gave the rope a mighty chuck. His hopes were immediately dashed by the descent of a huge loaf, which struck him on the forehead and knocked him into the ditch. As he strove to rise, the prey of bitter disappointment, he observed a pale man with very black eyes clambering over the fence on the far side of the road. When the stranger had successfully surmounted the obstruction, he crossed the road, and coming across to where Fursey lay, he stood looking down at Fursey's floundering attempts to get out of the ditch.

'You ought to be ashamed of yourself,' said the stranger. 'Drunk again.'

Fursey gaped up at him in astonishment. He immediately recognised the stranger as an anchorite, one of those holy men who retire to remote caverns, and having turned out the wild beasts dwelling therein, make such gloomy spots their habitation where they pass the rest of their lives on a sparse diet, praying for themselves and for mankind. The one who gazed down disapprovingly at Fursey, was an uncouth hermit covered with long, black, rusty hair. He was a living skeleton, yellow, haggard and hatchet-faced, mere cuticle and cartilage. In short, he was a hideous and dirty-looking apparition, clad in an inadequate piece of sacking, and the odour of sanctity that he shed around him was well-nigh insupportable.

'It's an ill wind that blows no one good,' said the gaunt stranger at last. 'I hate drinking alone. Get up and come with me.'

The astonished Fursey struggled out of the ditch.

'They call me "The Gentle Anchorite",' said the ascetic by way of introducing himself. 'Come along with me, but bring your loaf of bread with you. It'll pay for a drink.'

The two of them walked down the road together. Fursey wondered why he was accompanying the anchorite, but he told himself that he might as well go where the stranger was going, as go anywhere else. They had progressed some hundred paces when The Gentle Anchorite turned his dark piercing eyes on Fursey.

'Why are you holding your nostrils between your thumb and forefinger?' he asked.

'I cannot abide the stench,' replied Fursey.

'Nonsense,' said his companion. 'I am not conscious of any stench.'

'You're lucky,' said Fursey.

Fursey had noticed that his new acquaintance held something concealed under his left arm. The sacking which the anchorite wore, effectively hid it from sight. Fursey was too polite to pretend to notice, even when a muffled clucking became audible from the depths of the anchorite's habiliments; but when a hen suddenly thrust out her head and started to croak desperately, Fursey could no longer pretend that he was unaware of her presence. He stopped on the road and faced the hermit.

'You haven't been stealing poultry?' he asked. 'I cannot be a party to a crime.'

'No,' answered the hermit mildly. 'You can take my word for it. This bird is an offering from a client for whom I performed a miracle yesterday.'

'That's all right,' replied Fursey quite satisfied, and they continued on their way.

'I've had a gruelling day,' volunteered The Gentle Anchorite, 'and I feel myself much in need of refreshment.'

'Indeed?' remarked Fursey politely.

'You must know,' continued his companion, 'that persons like myself who are raised to an ecstatic intuition of the Sovereign Good, are much pestered by the servants of the terrible Emperor of Night. I refer to Satan, whom nothing tortures so much as the sight of a good man at his prayers.'

Fursey nodded understandingly.

'It's nothing unusual for me,' continued the anchorite, 'on waking of a morning to see my cavern flooded with a dismal light, and to find a devil sitting at the foot of my bed grunting like a pig. Sometimes they come as ghouls and harpies, and I have been followed around all day by a demon in the form of a water-dog. I have seen devils standing upside down, and I myself have been thrown by them into that unusual posture. But, praise the Lord, I am always well able for them, and I have no less than forty-eight demons tied down in moorland pools on the mountain on which I dwell.'

This speech seemed to Fursey unduly boastful, but politeness demanded that he make a sound indicative of his admiration. Thus, encouraged, the hermit continued his recitation.

'To-day I have had to struggle with a demon of more than usual agility and guile. I saw him first on awaking this morning. He was furry and had snouted jaws; he looked dazed and languid and was peering in at me through the mouth of my cavern. Strange to relate none of the usual exhortations or adjurations had the slightest effect upon him. I chased him all over the mountainside, and while he seemed lumbering and slow in his movements, he was surprisingly nimble in dodging. I caught him at last a couple of hours ago. I admit it was more by luck than anything else. He tripped over an outcropping rock. The creature seemed by then exhausted, and I had no difficulty in fastening him to the bottom of a bog pool convenient to my cave. I must examine him further to-morrow as I have never before seen a demon quite like him. The chase has left me in almost the same state of exhaustion myself. That is why we are proceeding to an ale-house, where I can recoup my strength.'

'Very interesting,' commented Fursey, hoping that his companion would not discover that he was a wizard.

They had by now come to a low-sized, thatched house with some writing above the door.

'Here we are,' declared the anchorite. 'I cannot read myself, but the legend runs "Cow's Head Select Tavern", which is the name of the place. The inscription is in the Latin language, and was carved by a parish priest from Donegal who had been drinking for a week and was unable to pay his score. The work was accepted by the proprietor, who is a man sensible of the value of culture, in full discharge of the debt. The building is a very ancient one. The same inscription may be seen carved vertically on the left doorpost in Ogham, which was the way the learned wrote before the intro-duction of Latin lettering into this country.'

Fursey expressed his admiration of these things, and the two of them bowed their heads and entered the low doorway. The interior was dark, but Fursey's eyes soon became accustomed to the half-light, and he saw that a long wooden counter ran down the middle of the room. Behind it stood the proprietor, who was bald and had neither beard nor eyebrows. There were several customers in the tavern in various stages of intoxication. They seemed upset by the entry of the anchorite and retired with one accord to the far end of the bar where they covered their mouths and noses with their hands. The proprietor hastily picked up a clothes peg from a neighbouring shelf and fixed it to his nostrils before approaching to enquire in what way he could be of service. The anchorite with-drew the hen from the depths of his clothing and placed her on the counter. From her long proximity to the holy man's person the bird seemed dazed and languid, and she seemed to find it difficult to keep her feet. She staggered once or twice and fell.

'The animal doesn't seem in very good condition,' remarked the proprietor diffidently.

'She's all right,' retorted the hermit. 'She's a stranger here, and she's shy. You'll find her good eating.'

The proprietor felt the bird's breast and wings while she gazed up at him mournfully.

'I'll allow you four beakers of ale or three of mead,' he declared at last.

'Very well,' replied the anchorite. 'Mark me up four beakers of ale. And this gentleman has a loaf.'

The tavernkeeper felt Fursey's loaf judiciously with his thumb.

'That's very good bread,' he declared. 'I'll allow you two beakers of mead.'

'Right,' said the hermit. 'Give us the ale first.'

At a signal from the proprietor a small boy whom Fursey had not noticed before, emerged from beneath the counter and with a piece of charcoal drew two columns on the whitewashed wall. In one of them he inserted four strokes and in the other two. He then crossed through two of the vertical strokes, and the proprietor produced two foaming beakers of ale and placed them on the counter. He then went to the door and drew in a few breaths of fresh air before replacing the peg on his nose and retiring to the furthest corner of the room. Fursey and the hermit took their beakers and seated themselves on a bench that ran along the wall.

'This is all of the highest interest to me,' observed Fursey. 'I have never been in a tavern before.'

The Gentle Anchorite took a long swallow of ale and scratched the black rusty hair on his chest reminiscently.

'It's a very efficient system,' he remarked, 'though I've been told that there are barbarous foreign lands too backward to appreciate its merits. They have instead some highly involved method which they call "coinage". They have little bits of gold and other metal, on which is engraved the head of the king; and in their benighted ignorance the backward inhabitants of those lands attach a disproportionate value to the tiny amulets and use them for all purposes of exchange.'

'I seem to have heard,' replied Fursey racking his brains, 'that there were at one time big territories called Greece and Rome which had some such complicated system.'

'There were,' agreed the anchorite triumphantly. 'And where are they now? Wiped from the face of the earth forever, while this country, the Island of Saints and Scholars, still endures.'

Fursey smiled happily and finished off the dregs of his ale. His companion nudged him sharply.

'Listen,' he whispered.

Fursey listened to the conversation which came up to them from the far end of the tavern. A small man who was the centre of an admiring group, was holding up to ridicule all writers alive and dead, punctuating his witticisms and sallies with bursts of cackling laughter which made Fursey shudder. As Fursey glanced in his direction, he recognised with alarm the gargoyle whom he had seen in Cuthbert's garden. The creature caught Fursey's eye and gave him a friendly nod.

'Oh, you know him,' remarked the anchorite apparently relieved. 'I feared from his appearance that he was a petty demon of the trickier sort.'

'I know him slightly,' responded Fursey nervously. 'He's a minor man of letters.'

'Oh, that explains it,' answered the hermit, and he arose to order another two beakers of ale.

Fursey glanced around the tavern covertly to assure himself that Cuthbert was not present. He told himself that the one person whom he must avoid above everyone else in the world, was the sexton of Kilcock Churchyard. Cuthbert's feelings towards him would certainly be not benevolent, in view of the disclosures he had made about Cuthbert at his trial before the Cathedral Chapter. It was bad enough to be burnt as a sorcerer, but it would be infinitely worse to be turned into a toad and kept indefinitely in a jar. But Cuthbert was not present. He had evidently turned the gargoyle loose on the world, or else the creature had escaped. Fursey washed down his relief with a long pull at his second beaker of ale.

'You can never be sure of whom you'll knock against,' confided The Gentle Anchorite. 'I was in here a few years ago, sitting where we are sitting now, having a drink with a most affable gentleman who insisted on paying for everything we drank. I was most favourably impressed by his demeanour and apparent piety, until glancing down suddenly I observed with some alarm that my companion had hands like the claws of a bird. Needless to say I immediately challenged him, and forthwith he turned into a spectre, badly-made and ill-dressed, very wicked-looking and stinking insupportably. His well-pressed cloak and kilt became all at once coarse black garments, dirty and singed by the flames. He made off through the doorway, and I would have followed him and transfixed him, had I not been prevented by the weight of the drink which he had forced me to consume. Nevertheless, the management was very grateful to me for having rid the house of him.'

Fursey smiled with the left side of his mouth, and ruefully contemplated the empty bottom of his beaker.

'What would he have done if you hadn't discovered him in time?' he asked.

'It's obvious that he came here to tempt me,' answered the hermit. 'No doubt after we had put down another few drinks, he would have invited me round the corner of the house to meet some lively and engaging female that he had conjured up. Or he might have attempted to dazzle me with the offer of a kingdom in exchange for my soul.'

'It just goes to show that a man must be very careful whom he talks to,' asserted Fursey.

'Oblige me by taking that grin off your face,' said the anchorite to Fursey, as he arose to indicate to the proprietor that it was time to serve the two beakers of mead.

'Was I grinning?' asked Fursey.

'Yes, ever since you began your second mug of ale,' replied the hermit severely. 'It's not at all dignified.'

As they sat in happy appreciation of the bouquet of the mead, Fursey watched with interest as a cow was driven into the tavern, and the small boy got a ladder and laboriously began to mark up a thousand beakers of ale on the wall, commencing high up in a corner near the ceiling. The cow was driven behind the counter, while her late owner, a melancholy-looking, ale-sodden farmer, sat down and began at once to reduce the number to his credit. A few moments later a little old woman entered, a shawl over her head, and placed two eggs on the counter. She was served with a half-beaker.

When The Gentle Anchorite had drunk his way through half his goblet of mead, he smacked his lips with satisfaction and plunged reminiscently into his life history.

'As a youth,' he began, 'I was a careless and indifferent fellow, much addicted to the sport of taws, a game played with round pebbles which one precipitates with the thumb, attempting to strike the taw of the opponent. Many a hen I stole from my mother's yard and gambled away at a taw-school. But I was saved early from a life of sin and entered the monastery at Cong. It was clear from the very first that I was marked out for a life of saintliness. As a novice my rapts and ecstasies alarmed the monks. It was not unusual for me during dinner in the refectory to be sometimes raised ten cubits from the ground, my spoon and knife still clutched in my fists, and landed in a height of passive contemplation where I experienced an ecstasy and an abstraction from the things of sense quite unobtainable by the less-favoured members of the community. At length the Abbot took me aside and advised me that I was far too pious for the smooth working of the monastery. I concurred with him in this: it was obvious to me that my extreme saintliness was leading my brethren into the sins of envy and jealousy. I wandered south and found a suitable cavern above the Cashel road. I drove out a family of wolves that had made it their habitation, and installed myself therein. I have been there nigh on forty years, and I can boast that never once have I indulged in the sensuous practice of washing.'

The anchorite raised a black claw and pulling back his sackcloth, bared his chest for Fursey's inspection. Fursey moved along the bench away from the holy man, seemingly overcome by such evidence of piety.

'I remember well,' continued the hermit, 'the first demon who attempted to harry me. I had just placed on the slab that serves me as table, the handful of acorns which was to constitute my evening meal, when I heard him snorting at the entrance to the cave. I admit that I was not without fear. It was my first experience of demons, and I didn't know whether he was intent on taking my life, or whether he would rest satisfied with a bout of harrowing and attempted seduction. Uttering a passionate cry for strength I went to the cavern's mouth to encounter him. At first I could see nothing, and then about ten paces away a sort of black phantom with horns and tail presented itself and began to gambol about before me. He was a demon with burning eyes and claws upon his hands, and as he skipped about, he turned from time to time and grinned at me furiously. The uncouth sight was too much for me: I retired precipitately into the furthest corner of the cavern where I fell on my knees and gave myself over to prayer for strength in the fiery trial of martyrdom and for help in the hotter fire of temptation. I was awakened from my devotions by a scream like that of a screech-owl, and on looking up beheld the horrible enemy squatting on his hunkers before my table from which he had swept my handful of acorns. He had placed a hunk of succulent meat upon the stone, and before my eyes he took it up with both claws and devoured it bones and all. Being of a quick understanding, I speedily appreciated that his object was to tempt me to the sin of gluttony. It was Eastertide, and a paschal taper stood to hand. I immediately seized it and broke it over his head. I cannot truthfully say which of us chased the other out of the cave, but the two of us coursed back and forward over the hillside the whole night through. My memory again fails me as to which of us was the pursuer and which the pursued, but I do remember most distinctly that every time I found myself within his reach, I received countless slaps and blows from a stick with which he had armed himself. His sportiveness abated just before sunrise, and I was found in a debilitated condition in a furze bush by some peasants on their way to market.'

'You must have been somewhat exhausted,' remarked Fursey.

'Somewhat exhausted!' echoed the hermit indignantly. 'I had just enough respiration left to prevent their burying me.'

'Our beakers are empty,' observed Fursey, who was beginning to tire of these reminiscences and was anxious to be allowed to speak himself.

'And likely to remain so,' replied the anchorite gloomily. 'We have nought left to trade for ale. Holy Poverty has its disadvantages.'

'Leave it to me,' said Fursey knowingly. He hitched his rope over his shoulder and made his way out of the tavern. He was back in a few moments, his arms loaded with foodstuffs, four loaves of bread, an aromatic cheese and a couple of pounds of best butter.

'Where did you get them?' asked The Gentle Anchorite suspiciously.

'Never you mind,' said Fursey.

'If they've been stolen —' began the anchorite virtuously.

He seemed less inclined to press the matter when a few moments later three glistening pots of mead were set in front of him.

Fursey took his own three pots from the counter in a wide embrace and carried them over to where his companion was sitting. For some moments no word was spoken while each addressed himself seriously to the business of emptying one of the pots. At length Fursey took his face out of his beaker and languidly wiped a few amber-coloured beads of the liquor from his cheeks and chin. He sighed and putting his elbow on the table, rested his head on his hand. For some time he regarded his companion pensively.

'You're a man of great learning and piety,' he said at last. 'Perhaps you can help me in my trouble.'

The hermit threw back the rusty hair that hung down over his face, so that he could see Fursey more clearly.

'If it's anything in the nature of a miracle,' he replied, 'I'll be glad to oblige you; but a small offering is expected. The labourer is worthy of his hire.'

'It's nothing like that,' responded Fursey. 'I only want advice.'

'Oh,' replied the hermit, and he seemed to be somewhat disappointed.

'Do you know anything about love?' enquired Fursey.

'Of course I do,' retorted the anchorite. 'By God's grace I can see as deeply into the abyss of love as any man.'

'How does one set about winning a woman's love?' asked Fursey.

'I haven't the faintest idea,' rejoined the anchorite haughtily. 'You don't appear to realise whom you're talking to.'

'I mean no offence,' explained Fursey. 'But there's an amiable young woman of my acquaintance, and I'm sore assotted on her.'

The anchorite groaned aloud in anguish. 'Seek not to follow after the daughters of iniquity,' he quoted.

'She's the daughter of a man called Declan,' replied Fursey.

'I don't care what her father's name is,' retorted the anchorite. 'I warn you that you're walking on the brink of Hell.' And he began to exhort Fursey to be strong in faith and put his confidence in God. Fursey only half-listened to his exhortations. The conversation seemed to him to have taken a wrong turning, but he felt too happy and dreamy to bring it back. His mind wandered to past events, and he found himself regretting that he had not made better use of his stay in Cuthbert's cottage. He should at least have remained until he had learnt the ingredients, composition and use of love philtres. Fursey sighed as he thought of his lost opportunities. Here he was a fully-fledged wizard, and the only sorcery he knew was how to fly on a broom and how to produce food by pulling on a rope. He fixed his eyes dreamily on the anchorite's long rusty beard and wondered if he pulled it, would a loaf of bread fall on to the table. Probably not, probably only a colony of bugs. His thoughts drifted to Maeve and the last time he had seen her, standing against the evening sky waving her hand to Magnus as he rode down the track from the cottage. The muscles of Fursey's body jerked convulsively as he tore his mind away from the image which was so acid in his memory. What was the use of wishing for further magical knowledge? Magnus had Maeve, and it was too late.

He sighed and forced himself to listen to the anchorite, who was droning some story from the life of a lady saint, in the apparent hope of edifying Fursey and winning him from carnal desire.

'... her eyes,' concluded the hermit, 'no longer lit up with the wild delight of the delirium of vice and bacchanalian orgies, but glowed softly with the blessed peace of conscious forgiveness.'

'This old fool wants to do all the talking,' thought Fursey. 'He won't let me get in a word at all. I'll show him.'

Fursey emptied his beaker and waited for the mead to subside in his stomach. Then he plunged into a rambling account, punctuated by hiccoughs, of the life and times of Blessed John the Dwarf, which he had heard read aloud in the refectory at Clonmacnoise. Between his hiccoughs and his faulty memory, the story of Blessed John, which should have been edifying and exemplary, became, as Fursey related it, very funny indeed. The good humour increased as The Gentle Anchorite also became afflicted with the hiccoughs, and Fursey had perforce to halt from time to time in his story to laugh at his companion. Merriment is infectious, and soon the hermit was emitting short melancholy barks, the sort of laughter one might expect to hear coming up out of a grave. He clawed his lank beard and asserted that Fursey was the pleasantest fellow he had ever met. Fursey slapped the anchorite jovially on the knee. A cloud of dust arose that nearly blinded both of them. As they staggered around sneezing and rubbing their eyes, their merriment nearly reached the stage of convulsions.

A couple of hours passed in this manner. Fursey could not afterwards recall the substance of their conversation, but he remembered that it was the best and most brilliant talk imaginable, scintillating with wit and good humour. When at last they agreed that it was time to go, the tavern was empty except for the proprietor asleep over the counter. They let themselves out, but when they gained the roadway, the fresh night air affected them powerfully. So uncertain was Fursey's gait that he had perforce to lean against a tree, and when he had secured its support, he was loath to leave it. He stood, a tubby figure propped against the bole, smiling blandly at the circular moon overhead, while The Gentle Anchorite capered in the middle of the road trolling forth a song of suggestive and improper import. When the hermit had finished his bawdy lay, he succeeded in detaching Fursey from the tree, and with old-world hospitality offered him accommodation in his cave for the night. Fursey thanked him earnestly and shook his hand; and the two of them proceeded unsteadily arm-in-arm down the road.

It was a night of filmy moonlight, the sort of night on which almost anything might well be abroad, one of those nights on which the dead yearn to look on the living and to accost them. The stark trees laid their moon-softened shadows here, there and everywhere. Overhead the moon sailed among her stars, suffusing the fields and the roads with soft blue light and silence. But Fursey was not afraid: one is not afraid when one has as companion a man with forty years' experience of tying down demons. Fursey told himself that The Gentle Anchorite's fame must have spread far and wide in the world of shadows, and it would be a hardy demon or spectre who would venture to approach him, especially when he was drunk and belligerent.

The road was long. It seemed to Fursey that they walked for hours before scrambling through a hedge and making their way over the bare hillside. It was another hour at least, an hour of weary struggling uphill through furze and bracken, before they came to the stony place where the hermit had his habitation. It was a spot bleak enough to satisfy the most exacting anchorite, a low cave in the rocks, and beyond it the bogs. The air was moist, and a small breeze blew steadily across the waste. Fursey could see here and there the glint of a moorland pool.

The hermit had grown quiet and seemed plunged in a deep melancholy. Mead is a heady brew, but its effect soon wears off with exercise. Fursey was by now more tired than drunk, and he grunted bad-humouredly when the anchorite took him by the arm and insisted that before retiring to rest, he must see the hermit's latest conquest, the strange, shuffling demon who had been captured and tied in a bog pool that afternoon. The pool was not far removed from the cave, and after a few minutes clambering between the rocks and through the bracken they stood at its edge. The anchorite stretched out a black claw and directed Fursey's attention to a huge rock incised with a cross, which lay at the bottom of the pool. Fursey bent over the edge and peered in. The water was only about six feet deep, and the head and four paws of some creature were discernible projecting from beneath the boulder. The creature lay spreadeagled on its back with all the weight of the rock on its chest. Fursey gazed with quickening interest — surely he had seen those bear's paws before and that body covered with black hair. A pair of red foggy eyes looked up at him pathetically. It was Albert!

Fursey stepped back quickly and allowed himself to be led back to the cave by the hermit, who repeated his account of the difficulty he had experienced in capturing the unusual demon. Of course, thought Fursey, Albert was impervious to religious adjuration and exhortation for the simple reason that he did not belong to the Christian order of things, but was a creature of an older religion. Fursey had not recovered from his surprise, and his thoughts were still scattered when they arrived back at the cave, and the hermit conducted him into its depths.

'Now for our evening meal,' said the anchorite. Going to a hole in the wall he drew out a couple of crusts and placed them on a flat rock. 'Seeing as how you are my guest,' he continued, 'we will make high festival,' and with the conscious air of being a generous host, he produced a hazel nut. 'We will divide it between us,' he said, placing it on the stone slab.

Fursey stared gloomily at this meagre fare and essayed to crack the crust between his teeth. His efforts did not meet with much success, and he replaced the crust upon the table and wiped the blood from the corner of his mouth.

'Try the nut,' advised the hermit, who was crunching his crust with evident appreciation. Fursey picked up the hazel nut and gingerly brushed off the green mould that covered it.

'Ah, you're losing the best part,' said the hermit deprecatingly.

Fursey smiled faintly and biting off half the nut, pushed the other half over to his companion. He found that it lent itself to easy mastication, and he sat ruminating on its unusual flavour until the hermit had finished his meal.

'Let us return thanks before retiring to rest,' said the holy man sinking on his knees. Fursey chose a smooth spot on the floor and knelt, resting his elbows on a rock and sinking his face in his hands. The hermit prayed for almost an hour in a loud and terrible voice, accusing himself and Fursey of all the known sins and imploring forgiveness, while Fursey on his knees slumbered fitfully. When the hermit had brought his orisons to a conclusion in a final wallow of abnegation, he directed Fursey's attention to a neat row of disciplines hanging on the wall. There were about a dozen, and they varied in size from a narrow, lithe whip to a broad, leathern thong in which were embedded a goodly number of nails and shark's teeth.

'We must do a little penance before we retire,' said the hermit, 'a couple of dozen lashes apiece. We can confer them upon one another.'

'I always do my penance in the morning,' replied Fursey hurriedly.

'You might be dead before the morning,' urged the hermit, 'and you will have lost this opportunity of acquiring grace.'

'I'll risk it,' said Fursey stoutly. 'Morning is my time for mortifying myself, and I'm not going to break the good habit of a lifetime.'

'Have it your own way,' answered the hermit huffily. 'I'm not going to forego my nightly mortification of the flesh. Oblige me by giving me twenty lashes.'

An odour of sanctity swept across the cavern like a wave as the holy man peeled off his upper garment and took up his stand, stripped to the waist, with his back to Fursey. Fursey inspected the row of disciplines.

'What size would you like?' he asked.

'One of medium strength,' replied the hermit.

Fursey examined the row of disciplines judiciously, then he turned and looked at the hermit's back. A sudden image had come into his mind, a picture of the unfortunate Albert lying at the bottom of the moorland pool with two tons of granite on his chest.

'I venture to suggest,' said Fursey, 'that the thick hair with which your back is draped, affords you considerable protection against a discipline of medium weight. In a holy matter such as this, you must play fair with God. I suggest a discipline of greater striking power.'

The hermit turned his head to gaze at Fursey. He seemed to think that his sanctity was being called into question, and his reply was short.

'Use your judgment,' he said testily, and turning away once more, he hunched his back to meet the blow. Fursey picked down the weightiest discipline and tested the shark's teeth and nails with his thumb. Then he rolled up his sleeves and let fly with all his strength at the hairy back of the hermit. The snaky thong whistled, struck with a resounding smack, and wound twice around the holy man's body. The Gentle Anchorite emitted a howl and capered madly up and down the cave.

'What's wrong?' asked the astonished Fursey. 'You told me to hit you.'

'I didn't tell you to take the skin and flesh off my bones,' gasped the anchorite, turning on Fursey eyes full of bale.

'I'll use another discipline for the remaining nineteen strokes,' replied Fursey comfortingly. 'There's a nice one here with broken bits of razor embedded in the leather.'

'I've had enough for to-night,' muttered the hermit between his teeth. 'Already I can feel my soul suffused and flooded with sanctifying grace, but in the morning,' and his eyes met Fursey's, 'I'll have the remaining nineteen when you are having your twenty. We shall confer them on one another. That is the most convenient.'

'Certainly,' agreed Fursey, quickly making up his mind that he would be gone before the morning.

The anchorite was still squirming as he indicated a heap of foul-smelling straw in the corner, which was to be their bed. He laid himself gingerly on his face as his back seemed to be still sore, and Fursey stretched himself alongside. Before long the cave was shrill with the hermit's catarrhal snores which forced their way through his beard in a muffled whistle.

Hour after hour Fursey tossed on the straw unable to sleep. When a man of determined sanctity has lived in a small cave for forty years, the insect life is apt to assume alarming proportions. Bugs, resigned for many years to the thin diet which the hermit's skinny frame provided, after one nip at Fursey scuttled off to tell their friends, and soon all the game in the cavern were making in his direction. They came in such myriads that for a moment Fursey thought that an attempt was being made to murder him. Plump fleas investigated different parts of his body in a series of gargantuan hops, while great strapping bugs fastened themselves to his arms and thighs. The smaller fry of the insect world, mites and the like, contented themselves with setting up colonies in unlikely corners of his anatomy where the competition was less keen. Fursey rolled and wallowed, but to no avail. To add to his discomfort The Gentle Anchorite woke up and seemed not only jealous of the attention his vermin were paying to Fursey, but to fear that there was a real danger of losing the external evidence of his forty years' sanctity, so he bent over from time to time to collect as many bugs as he could from Fursey's body and put them back on his own. This preposterous behaviour Fursey found in the highest degree exasperating. In his opinion it only encouraged the more mischievous of the bugs to greater liveliness, and it obviated all possibility of sleep. You couldn't possibly sleep if you were turned over every half-an-hour by your host and searched.

Towards morning the hermit's excursions became less regular, and he slept for longer intervals. When Fursey heard the muffled snores taking on a deeper note, he crawled from the straw on his hands and knees and dragged his wounded body through the mouth of the cave into the fresh air. There was a little patch of grey in the sky to the east, and realising that there was little time to spare, he hobbled quickly across the intervening space to the edge of the pool where Albert was imprisoned. He fell on his knees on the heather at the edge.

'Hello, Albert,' he whispered.

A stream of bubbles issued from Albert's mouth. As they broke on the surface they resolved themselves into a string of very bad language.

'Sh!' said Fursey. 'Don't curse.'

Albert made another effort, and the breaking bubbles indicated to Fursey that Albert was devoted to his service, that he was the best master Albert ever had, and for God's sake to get him out of the pool. Fursey cast a hurried glance over his shoulder to assure himself that the hermit was not yet abroad, before immersing himself in the pool, clothes and all. The cold water was a considerable relief to his bug-scarred body, and after Herculean straining at the boulder he succeeded in rolling it to one side. Albert immediately bobbed up to the surface where he floated on his back. He seemed intact, though a little flattened. Fursey clambered out of the pool and taking Albert by one of his bear's paws, hauled him on to the bank. Albert shook himself like a dog, scattering water in all directions; and then collapsed against a rock. He volunteered no word of thanks, but threw a terrified glance in the direction of the cave.

'If he comes out,' he wheezed huskily, 'order me to disappear. It's the only thing that will save me.'

'Come on,' said Fursey. 'It's time we got away from here,' and he set out at a trot down the hillside, with Albert staggering along at his heels. Fursey did not stop until they reached the road.

'I'm done up,' gasped Albert. 'You'll have to carry me.'

'We're safe now,' replied Fursey as he helped the exhausted Albert through the hedge. The familiar sat down in the dust of the road while Fursey seated himself on the grassy bank facing him.

'You should have ordered me to disappear up there at the pool,' complained Albert. 'Then I could have travelled down the hill with you in my capacity as an aetherial essence. It would have been far less tiring.'

'I didn't want to let you out of my sight again,' replied Fursey, 'until I had found out how you got into that predicament. I think you owe me an explanation.'

Albert looked uneasy.

'Come now,' said Fursey severely. 'I summoned you on the road yesterday, and you failed to appear. How was that? Don't you realise that you are bound absolutely to my service?'

Albert assumed a hang-dog look, and his eyes failed to meet his master's.

'It's all very fine,' he answered sullenly. 'If you had a rock as big as a mountain on your chest, you'd be slow in answering a summons.'

'Don't quibble,' said Fursey primly. 'It's not a question of slowness in answering a summons; you didn't answer it at all.'

'I couldn't come,' bleated Albert indignantly. 'That mad fellow up there, the long, thin fellow, had got hold of me and fixed me in the pool. I couldn't get out. You saw it yourself; what's the use of asking silly questions?'

'You're avoiding the issue,' retorted Fursey. 'You're bound to my service, and you're supposed to be at hand all the time, ready to appear the moment you're summoned. What were you doing gallivanting round the countryside getting into trouble?'

Albert fixed his foggy red eyes on his master and glared balefully, but did not reply. Fursey flushed and stamped his foot on the ground.

'If you don't answer me,' he said, 'I'll punish you. I'll think up something terrible to do to you. I'll turn you into something extraordinary, a lizard or something like that. You don't appear to realise that I've inherited The Grey Mare's powers, and I'm a very formidable wizard.'

'Garn!' interjected Albert contemptuously. 'You're the most hopeless wizard I've ever encountered. Why, you don't know how to do anything.'

'Don't be impertinent,' shrilled Fursey.

'If the marrows of an unbaptised babe were put into your hands,' said Albert raising his voice so as to shout his master down, 'I don't believe you'd know what to do with them. Can you even turn milk sour? Do you even know how to plough a field with four toads harnessed to the plough? Why, you don't even know how to do the simplest things.'

Fursey did not reply, but sat for a moment thinking of his deficiencies. When the eyes of sorcerer and familiar again met, both seemed rather ashamed of their loss of temper. At last Fursey spoke.

'How did it happen?' he asked simply.

'I'm that starved,' replied Albert sulkily, 'through your refusal to supply me with my proper meed of blood, that I became desperate. I wandered off hoping to find some quiet human whom I could have a nip at when he wasn't looking. I didn't expect to run into a wild character like the hairy fellow up above, who chased me around the whole afternoon shouting Latin at me.'

'Let it be a lesson to you,' said Fursey reprovingly. 'You shouldn't try to bite people.'

'It's all very well for you to talk,' growled Albert. 'You look well-fed enough, but I've grown that meagre that if I stand sideways you can hardly see me. Really, master,' he said with a throb of emotion in his voice, 'you'll have to do something for me. My coat is all falling out. Soon I'll look like an old, mangy, moth-eaten dog. Look.'

He put a shrunken paw to his chest and pulled out a handful of hair, which he held out for inspection. When Fursey answered, his voice was sad and far-away.

'Maybe, Albert,' he said, 'you won't be bothered with me much longer. I'm on my way to Cashel to surrender myself to the authorities.'

'Why should you do that?' asked Albert astonished.

'I've tried life,' said Fursey, 'and I've found it wanting.'

'So now you're going to try death?'

Fursey thought for a moment before replying.

'Aye,' he answered at last.

'You know that you'll be burnt?'

'Yes,' replied Fursey.

A look of genuine happiness spread over Albert's countenance from his red eyes to the tip of his snout, but he tried manfully to hide his satisfaction.

'Maybe it's best for us both,' he said consolingly. 'You'll be rid of the cares of living, and when you're dead, I'll be able to secure another master, some young wizard with a promising career ahead of him, who is fully cognisant of the care which he should bestow on his familiar.'

'I'll miss you,' said Fursey sadly. 'It's not that you're an engaging companion, but I've sort of got used to you.'

'You won't feel the sense of loss for long,' replied Albert somewhat impatiently. 'They'll have you burnt in a couple of days.'

'I don't imagine that we'll see one another again,' declared Fursey. 'I think farewells should be quick. It's best that way.'

Albert rose from his hunkers and held out his paw. Fursey took it and shook it sadly.

'Goodbye,' said Fursey.

'Goodbye,' replied Albert. 'Don't forget,' he added anxiously, 'that you've to order me to vanish.'

'Disappear,' commanded Fursey; and as Albert dissolved, Fursey waited to utter a final word of melancholy valediction to a single smoky red eye which hung alone in the air for a few seconds after the rest of Albert had gone. Then he turned hurriedly on his heel and made off down the road that led to Cashel.

Chapter X

About an hour later Fursey's unwilling feet brought him to New Inn Cross. A crossroads is at all times a place of foul repute, a point where watchful fiends are apt to lurk, and a spot likely to be used for nocturnal dances and all classes of witchery. Fursey would have hurried by, but he was suddenly rooted to the road at the sight of a familiar figure in black leaning nonchalantly against a gate. It was Cuthbert! A dark lock of hair hung over his forehead obscuring one of his eyes. The other eye was fixed upon Fursey. A witchhazel wand was propped against the gate beside the sexton. In his hand he held a silken bag, and a red cock was perched upon his shoulder.

Such was Fursey's terror that he stood in the middle of the road bereft of the power to move either forward or backwards: his legs had become like two rods glued to the ground. His heart gave one mighty whack in his chest and then seemed to stop beating altogether. He struggled to regain his breath, his mind the prey of the most painful imaginings. He saw himself turned into a toad and imprisoned in an earthen jar for the duration of Cuthbert's life; and on the sexton's demise, perhaps handed down to generation after generation of sorcerers as an interesting specimen. The intolerable boredom of such an existence was borne in powerfully upon him and filled him with the strongest disquiet. It might well be that many thousands of years would elapse before some accident occurred to break the spell and effect his release. Through a film of mist he observed the sexton detaching himself from the gate and sloping across the road towards him. He became aware that his limp hand had been lifted from his side and was being warmly wrung.

'My dear friend Fursey,' came the sexton's voice, 'you have no conception of the pleasure this encounter affords me. I located you in my crystal about an hour ago and travelled here to intercept you, as I desire to have some discourse with you in private.'

Fursey was not conscious of what happened next; but when he became once more aware of the world about him, he found himself propped against the gate while the sexton fanned him anxiously with his hat.

'That was a bad turn you took,' purred Cuthbert. 'My poor friend, wait here for a moment while I procure you a stimulant.'

The sexton grabbed Fursey's length of rope and hurrying to a neighbouring tree, flung it over one of the branches. He gave it a sharp jerk and deftly caught the cup of mead which fell from the foliage. He came running back without spilling a drop, and having prized Fursey's teeth open with his witchhazel wand, he poured the entire contents down Fursey's gullet. Fursey hiccoughed and recovered full consciousness.

'Are you all right?' asked Cuthbert.

'I'd like to sit down,' responded Fursey feebly.

Cuthbert helped him into a sitting position with his back supported by the gate, and stood over him cracking his fingers nervously. Fursey gazed disconsolately from the red cock perched on the sexton's shoulder to the small silken bag which swung from his hand. Then a seemingly interminable spate of words fell from Cuthbert's lips. Fursey's wits were too scattered to follow the sexton's flow of talk, which seemed to be about Fursey's health. Fursey was not concerned about his health: what he was worried about was his future; but as Cuthbert's deluge of words flowed over his consciousness, odd words and broken sentences began to form a sediment, which he turned over slowly in his mind and began to examine. The sexton appeared to be trying to explain away the part which he had played at Fursey's trial, and to convince Fursey that he felt for him only fraternal goodwill and benevolence. Fursey pricked up his ears and began to listen. Then he fixed his gaze on Cuthbert's face. There could be no doubt about it. The sexton's manner was ingratiating; the emotion that lit his countenance was the desire to please. Could it be that the tremor in Cuthbert's voice was due to fear?

'You understand,' concluded Cuthbert, 'that no other course was open to me. I had no idea that Satan held you in such esteem that he was prepared to conduct your defence in person.'

So that was it. Cuthbert, far from wishing to destroy him, was eager to placate him; not through any love for him, but because he was, as Cuthbert saw it, under the Archfiend's powerful protection. Fursey sat looking at his toes reflecting on the strangeness of things, while the sexton shifted his feet nervously, apparently anxiously awaiting Fursey's judgment. At length Cuthbert spoke.

'Tell me,' he begged, 'that you forgive me and that we are friends again.'

Fursey cocked his eye at Cuthbert's face.

'Yes,' he replied, 'I forgive you. Now, help me to my feet.'

Cuthbert hastened to comply and assisted in massaging the hinges of Fursey's knees, from which the weakness had not yet quite departed.

'Remember,' said Cuthbert, 'that if I can at any time be of the slightest assistance to you in any matter great or small, I am entirely at your service.'

'Thank you,' replied Fursey, 'I think I must be going now.'

'Not that I wish to imply,' continued Cuthbert, 'that a man of your lively and subtle temperament, who has the added advantage of being so highly connected, should ever stand in need of the assistance of a man in such a humble line of wizarding as myself. You are a man who has it in his power to confuse and dazzle tigers, but I shouldn't wish you to depart without realising to the full the depth of my esteem.'

'It's very nice of you,' answered Fursey, 'but I really must be going. I've an important appointment in Cashel.'

'Before you go,' protested Cuthbert, 'I insist that you honour me by accepting from me a small gift.'

Fursey looked at him uncertainly.

'What is the nature of the gift?' he asked suspiciously.

'You are going to Cashel, a place dangerous to such as you on account of the prevalence there of religious jugglery. I shall provide you with a protector so that none will presume to approach you, let alone lay hands on you.'

The sexton's eagerness was such that before Fursey could reply, Cuthbert had shaken on to the road from the silken bag which he carried, a variety of curious objects, human knuckle-bones, nail-parings, moles' paws and elf-shots, things which immediately suggested to the startled Fursey that an operation of a magical character was imminent. Cuthbert then seized the red cock which was perched on his shoulder, and before the luckless bird had time to do more than give an indignant croak, its neck was wrung and its corpse flung on the ground. In a twinkling the sexton had drawn in the dust of the roadway with his witchhazel wand a circle with four divisions and four crosses.

'Stand inside,' he commanded.

The trembling Fursey deemed it safer to obey. He watched with horror as Cuthbert deftly arranged the objects that had fallen from the silken bag.

'You have no occasion for fear,' the sexton assured him. 'I shall also draw with charcoal the Star of Solomon and the Sacred Pentagram.'

This operation was completed before Fursey found his voice.

'What are you going to do?' he quavered.

'I'm going to conjure up a poltergeist,' replied Cuthbert, 'and instruct him to accompany you everywhere you go, and cast around you the cloak of his protection. By magic I shall constrain him to appear.'

Fursey opened his mouth, but no sound came out.

'The thing to remember,' declared Cuthbert as he briskly completed his preparations, 'is that it is the double tail of the serpent which forms the legs of the solar cock of Abraxas.'

'I really have to go,' gasped Fursey.

'You can't go now,' said Cuthbert sharply. 'If you step outside the circle, you are likely to be subtly consumed and altogether destroyed. The terrible citizens of the spiritual world are all about us, and but for the judicious precautions which I have taken, I would not be able to answer for the safety of either of us.'

Fursey felt his knees weakening again. He closed his eyes and tried to pray while Cuthbert made mysterious passes with his wand and began to mutter strangely. Suddenly Cuthbert raised his two arms above his head and yelled three times in honour of triple Hecate. Fursey crumpled up and fell at his feet. As Fursey grovelled on the ground, he observed a thickening of the air at a spot just outside the circle. Something was slowly taking shape. At first the form was shadowy and strange, but before long it took on flesh, until it stood there in its entirety, a huge creature some eight feet in height with powerful, hunched shoulders. Its swinging arms were so long that the knuckles of its hands almost touched the ground. In general appearance it resembled a man, save only that it was green in hue. As its eyes, alight with hot, unholy fires, fixed themselves on Cuthbert and Fursey, its features became distorted in a sardonic grin. The creature was bald, and a fine stream arose from its polished green skull.

'Eminently satisfactory,' said Cuthbert rubbing his hands. 'What's your name, my good fellow?'

The grotesque creature answered with its tongue hanging half-a-foot out of its mouth.

'Joe,' it said. 'Joe the Poltergeist.'

'Very good, Joe,' said Cuthbert briskly. 'You see this gentleman here at my feet?'

'Ay,' replied the poltergeist.

'Well, listen carefully to your instructions. You will, when I tell you to do so, resume your invisibility and attach yourself to this gentleman as his protector. You are not to leave him for a moment. If aught menaces him, you will take immediate steps to ward off the danger. It is anticipated that it is from human beings that the danger will threaten. You will deal with those human beings as you think fit. Do you understand?'

'Ay,' said the poltergeist.

'Now, disappear,' ordered Cuthbert. 'Do you hear me? Disappear.'

Fursey clambered to his feet and got behind Cuthbert. When the sexton spoke again, Fursey was aware of a new note in his voice. It seemed to Fursey like a note of anxiety.

'I'm addressing you, Joe the Poltergeist,' enunciated Cuthbert with severity. 'I command you to vanish.'

For a moment there was silence, then as Cuthbert turned to him, the terrified Fursey saw that the poltergeist still stood in the roadway, with an obscene leer creasing his unattractive countenance and his long talons twitching alarmingly.

'Something has gone wrong with the spell,' muttered Cuthbert out of the corner of his mouth. 'He declines to vanish. For your life, do not stir outside the circle.'

The master sorcerer made several passes in the air, but they in nowise served to relieve the situation. The sexton seemed puzzled; then he turned and fixed a suspicious eye on Fursey.

'Have you by any chance,' he enquired, 'crosses or religious amulets about your person, which may have interfered with the smooth working of the spell?'

'No,' replied Fursey.

'Are you sure?' asked Cuthbert sharply as he noticed Fursey's hesitation.

'I admit,' faltered Fursey, 'I admit that I said a prayer while the spell was in the course of being woven.'

Cuthbert greeted this intelligence with a sharp intake of breath.

'Nice mess you've landed us in,' he hissed. 'Such a *contretemps* is altogether outside my experience. I haven't the faintest idea how we'll get rid of him.'

'Couldn't we make a run for it,' suggested Fursey hopefully.

'Don't attempt anything of the sort,' snapped Cuthbert. 'If we as much as put a foot outside the circle, he'll tear us in pieces.'

Fursey shivered as the poltergeist began to lumber around the edge of the circle grating his teeth horribly.

'It's a tricky situation,' commented Cuthbert. 'Of course I could try to undo the spell by reciting it backwards, but such an operation is fraught with danger. The magic is liable to stick in one's throat. I think the best thing that I can do, is begin again and weave the spell once more, and we'll see what happens.'

'Is there not a danger that if you pursue such a course, the net result may well be that we shall have two poltergeists to contend with instead of one?'

'There is wisdom in what you say,' answered Cuthbert thoughtfully. 'There's really only one thing to do. I shall have to fly home on my witchhazel wand and consult my books. I have no doubt but that Camerarius will have something to say in the matter.'

'Can't you take me with you?' enquired Fursey anxiously.

'I regret that my wand is too light to carry two,' replied Cuthbert. 'You can await my return in perfect safety provided you remain within the circle. I expect that I shall be back before night-fall. Do not let the phantom coax you into leaving the circle.'

'You need have no anxiety on that score,' Fursey assured him.

'Very well,' said Cuthbert, and throwing his leg nimbly across his wand, he shot vertically into the air to a considerable altitude. Fursey saw him peering to left and right to get his direction before making off over the tree-tops towards the north. Joe the Poltergeist was apparently taken by surprise, and he manifested in no un-certain manner his chagrin at the loss of one of his prey. For some minutes he ran up and down roaring horribly, then to relieve his feelings he pulled up a couple of trees by the roots and tried to tear up a length of road. At last he came back and opening his mouth, displayed before the quaking Fursey two magnificent sets of grinders, which he gnashed horribly.

How long Fursey could have endured the proximity of the dreadful creature without breathing his last through sheer fright, it is impossible to say; but at that moment the sound of many voices striking up a hymn was heard from round the bend of the road. All at once the poltergeist seemed to forget Fursey, he turned immedi-ately on his heel and lumbered off to investigate. The moment he had turned the corner and was out of sight, Fursey shot like a bolt from the circle, burst through the hedge without seeing it, and made off across the fields.

A party of a dozen monks from Clonmacnoise, pilgrims to the shrine of the saintly Gray Mare, moved slowly along the southern road. They had walked twenty miles since morning; and as they plodded along, they leaned wearily upon their staves. It was with a view to whipping up their flagging enthusiasm now that they were nearing their destination, that the Master of Novices, who was in charge, ordered them to strike up a hymn. The monks sang lustily, for the hymn was well-liked, having a jovial swing. As they approached a bend in the road, little Brother Patrick made frantic attempts to pitch his voice above the musical baying of Father Sampson, so as to convey to his brethren the alarming intelligence that he had just espied a flying wizard in career over the tree-tops. But Brother Patrick failed to make himself heard, and the hymn continued for several minutes until it was brought to a sudden close by the appearance of Joe the Poltergeist round the bend of the road. The band of pilgrims stopped dead and stood huddled together in the centre of the track as the grotesque monster lumbered in their direction. Their first instinct was to take to their heels; but the Master of Novices, always a cool man, succeeded in staying the panic. A small stream crossed the road about fifty paces from where they stood. The ungainly stranger continued towards them until he reached the middle of the stream, and there he took his stand facing the pilgrims, a horrid and fearsome sight with the water flowing over his hairy, green ankles. It was apparent from his menacing demeanour that it was his intention to oppose their progress. In the unearthly silence that seemed suddenly to have fallen over the entire countryside, Brother Patrick at last made himself heard. His report of the flying wizard did nothing to allay the apprehensions of his brethren, who shifted nervously as they realised that there was devilry afoot.

'What is he?' asked Father Placidus in a thin voice. 'Is he an arch-vampire?'

'A poltergeist by the look of him,' replied Father Sampson.

This opinion was substantiated a moment later when the horrid spectre stooped down suddenly and, picking up an armful of stones, began to pelt the monks mercilessly.

'Stand where you are,' commanded the Novice Master. 'In a struggle between Good and Evil, the Good must never give ground.'

'I observe that he has taken his stand in south-flowing water,' said Father Sampson, who had an eye for strategy. 'I doubt if we shall succeed in overcoming him with spiritual weapons, for it is a well-known fact that south-flowing water has magical properties.'

'We can only try,' answered the Novice Master, and taking his book of exorcisms from under his arm, he advanced ten paces towards the poltergeist.

The exorcism was unsuccessful. The poltergeist laughed uproariously during the first part of it; and before the Master of Novices had got as far as the adjuration, Joe swept the book from his hand with a well-aimed lump of rock. The Novice Master retreated precipitately to his brethren on the roadway.

'Perhaps we should essay the fulmination of an anathema,' said Father Placidus, who was so beside himself with terror that he scarcely knew what he was talking about. In fact, the general fright was such that the monks would very likely have bolted only for the powerful influence of Father Sampson. The ex-wrestler was not only unafraid, he was spoiling for a fight. His ire increased when he received a blow of a stone on the forehead. He tore off his monk's habit and revealed a frame knotted with muscle.

'Father Novice Master,' he begged, 'give me leave to assail this offensive demon. I am confident of my ability to weaken and annihilate him.'

The Novice Master blenched. 'It is a perilous undertaking —' he began.

'When I was a wrestler at the Court of Thomond,' snarled Father Sampson, 'no man, save only Father Furiosus, ever stood successfully against me. Why did God give me bodily strength, save only that I should use it in His service?'

'I must admire your manly and aggressive spirit,' replied the Novice Master, 'but I should not wish you to lose your life.'

'Please,' begged Father Sampson. 'I assure you that my many years' experience as a wrestler has given me a suppleness of limb which almost places me in the contortionist class. I'm confident of my ability to apply as efficacious a stranglehold as in days gone by. All the more effective methods of choking an opponent are very well known to me.'

'Bravo!' shouted Brother Patrick, who loved the sight of blood, having been much addicted to attendance at cockfights in his youth.

The Novice Master hesitated. 'Very well,' he said at last. 'Our blessings will go with you. In the meantime we others will intone a hymn by way of encouraging you and confusing the demon.'

Brother Patrick gripped Father Sampson by the arm.

'Try and get him with a hammer-lock or a crutch-hold,' he

advised, 'and then when you have him, kick him in a vital spot.'

As Father Sampson, clad only in his singlet, moved down the road to meet the poltergeist, the monks under the direction of the Novice Master began a heartening hymn. All sang lustily, save only Brother Patrick, who was too excited to join in. The diminutive lay brother capered up and down wrestling with an imaginary opponent.

For some time the monk and the poltergeist circled one another warily. Then Father Sampson suddenly closed and attempted to trap the poltergeist's torso between his legs in the scissors-hold, but the demon, gripping the monk's foot, hugged the captured leg closely to his chest before passing it around the back of his neck and throwing Father Sampson heavily. Quick to seize advantage, the poltergeist tore a block of granite from the bed of the stream and flung it at his opponent, missing the latter by inches.

'Dirty foul!' screeched Brother Patrick. 'Play the game, you filthy demon!'

Father Placidus shook his head despondently. 'And there are some,' he remarked, 'who impudently proclaim that it is folly and ridiculous beyond words to believe these marvellous happenings.'

Father Sampson was again on his feet and had delivered a couple of rabbit punches before the poltergeist realised what was happening. Then the monk essayed some of the traditional strangleholds and chokelocks, but the extreme pliability of his opponent's body made it extremely difficult to keep him in a tight grip. Joe seemed to be able to slip out of everything. At one moment Father Sampson had the demon's head trapped between his knees and was essaying a simultaneous three-quarter nelson and a kidney-squeeze, but the poltergeist escaped by making a half-turn so that he rolled over the back of his opponent. While they faced each other again, the monks shouted the final verse of the hymn and began another without pausing for breath. Both adversaries were covered with sweat and breathing heavily. Father Sampson was apparently planning to cross-buttock the phantom with his left leg, but Joe rushed in first and succeeded in trapping the monk's forearm under his left armpit. Father Sampson replied with a short-arm scissors followed by an ingenious toe-hold, and in a moment both of them had fallen and were involved in a struggle in the bed of the stream. At first Father Sampson was content to apply pressure with his thumb against a point immediately below the lobe of the demon's ear, but then with a quick movement he succeeded in capturing his opponent's right leg. For some minutes he worked on the leg to the extreme discomfort of the demon, who yelled hideously. The excitement was too great for Brother Patrick. He burst away from the band of monks and, running to the stream, gave the poltergeist a resounding kick in the ribs before scuttling back to safety.

It was obvious to the onlookers that the struggle was between the skill of the trained wrestler and the brute strength of the poltergeist. At one period things looked bad for Father Sampson. The demon sprang into the air and landed heavily seated astride the monk's chest. With his foot on Father Sampson's face he dug his thumbs into the monk's windpipe as an additional means of persuasion. But Father Sampson escaped from his perilous situation by bending the demon's arm back in a painful angle so that Joe had perforce to release him. When they faced one another again, the green sweat was running down the demon's face. With a sudden forward movement Father Sampson gripped the poltergeist by the wrist and in a moment had flung him backwards over his head. The demon landed on his back with a sickening crash. It was the famous Irish Whip! A wild shout of applause arose from the watching monks, and they started to run down the road towards the stream. Joe the Poltergeist lay among the rocks totally uninterested in the subsequent proceedings. The monks under the direction of Father Sampson strained at a huge rock and strove to roll it over on top of the poltergeist so as to pin him down for all time; but before they could complete the operation, the demon struggled to his feet, and assuming the form of a water spaniel with the head of an ox, he ran limping down the road, pursued by the maledictions of the whole body of clergy.

*   *   *

When Fursey arrived at the southern gate of Cashel, the guards on duty took to their heels. No attempt was made to oppose his entry into the settlement, nor was his progress through the streets impeded. The inhabitants fled before him, spreading on all sides the terrible news that the arch-sorcerer was once more in the city roaming about seeking whom he might devour. This dire intelligence caused a considerable exodus of citizens through the northern gate. Before taking to flight some hurried to their cabins to collect their few possessions. Aged parents were dragged from their inglenooks and flung across the broad shoulders of their sons. A stream of refugees, bowed beneath these burdens, poured through the northern gate, their eyes bloodshot, their only anxiety to put as great a distance as possible between themselves and the terrible Fursey.

The sorcerer himself plodded through the streets unaware of the commotion of which he was the cause. He observed that the settlement was singularly deserted, but he was too taken up with his own affairs to ponder overmuch on such matters. At the foot of the incline which led to the Bishop's Palace, he hesitated, but it was only for a moment: then with a thumping heart he began to climb the hill. When he reached the head of the track, he knocked timidly on the Bishop's door. The bronze panels opened before him, and it became immediately apparent that the news of his advent had preceded him. The hall was lined with armed men; in the centre stood Father Furiosus with Bishop Flanagan trembling behind him. Fursey observed that the friar was well-equipped with spiritual weapons. On his right was a cask of holy water, and half-a-dozen underlings stood by with buckets, ready at a moment's notice to form a living chain so as to keep it replenished. On the friar's left stood a table with an open book of exorcisms upon it. The table was piled also with crosses, handbells and other evidences of an extensive religious armoury. But most formidable of all was the red-faced friar himself as he stood in the centre gripping his blackthorn stick menacingly. For a moment no one spoke. Then Fursey stepped forward.

'I have come,' he said haltingly, 'I have come to surrender myself to justice.'

As he spoke, he gazed anxiously at the friar's hard, green eyes set deep beneath his ginger eyebrows, eyes that seemed to Fursey to resemble the points of two screws already in position to bore into his brain. Father Furiosus returned his gaze unwinkingly. Fursey's eyes dropped, and he contemplated the blossoming, strawberry-like nose of the friar and the thin lips drawn tight across the determined jaw. The phrase 'The Church Militant' came to his mind, and he shuddered.

'How are we to know,' said the friar at last, 'that you have not been guided here by demons with the object of further wizardy and malice?'

'You have only my word,' replied Fursey, 'that I've come here and placed myself in your power of my own free will. Witchcraft is as detestable to me as it is to you.'

'Why have you come?' asked the friar.

'I've come that I may be released one way or another from my present unhappy state, the state of being a wizard.'

'So you admit that you're a wizard?'

'Yes, I freely admit that I'm a wizard, an unwilling one, but nevertheless a wizard.'

'Come into the other room,' commanded Furiosus. 'We will talk further.'

As they moved into the interior of the Palace, the Bishop plucked the friar's sleeve nervously.

'If this goes on much longer,' he whispered, 'we'll all fall into a lunacy. Why not have him put to death forthwith?'

'I'm managing this,' replied the friar roughly. 'It's a most involved case. I must probe it to its depths.'

The Bishop's Adam's apple vibrated anxiously.

'But if we permit him to move about thus freely, how shall we escape his devilry? Let me have him well thrashed and pelted with stones while the fire is being prepared.'

'No,' said Furiosus shortly.

'Well, don't blame me,' snarled the Bishop, 'if he suddenly throws a bridle over your head and changes you into a horse. I observe that at the present moment he is mumbling something which may well be a spell.'

They had reached an inner room, and the three of them were now alone. Father Furiosus glanced sharply at Fursey.

'What are you saying?' he asked.

'A prayer to blessed Kieran for help in my affliction,' replied Fursey. 'I hope you don't mind.'

The friar motioned Fursey to a chair and then sat down himself. Bishop Flanagan declined to sit, but hovered in the neighbourhood of the door lest it should be necessary to summon help.

'I may as well tell you,' began the friar, 'that his lordship and I have on many occasions during the past month discussed your case with Abbot Marcus of Clonmacnoise. The Abbot is fortunately in Cashel at present; and on receiving intelligence of your arrival, I sent a slave across to the library with a request that he should attend here as soon as his studies permit. So we may expect him at any moment.'

'I see,' said Fursey.

'It may interest you to know,' continued Father Furiosus, 'that your case is bristling with difficulties. For instance, you told us just now that you have voluntarily surrendered yourself; but how am I to know whether that statement proceeds from Fursey, late monk at Clonmacnoise, or from the demon that possesses him?'

'But I assure you that I'm not possessed by a demon.'

'That's all very well,' said the friar carefully, 'but if you are possessed by a demon, I should expect him to deny his presence, for lies would come more naturally to his tongue than truth.'

'It's a clear case of deadlock,' interjected the Bishop impatiently. 'The truth in the matter is not obtainable. In the meantime we cannot have you moving around the countryside roaring after your prey, or at least inflicting an innocent peasantry with wasting diseases and fits.'

'I wish you wouldn't interrupt,' said Father Furiosus.

'It's all very well for you,' retorted the Bishop. 'A roving friar has few responsibilities; but I'm bishop of this diocese, and I have responsibilities to the lambs of my flock. This man Fursey is a self-admitted sorcerer. His contention is that his dread powers were innocently acquired. Be that as it may, he has those powers, and he must be burned before he turns them to malefic ends.'

Father Furiosus seemed determined to ignore the Bishop. He turned his steady gaze on Fursey once more.

'How did you escape from your prison?' he asked. 'By sorcery?'

'No,' replied Fursey. 'Satan got me out.'

'Satan!' ejaculated the friar.

'Yes,' admitted Fursey. 'I've always found him very helpful, though a little headstrong.'

The friar's eyes widened, but he made no comment. Bishop Flanagan vented a horrified moan and edged nearer the door. The friar continued his examination.

'Is it the case that on departing from this city you stole all the gold so generously donated by Prince Apollyon of Byzantine, together with a high-stepping hound of superior pedigree which was my particular possession?'

'No,' replied Fursey. 'The gold was spectral gold and vanished with Prince Apollyon, who was Satan himself. The hound to which you refer, was no doubt one of the lower orders of imps, and, I expect, followed his master, as is proper.'

Nothing was said for a few moments while the friar and the Bishop tried to grasp the implications of this alarming intelligence. They had the information only half-digested when there was a sudden stir at the door, and Abbot Marcus entered. He bowed gravely to Bishop Flanagan and Father Furiosus, and nodded kindly to Fursey. Fursey in his chair felt suddenly uncomfortable.

'This wretched man,' gasped Bishop Flanagan, 'has just had the effrontery to inform us that the noble and generous Apollyon, Prince of Byzantium, is none other than the Archfiend Lucifer himself. Did you ever hear such nonsense?'

'I'm a man,' replied the Abbot, 'from whom the years are creeping away faster and ever faster. What avails me my coming old age unless it finds me wise? A lifetime's study and observance has convinced me that in the land of Ireland anything may happen to anyone anywhere and at any time, and that it usually does.'

'But such a preposterous suggestion!' exclaimed the Bishop. 'Apollyon is a man of great wealth and influence, most solicitous for the well-being of the Church, and most generous in his contributions to the support of its pastors —'

'I suggest,' interrupted Marcus, 'that we three seat ourselves here and listen carefully to Fursey's story of all that has befallen him since he first made acquaintance with the forces of Evil in his cell at Clonmacnoise. Let him relate all, bringing his narration up to the present moment.'

Thus encouraged, Fursey related his strange story. Father Furiosus listened intently, nodding his head occasionally at some marvellous happening or impish trick which was borne out by his own experience of the world of shadows. The only time he manifested impatience was when Fursey recounted his experiences in the cottage of The Gray Mare. The friar's impatience at this part of the story was understandable, for it was obvious to any man of sense that the martyred lady, at whose shrine so many miracles had recently taken place, could not possibly have been guilty of the unprincipled behaviour which Fursey attributed to her. Again the friar shook his head doubtfully when he heard Cuthbert accused of being a sorcerer of a hue deeper than is usual. Cuthbert was so obviously a man of sterling piety; and by private enquiry the friar had ascertained that Cuthbert performed the responsible duties of sexton with diligence and probity. It was hard to understand for so much of what Fursey related had the ring of truth. The friar began to wonder whether in these two matters of The Grey Mare and Cuthbert, Fursey was perhaps the victim of hallucination. When Albert came to be spoken of, the Abbot interrupted the flow of Fursey's tale.

'So you govern and maintain a familiar?' he said with interest.

'I've attempted to govern him,' replied Fursey, 'but unfortunately he's not readily amenable to discipline. As for maintaining him, I fear that I have not. The poor fellow has shrunk to a mere shadow of his former self.'

Fursey continued the faithful relation of his experiences, save only that when he came to speak of the employment he had obtained in Declan's cottage in The Gap, his heart failed him; and he forebore to mention that there had lived in the cottage as well as Declan a good-natured girl who was always laughing. He left Maeve out of his story altogether.

Bishop Flanagan evinced the greatest impatience during Fursey's recital. He shifted constantly in his chair, his underlip twitched, and his Adam's apple was in constant motion in his throat. It was obvious that he considered Fursey's story to be no more than the recital of unnecessary and uninteresting detail. To his mind, the only important point was that Fursey was a sorcerer, and as such should be burned. When Fursey brought the tale to a conclusion, the Bishop could no longer contain his impatience.

'How long must we listen to this creature's maunderings?' he burst out. 'Let us proceed at once to bring his wicked career to a conclusion before he has us all wasted and consumed.'

There was a moment's silence, then the Abbot spoke.

'Strange and wonderful as is his story, I believe that Fursey is telling us the truth.'

Fursey threw a look of dumb gratitude at the Abbot, and his eyes brightened with tears. It was obvious that Father Furiosus respected Abbot Marcus' opinion, for when he had contemplated the Abbot for a few moments, he too spoke, slowly and gently.

'I'm inclined to agree with you. I believe that while this unfortunate man is suffering from a moistening of the brain in regard to certain persons and incidents of which he has spoken, his intention is good, and he has striven to tell us the whole truth. He's to be pitied, not condemned.'

The Bishop squinted from the Abbot to the friar, and then across at Fursey. He opened his mouth as if to speak, but he ran his tongue across his lips instead and said nothing. Father Furiosus sat for some moments in thought before turning again to Fursey.

'I'm convinced of your penitence,' he said, 'and I'm sure that you are afire with anxiety to make amends to Heaven for your sins. Isn't that so?'

'Yes,' replied Fursey carefully.

'Well, an opportunity for atonement is at hand. Abbot Marcus and I are practical men, and we have discussed at length measures whereby this land may be rid forever of the pestilential demons which everywhere infest it.'

'Are things as bad as that?' asked Fursey, hoping to gain time, for he had an uneasy feeling that he was cast for a leading part in the task of purging the land of its unwelcome visitors.

The friar's brow furrowed.

'Things are very bad. Only yesterday a parish priest not two miles from here eloped with a visiting vampire. Great scandal has been caused, for he was much respected by his flock, being a man of outstanding piety and one of the largest bullock owners in the territory. The carcase of the unhappy man, sucked dry of blood, was found this morning in a ditch, where his phantom paramour had flung him. In the trading towns on the western seaboard there has been a deplorable outbreak of loose living, and I don't doubt that it is Hell-inspired. The "bad disease" is so rampant that if you enter a house in those territories and clap a citizen on the back, all his teeth fall out on the table.'

'It seems a perilous thing to be alive at all,' murmured Fursey.

'The worst feature,' continued Furiosus, 'is that the demons which lately infest the land, are all of foreign origin. It's a well-authenticated fact that the native Irish demons, whether they be banshees, fairy pipers, leprechauns or pookas, are far superior to the foreign brands. Our demons may be mischievous, but they are admitted all the world over to be as upright and pure in their manner of living as demons can be. The chastity of the Irish demon is well-known and everywhere admitted.'

Fursey nodded patriotically.

'Unfortunately the same cannot be said of the foreign demons which are now rampant. They are not only clad in a manner offensive to decency, but they seem to specialise in inciting men to lechery. It is therefore,' continued the friar, 'a national as well as a religious duty to rid the land of these pestilential hordes. That is where you can help.'

'Me?' said Fursey.

'Yes, you. From evil will come good. We must cash in on your friendship with Satan. It will be necessary for you to get in touch with him at once and persuade him to lead his entire forces to a lake in the north called Lough Derg. In that lake there's a small island known as Saint Patrick's Purgatory, on which you must persuade Satan to encamp with all his forces, two-legged, four-legged and those that crawl on their bellies. When you have done that, the clergy of Ireland who will be lying in ambush, will surround the lake and bless it, thus converting the entire lough into a vast stoup of holy water. The happy result will be that Satan and his angels will be imprisoned for all time on that island, and will therefore be no longer in a position to range abroad seducing the faithful from their allegiance.'

The sweat broke out on Fursey's forehead.

'How am I to get them on to the island?' he squeaked.

'By the exercise of ingenuity. You can think up a plausible plan at your leisure. You might suggest, for instance, that it would be a safe base from which they could harry the surrounding monasteries and settlements.'

'I see,' said Fursey.

'If you do this,' put in the Abbot, 'we can promise you your pardon and a safe berth in a monastery.'

'We might even be able to arrange a canonry in the Chapter,' said the Bishop eagerly. 'Think of that, the best of feeding and drinking and no more work for the rest of your life.'

'It will be a resounding victory for the Irish Church,' concluded the friar, 'and such a good act on your part will no doubt obtain for you divine forgiveness for your sins and sorceries.'

'Suppose,' said Fursey, 'that before the operation is complete, they discover that I'm not playing straight with them?'

'Then you will die a blessed martyr. What more could any Christian ask for?'

'It's a good plan,' commented Abbot Marcus. 'We three have discussed it during the past month, but the difficulty was how to coax the demons on to the island. Your advent offers the ideal solution and seems to solve the problem.'

Fursey grew alternately hot and cold. It seemed to him that the ecclesiastics were underestimating the difficulties inherent in assembling some thousands of fearsome creatures and then persuading them to take up their abode on a minute island on a small lake; but the word 'forgiveness' had been used, and Fursey's heart bounded at the thought of escaping the funeral pyre, which certainly awaited him if he refused. Moreover, he was filled with a great exaltation at the thought of being once more on the side of Good in the battle with Evil. And even if he fell, wrestling manfully with a score of cacodemons and hippogriffs, it would be a glorious end and one befitting a Christian.

'I'll do it,' he said sticking out his chin determinedly.

'Well said!' commented Abbot Marcus, smiling across at him.

'You won't forget,' added Fursey anxiously, 'to rescue me from the island before you pin the demons there forever?'

'That will be attended to,' answered the friar placing a friendly hand on Fursey's shoulder.

At that moment a flourish of trumpets was heard and a sudden cheering. Before the ecclesiastics had time to enquire as to the cause of the commotion, an excited slave burst into the room.

'My lord Bishop,' he announced breathlessly, 'the noble and most generous Prince of Byzantium has entered the city.'

With one accord the three ecclesiastics hurried to the door of the Palace. Fursey trailed along behind them, his heart thumping like a hammer. From their vantage point in the doorway they could see Prince Apollyon approaching down the street, gracefully casting handfuls of gold to the frantically excited populace. Now and again he paused to pat a child on the head or to enquire courteously as to the present state of some old gaffer's rheumatism. Then he proceeded on his way bowing left and right to his frenzied admirers. Bishop Flanagan's eyes nearly fell out of his head as the debonair figure began to ascend the incline towards the Palace.

'Such generosity!' he breathed. 'Every inch a gentleman!'

'He can well afford it,' muttered Fursey. 'They'd be well-advised to spend that gold quick before it disappears.'

This remark of Fursey's jarred the ecclesiastics considerably, reminding them of Fursey's assertion that the noble stranger was none other than the Prince of Darkness himself. Furiosus and the Bishop glanced doubtfully from Fursey to the approaching Prince. Fursey felt a slight pressure on his arm and, looking around, he saw that the Abbot Marcus was close beside him. The Abbot drew Fursey back a couple of paces from the others.

'Tell me the truth, Fursey. Is this gentleman really Lucifer, the terrible Emperor of Hell?'

'Yes,' replied Fursey; and for some reason the word seemed to stick in his throat.

The Abbot regarded him doubtfully.

'If that's so, I wonder why he has come.'

'I know why he's come,' ejaculated Fursey with a sudden sob. 'He knows that I'm in danger, and he's come to rescue me once more. He's the only one who really cares what becomes of me; and I've repaid his kindness by undertaking to betray him.'

Slow horror crept across the Abbot's face.

'Fursey, you owe allegiance to Heaven, not to Hell.'

The Devil would have been a fool indeed if he had failed to notice that his welcome was a lukewarm one. The Bishop shrank back behind the door, and even Father Furiosus was pale as he took the demon's proffered hand. The Abbot contented himself with a distant bow, and the face which Fursey turned to his old acquaintance, was streaming with tears.

'Let us go inside and talk,' said Apollyon quietly, and he led the way into the inner room. As the ecclesiastics followed, Father Furiosus dexterously hooked a stoup of holy water with his forefinger from the table in the hall, and carried it in concealed behind his back. The ecclesiastics seemed still doubtful of Apollyon's real identity, but the first words which he spoke, confirmed their worst fears. Apollyon was the only one of the five who was wholly at his ease. He crossed the room and seated himself in the Bishop's favourite chair.

'You've no occasion to weep, Fursey,' he said quietly. 'I know that you've betrayed me, but you forget that I'm the Father of Lies, Deception and Double-dealing. Your conduct in that regard affords me the highest pleasure. I find myself in the debt of these gentlemen: they have thrown you and me closer together.'

Fursey's mouth fell open, and he sat down suddenly in a chair. Father Furiosus produced the stoup of holy water from behind his back and began shakily to take aim.

'Please,' remonstrated the Archfiend. 'Do not forget your country's age-old reputation for hospitality. Oblige me by putting down that weapon. I'm not here as an enemy. I've come to make terms with the clergy of Ireland.'

Father Furiosus did as he was bid and sat down looking rather dazed.

'Abbot Marcus,' continued the Devil, 'you seem to be the only one who is retaining his wits. Oblige me by summoning the canons of the Chapter. I'm satisfied that they and you three gentlemen are sufficiently representative of the clergy of this country to ensure that any treaty I conclude with you, will be acceptable to the clergy as a whole. In the meantime, perhaps his lordship Bishop Flanagan will bestir himself and see that food and drink are provided for his guests.'

The Bishop staggered to the door and gave a few husky commands. When the ale and meats were borne in, the Bishop retained only enough presence of mind to see that Fursey got nothing except a plate of hard food. One would have imagined that natural curiosity would have constrained the canons of the Chapter to hurry over to the Palace to see such an important personage as the Archfiend, of whom they had read and heard so much; but a strange reluctance on their part manifested itself when they received Abbot Marcus' message. It needed all the Abbot's powers of persuasion and his insistence that perhaps the future of the Irish Church was at stake, before they climbed the hill to the Palace and came sidling round-eyed into the room in which the conference was to be held.

'My Lord Bishop and very reverend fathers,' began Satan. 'I'm well aware that you regard me with a certain prejudice. Nay, do not, in the excess of your courtesy, shake your heads and strive to look as if it were otherwise. Let us be honest and face facts. You don't approve of me. Isn't that so, Canon Pomponius?'

The broad-bellied doyen of the Cathedral Chapter manifested considerable alarm at being thus singled out. He shifted jerkily from one expansive ham to the other.

'You must make allowances, sir, for our upbringing — the tales remembered from childhood — the effect —' His voice trailed away into a whisper.

The Devil sighed understandingly.

'Let me explain myself,' he said. 'I'm a person cursed with a sense of freakish humour. I'm well aware that it interferes seriously with my effectiveness as a demon. You may assert that my humour is depraved. I freely admit that it is. For centuries it has spoiled my best-laid plans. I cannot conquer this boyish desire of mine to see monks, anchorites and other holy men startled out of their wits by an apparition, preferably a female one. It affords me the keenest amusement, but it's a vice which is rendering me more and more ineffective as a demon. While I'm splitting my sides laughing, the gentleman whom I'm tempting, has immediate recourse to prayer and other spiritual weapons, the very last thing which I wish him to do. The net result is that he always wins, and when I've recovered from my paroxysm of merriment, I find that there is nothing left for me to do but retire chagrined and baffled.'

The canons shifted uncomfortably, moistened their dry lips and wondered what was coming next.

'Father Furiosus,' said the Demon ingratiatingly, 'answer me a question. Which is the greatest of all sins?'

The friar's honest face betrayed his embarrassment.

'Everyone knows that,' he replied. 'It's not considered proper among decent people to put a name on it.'

The entire body of clergy nodded in agreement.

'We're all adult men,' said the Demon persuasively. 'We're not likely to incur injury by mention of the mere name.'

The canons shook their heads doubtfully.

'Come now,' urged Apollyon. 'Tell me which is the most grievous of all sins, so that the conference may proceed.'

The friar flushed slightly.

'The most heinous of all crimes,' he said, 'are those which may be summed up by the word "sex".'

The assembled clergy nodded in agreement, and then looked uncomfortably at the walls and ceiling.

'Exactly,' said the Archfiend with a sudden quick glint in his eye. 'Well, I offer this country immunity from such temptation, if you on your part promise me something in return.'

The clergy sat up in their seats and for the first time looked really interested.

'What do you want in return?' asked Father Furiosus carefully.

'I should expect that the clergy in their teaching would not in future lay undue stress on the wickedness of simony, nepotism, drunkenness, perjury and murder.'

'These sins which you mention,' said the friar after a long, cautious pause, 'are but minor offences when compared with the hideous sin of sex. What you somewhat exaggeratedly term drunkenness, perjury and murder are perhaps but the exuberance of a high-spirited and courageous people. Nepotism is, after all, merely an offshoot of the virtue of charity. As for simony, we know all about that. The cry of simony is usually raised by evil-minded persons who are unwilling to subscribe to the upkeep of their pastors.'

'You think then that we can perhaps do business on these lines?'

Before replying Father Furiosus glanced along the rows of eager ecclesiastical faces.

'I think we can,' he said at last.

The conference dragged on hour after hour. Fursey fell asleep and when he awoke, Apollyon was delivering his final oration.

'I promise the clergy of this country wealth and the respect of their people for all time. When a stranger enters a village, he will not have to ask which is the priest's house. It will be easy of identification, for it will be the largest house there. I promise you that whenever priests are sought, it will not be in the houses of the poor that they will be found. And as a sign that I will keep my part of the bargain, I will stamp the foreheads of your priesthood with my own particular seal — the seal of pride.'

The Archfiend's voice was lost in the tumult of applause, and the assembly broke up. The Canons of the Chapter left the building in small groups chattering excitedly to one another. Every face was aglow with animation save only that of Abbot Marcus, who sat crouched in his chair, his face shadowed with doubt and indecision.

'They have compromised with Evil,' Fursey heard him muttering. 'They have compromised where there can be no compromise.'

Father Furiosus and the Bishop had walked out into the hall with the canons, and Fursey found himself alone with Apollyon, alone except for the motionless figure of the Abbot sunk in his chair in a far corner of the room. The Archfiend seemed tired as he moved towards the door with Fursey.

'Well,' he said pausing on the threshold, 'it's over now — a most satisfactory arrangement, in which both sides are convinced that they have gained substantial benefits. Do you realise what has happened, Fursey?'

'No, I was asleep.'

'Well,' said the Archfiend carefully, 'unless my sense of humour has again betrayed me, I appear to have the souls of the Irish clergy in my bag for all time. It'll give Hell a considerable Irish ecclesiastical character, and I suppose the other damned won't like it. They'll say that they've enough to put up with as it is.'

He sighed and seemed to become very depressed as he meditated on the future.

'Life will be very difficult in the coming centuries,' he said. 'Before long Hell will hardly know itself. It will bear an extraordinary resemblance to an Annual General Meeting of the Catholic Truth Society. It's a terrible prospect for a demon of sensitiveness and breeding like me.'

Fursey had not the slightest idea what the Archfiend was talking about; but as politeness demanded it, he made a sound indicative of his sympathy. The Devil started suddenly, possessed by a new idea.

'Fursey,' he said eagerly. 'I've a proposition to make to you. I have the Irish Church in my bag for all time. I'll exchange the souls of all of them, born and unborn, for your soul.'

'No,' retorted Fursey. 'Certainly not.'

The Devil's face fell. 'I suppose you're right,' he replied gloomily. 'Your soul is the only thing which your country has left you, and I suppose you're right to stick to it.'

Grimly he hummed one of the psalms backwards for a few moments. At last his face cleared, and he turned to Fursey once more.

'It's unlikely that I'll see you again. Before I go, I'd like to know how you're placed for the future.'

'I don't know. I expect they'll let me back into Clonmacnoise.'

'I'd advise emigration,' said the Devil. 'The future of the Irish race lies in emigration.'

'Ah, the country isn't as bad as all that,' protested Fursey.

'The country is all right,' replied the Devil. 'The only thing that's wrong with it, is the people that are in it.'

'I don't agree with you,' said Fursey patriotically.

'Maybe,' sighed the Devil, 'maybe I should have said that the country and most of the people are all right; what's wrong with this land is the hard-fisted few that have and hold it. Forgive me if I seem to be carping,' he continued, 'but I'm rather out of patience with the Irish race. Your countrymen have no real sense of humour as the phrase is understood by other peoples. They never laugh at themselves.'

'Maybe,' replied Fursey.

'Goodbye now,' said the Devil, 'and don't get yourself into any further trouble.'

'I won't,' said Fursey. 'Are you not going out through the front door?'

'No. I'll take my departure through the smoke-hole in the roof. I don't want to have to shake hands with Bishop Flanagan. Damn it, I have my pride.'

The Archfiend waved his hand to Fursey in melancholy valediction, and streaking up to the ceiling, made a perfect exit through the smoke-hole, just as Father Furiosus and the Bishop re-entered the room rubbing their hands and evincing every sign of satisfaction.

'Is our friend gone?' asked the friar.

'Yes,' replied Fursey pointing to the ceiling. 'He went that way.'

The Bishop laughed tolerantly as if the Devil's choice of exit was an understandable boyish freak. He turned genially to Furiosus and the Abbot.

'Well, everything is fixed,' he said, 'most satisfactorily. The only thing that remains to be done, is to burn Fursey.'

Fursey glanced incredulously from the Bishop to Father Furiosus. When he saw the friar nodding gravely, he turned and fled to the far corner of the room where Abbot Marcus was rising stiffly from his chair.

'Father Abbot,' he cried, 'they say that they're going to burn me. It's not true, is it?'

The Abbot looked at him sadly.

'Of course it's true. You know as well as any of us that the only way to cure a sorcerer is to burn him. I understood that you appreciated the position when you surrendered yourself. After all, we can't allow a wizard to be at large in the territory, nor can we allow your soul to be eternally lost for the want of a little cleansing fire.'

'That's all very well,' quavered Fursey, 'but I thought that now that everything is fixed —'

Before he could utter another word Father Furiosus, who had approached him from behind, seized him suddenly by the arms and flung him forward on his face on to the floor.

'Call the guards,' commanded the friar.

Fursey, not unnaturally incensed at this high-handed proceeding, bounded to his feet, and before the three ecclesiastics, who apparently did not expect resistance on his part, had grasped what he was about, he darted through the door into the hall. A damp-souled serving-man was gloomily sweeping the floor with a broom. Fursey did not stop to ask his permission, but snatched the broom from him; and running to a corner, tore the box of ointment from his pocket. He had thoroughly smeared the shaft before the clerics burst from the room into the hall.

'Stop!' shouted the friar.

Before they could reach him, Fursey had flung his leg over the broom and shot towards the ceiling. As he flew in circles around the hall, his head brushing the rafters, Father Furiosus sprang from table to table aiming blows at him with his blackthorn stick.

'Resistance will avail you nought!' shrilled the Bishop.

Fursey did not answer: he was too preoccupied in steering the broom in the limited space available so as to avoid collision with the walls. It was a difficult task, for the constant circling made him dizzy.

'Come down, Fursey,' urged the Abbot. 'These antics can have only one end. Please come down.'

'Yah!' retorted Fursey. 'Come down and be burnt! What kind of a fool do you think I am?'

The Bishop tore open the great door of the Palace with the apparent object of summoning assistance. Fursey saw his opportunity. He swooped suddenly, snatched a flint and taper from a table, banked sharply, and shot through the open doorway like a bullet. When he reached the open air, he swerved once again and alighted on the roof of the Palace. A large crowd of townspeople who had waited for hours before the Bishop's dwelling in the hope of further financial benefit from the visit of the generous Prince Apollyon, raised a shout of surprise as they beheld the marvel and saw Fursey perched on the ridge of the roof. Their astonishment changed suddenly to rage as they beheld Fursey lighting the taper and setting fire to the thatch of the roof in half-a-dozen different places. It was borne in powerfully on the citizens that it would be incumbent on them to contribute generously for a new palace for their pastor. A storm of maledictions was hurled at Fursey, but the more practical were quickly disciplined by Father Furiosus and ran in all directions for ladders and buckets. Fursey regarded the creeping flames with satisfaction, then a thought seemed to strike him. He peered down at the howling mob as if to select a victim. His eye fell on a small, flaxen-haired slave on the edge of the crowd, who was gaping up at him with his mouth open. Fursey flung his leg over the broom once more and suddenly swooped. The crowd panicked and gave way before him, allowing Fursey as he swept over their heads, to grip the diminutive slave by his long hair and fly back with him on to the roof of the Palace. The slave lay across the ridge of the roof with his eyes turned up to Heaven, fully convinced that his last hour had come. Fursey took him by the throat.

'What day of the week is this?' demanded Fursey.

'What's that you said, sir?' gasped the slave.

'I asked you what day of the week it was.'

The slave closed his eyes and started to say his prayers. Fursey thumped his head a couple of times against the crossbeam so as to make him stop. The treatment was efficacious. The wretched creature was silent and looked up at Fursey with his eyes bloodshot and his tongue hanging out.

'What day of the week is it?' repeated Fursey applying additional pressure to his gullet.

'Saturday,' gasped the slave.

'I thought so,' muttered Fursey grimly, and with a mighty heave he yanked his prisoner into a sitting position.

'Point out the position of Kilpuggin Church,' snarled Fursey, baring his teeth.

The slave raised a trembling hand and pointed.

'Thanks,' said Fursey, immediately releasing him.

There was a howl of horror from the crowd as the slave slid down the roof and fell to the pavement below with a crunching sound that spoke of broken limbs. The flames were crackling merrily as Fursey once more mounted the broom and sped like a bolt across the housetops of the settlement and away over the green fields. Not once did he falter in his course until he sighted the little church of Kilpuggin. He circled the building once to reconnoitre. He saw horses tethered outside, but there were no human beings. He made a second circuit just for safety, and then made a smooth landing at the church door. He propped his broom carefully in the entrance, and tiptoed in. It was as he had hoped. In the nave in the centre of a small group of friends stood Magnus and Maeve, and behind them Declan and the Widow Dykes. The double wedding had not yet commenced.

'Why, it's Flinthead come to my wedding!' cried Maeve. 'Welcome, Flinthead!' and she advanced a pace to meet him. Fursey brushed by her, his eyes fixed on Magnus, who was smiling down at him in amused contempt. Fursey did not waste any words, but promptly kicked the bridegroom in the stomach and sent him sprawling. Phineas the Clerk pushed himself forward through the horrified group of guests.

'Flinthead!' he exclaimed. 'Are you mad?'

'I'm not Flinthead. I'm Fursey, the most powerful and terrible sorcerer that this land has ever known.'

'I always knew that there was something strange about you,' breathed Maeve.

'Are you mad?' repeated Phineas shrilly.

'Look through the door,' shouted Fursey, 'if you don't believe me. I've just set fire to the Bishop's Palace, and the flames of Cashel are roaring into the sky.'

Magnus sat up on the floor, more astonished than angry, until Fursey put him once more into a recumbent position with a deft kick under the chin.

'I'm now going to turn you all into toads,' asserted Fursey, 'and keep you in jars for my amusement.'

There was a gasp of horror, and the little group withdrew a couple of paces.

'Nonsense,' declared Declan, coming forward and peering closely into Fursey's face. 'You're not a sorcerer. You're Flinthead, my farm-boy, who ran away last week with a suit of my second-best clothes.'

'What would you like for your wedding?' asked Fursey fiercely. 'Wine?'

'Yes,' replied the old man.

Fursey swept the coil of rope from his shoulder, and flinging it over a beam in the roof, jerked it sharply. An immense beaker of wine fell out of nowhere and smashed in pieces on the floor at his feet. The guests retreated precipitately with cries of horror, save only Declan, who clambered on to a chair and began to inspect the rafters to see whether there was anything else concealed there. A priest had appeared among the startled guests. Fursey heard the word 'weapons' and saw that the men were scattering towards the back of the church. He immediately seized Maeve by the arm and ran with her to the door.

'Oh, Flinthead,' she gasped. 'What are you doing?'

'I'm eloping with you,' explained Fursey. 'We're going to a better and a freer land.'

'But I can't elope with you,' she said. 'I've got to marry Magnus.'

'You can't want to marry that big, boastful bully,' insisted Fursey.

'But the priest has been paid and all the guests invited,' she objected faintly. 'What will people say?'

'Let them say what they like,' asserted Fursey stoutly. 'Your friends have run for their weapons. You wouldn't want to see me cut to pieces at your feet.'

'Of course not. But I can't marry a sorcerer.'

'Why not? It's as good a profession as any other.'

'But what would we live on? You've no property.'

'We'll fly to Britain,' declared Fursey, 'and open a grocer's shop. It's the easiest thing in the world, I'll spend the mornings pulling on the rope, and the afternoons selling off the goods.'

'I hear them coming,' declared Maeve, throwing a terrified glance over her shoulder.

'If you don't come with me,' declared Fursey, 'I'll have to stand here and fight them; and however manfully I fight, I'll be cut to pieces.'

'But have we a steed on which we may escape?'

'Yes,' replied Fursey, producing the broom.

'You're such a precipitate man,' gasped Maeve.

'The man of action rules the world,' declared Fursey. 'Throw your leg across.'

'Oh, I couldn't,' said Maeve modestly, 'I'll ride side-saddle.'

As the guests burst from the church clutching their swords, they saw Fursey bent intently over the broom as it rose, while Maeve sat behind, clinging to him desperately and emitting little terrified screams. Thrice Fursey circled the church shouting derisively, while the terrified guests ran hither and thither. Then Fursey, fearing that they might start ringing the church bell, and so bring him to earth, rose high into the air and turned his face towards the east. He glanced over his shoulder only once to gaze with satisfaction at the billowing smoke that crept upwards into the sky over Cashel. Then he flew eastwards, over the grey-green fields, the crooked roads and the sluggishly rolling mountains of Ireland, the first of many exiles for whom a decent way of living was not to be had in their own country.